SPECIES OF THE GALAXY

Devorans

Homeworld: Devorus
Lifespan: 1,000+ Standard Years
One of the older space-faring species and members of the Galactic Confederation, Devorans possess a reptilian appearance and lay eggs but are warm-blooded. The Devoran homeworld is at the heart of the largest conglomeration of planets in the galaxy, the Devoran Union.

I0552812

Ersidians

Homeworld: Ersid
Lifespan: 150+ Standard Years

A hulking, bear-like member species of the Galactic Confederation, Ersidians believe strongly in honor and that their ancestors watch over and guide them. They have colonized many systems in their local space. Their home planet is the capital of a small network of colony worlds. The current President of the Galactic Confederation is Ersidian.

Humans

Homeworld: Earth
Lifespan: 125+ Standard Years
Humans are the dominant species in the Earth-Alpha Centauri Alliance (EAC). They're more or less like you and me. Thanks to the marvels of modern medicine, humans can remain active well past their one hundredth birthday. Human civilization has expanded to included colonies on most of the inhabitable planets within ten light years.

Kerrolians

Homeworld: Kerrola
Lifespan: 100+ Standard Years

Kerrolians, close relatives of Traxians, average shorter in height than humans and are covered with fur, have pointed, upright ears (like a wolf or cat), digitigrade locomotion, have elongated snouts and prominent canines (though most don't protrude), and bushy tails. Their homeworld is part of the Traxian Domain and is not a member of the Galactic Confederation.

Ryll

Homeworld: μ (Mu) Arae
Lifespan: 65+ Standard Years

Ryll are an amorphous species resembling giant amoebas. They typically wear bulky environmental suits as they are unable to interact with most technology otherwise, though they do possess contact telepathy. Their suit translators are

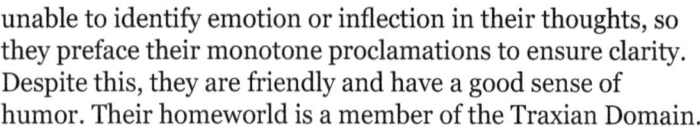

unable to identify emotion or inflection in their thoughts, so they preface their monotone proclamations to ensure clarity. Despite this, they are friendly and have a good sense of humor. Their homeworld is a member of the Traxian Domain.

ZACK JACKSON
& THE SECRET OF VENUS

This is a work of fiction. All characters and events portrayed in this book are fictional, and any resemblance to real people or incidents is purely coincidental.

Print Edition by CreateSpace
ISBN: 978-1-944999-05-6

Copyright © 2018 by Hans Cummings

All rights reserved, including the right to reproduce this book or portions thereof in any form.

Learn more about this and other works by the author at:
http://vffpublishing.com
Use Twitter? Follow the author @hccummings

Edited by Cynthia Shepp
http://cynthiashepp.wordpress.com/

Cover Art by Joshua Pinka
http://www.truepinkas.com/

Interior Art by Hanae Ko
http://hanaeko.com/

Cover Design by Eric Hubbel
http://www.erichubbel.com/

Kindle edition available through Amazon.com

*For Tink, without whom this would not have been possible,
and our little shadow, Callie, RIP my sweet kitty
(2001 - June 25, 2018).*

Special thanks to Tabitha Whitehead, Cindy Whitehead,
Penny Williams, Scott Schwartz, Dave Paul, and Keith Mingus
for their feedback on this novel.

Dedicated To
The men and woman of the Mercury, Gemini, and Apollo
space programs. Your spirit of discovery and sacrifice will fuel
dreams of exploration for countless generations.

Dr. Stephen Hawking, Dr. Carl Sagan, Dr. Brian Cox, Dr. Phil
Plait (The Bad Astronomer), Dr. Neil deGrasse Tyson, and Bill
Nye (The Science Guy). You taught me that the real universe
can be just as wonderous as that of our imaginations.

Gene Roddenberry, George Lucas, the cast and crew of Doctor
Who, Bioware, Steve Winter & the TSR Staff who created
Star Frontiers, and Posthuman Studios. You created fantastic
worlds in which to play that grew my imagination in more
ways than I can count.

Inspired By
The universe of Zack Jackson was inspired by numerous
sources:
Star Trek
Star Wars
Doctor Who
Mass Effect
Star Frontiers
Eclipse Phase
The Honorverse
Through the Wormhole
Firefly

The Zack Jackson Series
Zack Jackson & The Cult of Athos
Zack Jackson & The Cytherean Academy
Zack Jackson & The Hives of Valtra
Zack Jackson & The Secret of Venus

Uurts
Homeworld: Ersid
Lifespan: 100+ Standard Years
Resembling centaurs from Earth mythology, Uurts share Ersid with their cousins, the Ersidians. Where the Ersidians historically dwell in the mountains, Uurts roam the plains of their homeworld living as nomads. Of course, in the modern era, they share cities all over the planet and on their colony worlds. There are still some Uurt tribes who live a nomadic life, though they are comfortable with technology.

Valtraxians
Homeworld: Valtra
Lifespan: 35+ Standard Years
Valtraxians are an eight-legged insect-like species often described as a cross between a grasshopper and a praying mantis. Their species possess four genders: male, female, drone, and incubator, and they live in communal hives, much like bees or ants. Despite their short lifespan, many become brilliant engineers. Valtra is a member of the Galactic Confederation.

Chapter 1

The shuttle swooped through amber clouds, banking to avoid a dark thunderhead pouring acidic rain on the hellscape below. From his seat just forward of the shuttle's swept wing, Zack regarded a multi-domed structure in the distance, partially obscured by the dun-colored haze.

As the shuttle hit a pocket of turbulence, one of Zack's roommates, Ix, chittered and shifted in its seat as it secured its green felt fez. Zack clutched the armrests as the cabin lurched and dropped.

"Do not worry, Zack." The Valtraxian cocked its head, the translator embedded in its upper thorax converting its chitters into words he understood. "If we fall, the emergency balloons will deploy and arrest our descent before we are crushed by the atmosphere."

"I'm not worried." Zack loosened his grip on the armrests. Grabbing them was a reflex. Previous flights to Cytherea well acquainted him with the bumpy nature of traveling to the floating city. Other passengers, mostly students, chatted among themselves as the shuttle leveled off and made its final approach.

Zack reached forward and switched on the screen installed in the seatback in front of him. He adjusted the picture until it displayed the shuttle's forward view of its Cytherean approach. Half-a-dozen domes contained the upper levels of the city. Suspended in the clouds of Venus, it resembled a fairy-tale castle.

A flight of single-seat aircraft blasted past the shuttle, banking to approach one of the military hangars on the far side of the city. The Earth-Alpha Centauri Alliance maintained a small garrison on Cytherea, mostly for show.

Although the amount of air traffic around Cytherea seemed high to Zack, it occurred to him that his observation during last year's arrival could have been the anomaly. Two years at Cytherean Academy did not make him an expert on local air-traffic patterns.

A rote affair, docking and disembarking moved swiftly, unburdened by complications. Automated luggage handling

1

and modern fabricator units installed in each dormitory made traveling easy; Zack packed only enough clothes to wear during the journey from Earth to Venus.

He hefted his new blue-striped black duffle bag over his shoulder as he waited for Ix. The Valtraxian required only that which fit in its scant pouches, making Zack's traveling light look like overpacking.

Once Ix joined him, the pair made their way through the arrival terminal past the lines of first-years awaiting orientation. Zack spotted his counselor, Mr. McPheely, speaking to a group of students. The older man acknowledged his wave with a nod and a smile.

"After we drop off this stuff in our room, do you want to get something to eat?"

Ix chittered to itself for a moment. "I cannot. I have an appointment in forty-two minutes to discuss this year's accelerated schedule."

"You're connected to the school's Hypernet, right? Have you found where we sign up for extracurricular activities?" When they were on Valtra, Zack and his Devoran friend Dravs promised to attend a martial arts class with Xal. It felt like the best way to help their Ersidian friend gain some self-confidence.

"I have not. If I see it, I will send you a link."

"Thanks."

They made their way to the transport-pod platform, located near the docking bays and arrival terminal on one of the lower levels of the city. The distance between the terminal and Hathor Dome made walking to their dorm impractical. Over the public-address system, a melodious voice greeted new and returning students.

"Welcome to Cytherea where all the domes are named after goddesses of beauty and love from Earth mythology, in honor of the planet Venus itself. We invite you to visit all the plazas during your stay."

Zack faced Ix. "That's new, isn't it? They didn't have that kind of announcement last year, did they?"

"Not that I recall. Perhaps the information is intended for the large number of new arrivals this year."

The pod whisked them away from the arrival terminal. Within a few minutes, they entered the lift in Hathor's lower level that took them to their dorm. Each dorm suite in Hathor Dome comprised three, four-student bedrooms joined by a common area. Ix and Zack walked past half-a-dozen suites after exiting the elevator before arriving at the one they shared with Mickey, Steve, and four other students. As they approached, Zack noticed the door stood ajar, doubtless from other students moving in after the semester break.

As they entered, Victoria and Susan greeted them amidst their reorganization of furniture in the common area. Susan pointed toward the grey, sharp-angled sofa. "You boys are just in time!"

"I am not a boy." Ix cocked its head.

Victoria lifted one end of the sofa while Susan grabbed the other. Susan grunted as she raised her end. "I didn't mean it literally."

Zack set down his backpack and helped Victoria with her side. Ix helped Susan. The four of them repositioned the sofa to face the room's main holoviewer.

"Why are we rearranging the furniture?" Zack leaned on the sofa back and regarded the holoviewer. The sound was muted, but he determined from the images it was set to a nature program of some sort focused on Ersidian wildlife.

"Because Steve and Mickey rearranged it last time, and it was wrong all year!"

Scrutinizing the room, Zack failed to see improvement gained with the new arrangement. "Oh. Have Polly and Barbara shown up yet?"

The two young women giggled. "Your girlfriend isn't here yet."

"She's not my..." Zack noticed neither paid attention to him. The girls retreated to their room. Their giggles faded as they lost interest in Zack's relationship, and he overheard them discussing dinner instead. Zack followed suit, and he and Ix passed through the doorway into their room.

Zack sighed as he threw his duffle bag onto his bed. It bounced on the tight, cream-colored blanket. The summer passed far too quickly for his liking, particularly after returning home from his Junior Ranger trip to Valtra.

The dorm room appeared different. He scanned the area. Ix's nest, a pile of green and brown blankets, still sat next to his bed. Mickey's bunk, unkempt as usual, featured blankets and

3

sheets pushed toward the wall as if someone had just rolled out from beneath them. The neck of a guitar protruded from under the multicolored-striped blankets, and his tablet sat perched precariously on top of a stack of clothes on his desk.

Both Steve's bed and his desk appeared in a factory-fresh state; new sheets and blankets covered the mattress, and the desk area appeared neat and clean. No trace of Steve's belongings remained. Ix skittered past and placed its pack on the floor next to its nest.

"Hey, Ix, do you know what happened to Steve?"

The Valtraxian chittered and cocked its head as it examined the dormitory. "No, I have heard nothing."

"Well, that's strange." Zack opened his duffle bag and removed his effects, haphazardly shoving them into desk drawers. When he reached the iron sphere given to him by Professor Gladstone, he paused, rotating it in his hands as he examined its flawless surface. Reportedly a fragment from an iron star, an astronomical impossibility according to the good professor, the sphere's clear, synthetic case protected it from corrosion.

Zack placed it on his desk.

"Oh, uh, hey, Zack, Ix." Mickey entered the room and moved his guitar before plopping on his bed.

"Hey, Mickey." Zack raised his hand in greeting before gesturing toward Steve's bed. "Do you know where he is?"

The musician grunted as he retrieved the tablet from his desk and then tapped the screen. "He moved dorms."

"Why?"

"Uh..." Mickey shrugged and flipped through pages of sheet music on his screen, "He said something about his parents making him. They wanted him staying with his sister."

Zack perked up. "He has a sister? I didn't know that." He withdrew the sculpture Polly gave him on his birthday last year and placed it next to the iron star fragment. He turned the bust, so it didn't stare directly at him. He found the accurate detail of her rendition of his head unsettling at times. As much as Polly annoyed him, she possessed talent in sculpting.

"Yeah, she wasn't here last year. I guess she just transferred. Steve was bummed out about it."

4

"Will we welcome a new roommate, or may we utilize the extra space?" Ix rummaged through its pile of blankets, like a chef tossing a salad.

Mickey scrunched up his face as he stared at Steve's former bed. "New roommate, probably. Maybe a Devoran. Have you been to Ishtar Plaza yet?"

"No, we came straight here from the ship." Zack hefted his duffle. "I had to unpack. This thing was heavy. Did Steve say anything else? Which dorm is he in?"

Mickey shrugged. "He was pretty mad. We'll probably see him around."

"I must leave." Ix finished unpacking and touched Zack on the shoulders as it passed. "Professor Eckstein is expecting me."

"Uh, I have to go, too." Mickey shut off his tablet and left it behind on his bed. "See you later!"

Zack glanced around his now-deserted room. He pursed his lips. He knew sticking around would likely land him in a situation involving more physical labor with Victoria and Susan.

Maybe Jenny's around. He activated his Personal Digital Assistant, once again pining for the day when he would be eligible for implants. "Skip, send a message to Jenny and see if she wants to meet in the plaza for dinner."

"Acknowledged, Zack."

He had named his PDA's Artificial Intelligence Skip as a hasty mistake, intending it as a temporary placeholder, but he never thought of a better name.

Zack rearranged the items on his desk while he waited for Jenny's response. They corresponded last while she was on her way to Cytherea, having caught an earlier flight to get away from her overbearing grandparents. His parents had instructed him to give her space in consideration of her parents' accident, but that didn't seem right to him.

His PDA pinged when Skip relayed Jenny's response. "Reply from Jenny: 'Sure, I'll meet you in front of the Neutron Café.'"

He peeked out of his room into the common area. The girls were nowhere to be seen, so he sped into the hall. More students filled the corridor now, all in the process of moving in after the term break. He passed Ian and Ben, two of the

5

boys who shared his dorm cluster, in the hallway. They paused their conversation long enough to grunt greetings in Zack's direction, but neither stopped to chat.

As he stepped into the lift to take him to Ishtar Plaza, Zack's PDA pinged with another incoming message. This time, it was from his Junior Ranger Troop Leader, Bariss. "We need to talk about the Valtra situation, ASAP."

Chapter 2

Jenny stared out the observation window. As always, she saw only the thick, sand-colored clouds below and the expanse of beige sky above. Still, it beat sitting in her windowless dorm room, and with students just now arriving for the new school year, this spot possessed something her room didn't—quiet.

Returning to Cytherea early gave her a chance to get away from her hovering, smothering grandparents. In relative peace, she could deal with the kaleidoscope of emotions whirling through her mind. Being able to live on her own schedule made leaving Earth the best idea she had in months.

Following the accident, Jenny wanted more than anything to speed to Vilicus, the Ringworld of Sol, where her parents underwent reconstructive surgeries and convalesced from the crash that almost claimed their lives. Her father suffered the worst injuries. Even now, he could not effectively communicate without electronic aid. Her mother Amélie fared better, although she still needed daily physical therapy to learn how to walk again with the aid of cybernetic muscle stimulators. Unfortunately, travel times made visiting her parents in person impractical without affecting her attendance at school. Her mother assured her they understood and stressed that her continued education was more important than sitting idle in a hospital room.

Despite the cloudy haze, Jenny watched shuttles transport students from the ship that recently entered orbit. She thought it was *Hermes*, also known as the Venus Express, but she hadn't bothered to check. If that was indeed the case, then she would at least be reunited with her friends, Zack and Ix. Though it had only been a few months since their trip to Valtra together, the time spent without them felt like agony in the wake of her parents' accident.

By now, her roommates—Cait, Gabrielle, and Astrid—were sure to have arrived, unpacking and catching up on what they did during the school's designated summer break. Jenny had no desire to be in the middle of that. She liked her roommates, but the three of them together, especially cousins Gabrielle and Astrid, were a hurricane of insanity at times. The commotion of the other students arriving and unpacking in her dorm cluster added to the chaos, noise, and aggravation.

7

In the periphery of her vision, she saw an incoming message from Zack, routed through his old-style, handheld PDA, asking if she wanted to meet for dinner. She sent off a reply, relieved she had an excuse to do something other than return to her room and listen to her roommates chatter.

She followed the promenade around the perimeter until she reached an elevator. A pair of older students held hands as they exited. Jenny greeted them as they walked by. "Daniel. Mercer."

They nodded in acknowledgement and continued talking in low voices as they passed. She recognized them from one of her science classes the past year. Jenny made her way down to Ishtar Plaza. Another message popped up in her periphery. From Bariss. "We need to talk about the Valtra situation, ASAP."

Jenny composed a quick response. "Zack and I are headed to dinner. Talk after?"

She hoped whatever Bariss had to say could wait until after she'd eaten. While wallowing in self-pity, Jenny had forgotten to eat lunch, and the knots in her belly reminded her in no uncertain terms that this transgression would not go unanswered. A location followed his acknowledgement— *Shakti Dome, Toumba level, Atalanta Arms*—presumably, his apartment.

The doors to the elevator opened, revealing Hathor Dome's main transit hub. A short corridor, as wide as a city street, led to Ishtar Plaza. From there, she heard rhythmic drumming accompanied by Devoran horns and guttural singing. The central park area of the plaza resembled a festival, dotted with tents and pavilions, curved graceful Devoran-style structures.

Jenny had heard there would be an increased number of Devorans on Cytherea for the next several months, but she hadn't realized they would be so visible and present. A crowd of Devorans lined the edge of the park and cheered. She noticed a brilliant emerald-and-sapphire-hued Devoran standing a head and shoulders taller than the rest of the crowd, a female, Jenny assumed from the traditional ivory-shell-and-feather adornment on her frill. *She must be standing on a podium.* Jenny turned to move in the opposite direction as the Devoran bowed her head. Being caught in a fervent crowd would unacceptably delay her dinner.

She didn't see a human face among the throngs of Devorans assembled in the plaza until she traveled halfway around the promenade toward the Neutron Café. She encountered students agog at the spectacle in the park, while adults appeared indifferent to the commotion, or, in some cases, seemed annoyed. A squad of Devoran soldiers marched past, patrolling the plaza. While observing them, she spotted Zack standing in front of the café, his hands jammed in his pockets.

"Zack!" She waved as she approached him. He returned her wave. She noticed he stood stiff, as if afflicted with rigor mortis, when she hugged him.

"Bariss wants to talk to me about what happened."

"Me too." Jenny peered into the café, packed wall to wall with diners. "Can we go somewhere else? It's too busy in there."

Zack turned and nodded. "Where? I passed the Positron Café on the way here. It's busy, too."

Jenny chewed her lip and pointed down the hallway to the nearest elevator. "Next level down. There's a place I know. Have you ever been to Bit Bytes?"

"No, I heard some other kids talking about it. It's some sort of virtual reality place?"

She led him down the hallway to the lift. "If you have AR implants, you can select several different types of scenery, depending on your mood." During her first year at school, Jenny had configured her augmented reality implants, a component of the ocular implants she received several years ago, to access Bit Byte's systems as well as Cytherea's. Even before they approached it, the heads-up display indicated a two-minute wait until the elevator arrived on their floor.

As they waited, Zack shuffled his feet as he regarded the crowd. "Do you know what's going on? I've never seen it this busy, not even when they redecorated the whole plaza for our holidays last year. There seem to be a lot of Devoran Defense Force troops here, too."

Jenny held up a finger to indicate Zack should wait while she searched through Cytherean News. A twinge of guilt gnawed at her. She should already know current Cytherea events, but preoccupied with her parents' recovery, she paid little attention to things that didn't directly affect her.

9

Found it. "It says Cytherea is being used as a staging area for Confederation citizens who are relocating to Vilicus from Al-Gehara. I don't understand why they're all crowded in Ishtar..."

Jenny whistled. The door to the lift opened, and two bear-like Ersidians exited. She recognized them as students whose parents worked on Cytherea, but she didn't know their names. She and Zack stepped aside, allowing them room to pass.

After they entered the lift and pressed the button to take them to the next level, she turned to Zack. "It looks like the former royal family of Devorus has been allowed to erect a temporary pavilion in Ishtar Plaza."

His eyes widened. "Royal family? Didn't the civil war happen hundreds of years ago?"

From the perspective of the Earth-Alpha Centauri Alliance, formation of the Confederation seemed akin to ancient history. The Devoran civil war, a relatively small conflict as it related to Confederation history, didn't directly affect the EAC, so the subject received little attention in classes not focused specifically on Devoran history. Teachers spent so little time on the war, all Jenny could say for certain was before it occurred, the Devorans lived in the Devoran Empire and after it ended, the Devoran Union.

Jenny tucked a stray lock of hair behind her ear. "I remember reading that members of the family, particularly the former emperor and empress's daughter, still have a lot of political influence, even though they abdicated and renounced their royal status."

Jenny then realized why the Devoran female she saw appeared so tall—the Devoran royal family originated from a sub-species commonly called Noble Devorans and stood at least a head taller than other Devorans.

"Wow, bigwigs here. Maybe that's why all the soldiers are here, too. How long are they here for?" Zack allowed Jenny to exit the lift first and followed her as she led him to Bit Bytes.

"Until the relocation is complete, I guess. A few months, maybe?" As they approached the restaurant, Jenny's AR software kicked in. Beyond the doors, she perceived, through her implants, a Parisian café in the style of earth's early 20th century. In reality, she observed a visual overlay that changed the appearance of furniture and decorations, fooling her brain with its flawless effect.

"Huh. I expected something more... digital, I guess." Zack glanced around the café. Jenny knew from experience he viewed rather ordinary white tables and chairs. She turned off her AR overlay once, and the drab experience convinced her that augmented reality was much more interesting.

"It's a whole different world if you have ocular implants with AR." Jenny took a seat at small round table in the corner. Her implants showed her a window seat overlooking the Seine with the Eiffel Tower in the distance. "It looks like Paris to me."

"I can't wait." Zack reached toward the middle of the table and pressed the button to call a server. An early model bioreplicant lurched toward them.

After placing their orders, Jenny updated Zack on the latest news of her parents. "Papa still can't talk without a machine to help him, but his reconstruction is finished. They still have more work to do to make him look human again."

"So, he has a bunch of metal bits showing where they fixed him?"

Jenny closed her eyes to will away the image of her father's cybernetic visage and nodded. "His face was shattered, and his torso was crushed, so there was a lot of work to do. Mama mostly needed her arms and legs fixed. She's still learning to walk again, and they have her hooked up to some temporary cybernetic muscle stimulators. They're stuck in the hospital on Vilicus until they can travel on their own again."

"Oh." Zack chewed on his lip. "How long will that be?"

"They couldn't say. Another couple of months, I would think. Maybe longer."

Once their meals arrived, they ate quickly, making small talk about their classes in the upcoming semester. Then, Zack and Jenny headed for the transport hub to pick up a travel pod to Shakti Dome. A squad of uniform-clad Devorans exited the pod and marched down the corridor toward the plaza. Jenny assumed they were protection for the nobility.

The travel pod whisked them away. As Zack droned on, fretting over his family's impending move to Vilicus, Jenny's thoughts strayed to a face half-covered with gleaming metal and red eyes glaring at her, yet, showing no sign of recognition— her father trying to remember he had a daughter.

Chapter 3

The apartments in Toumba level of Shakti Dome occupied squat, curved-facade buildings that surrounded a small park. Short-cropped grasses and ornamental shrubs of the grounds framed a double-lobed pond. Fish splashed in the pond as tall, yellow, and violet flowers swayed in the slight breeze provided by the city's air-circulation systems.

The plaza directory showed Zack and Jenny the route to Atalanta Arms. The tallest building surrounding the park, it reached to the top of the dome. Balconies overlooked the greenery, and the two young humans observed families enjoying each other's company in the warm evening air.

For evening, the city's systems darkened the photovoltaic panels at the top of the dome to restrict the amount of light allowed through. Days on Venus, two hundred forty-three Earth days to one Venusian day, were so long Zack had never actually seen night. From what he understood, however, the way the thick atmosphere scattered light around the planet, little variance in luminescence separated night from day.

"Nice place. Way better than our dorms."

Jenny nodded. "It reminds me of our apartment building on Messier Habitat. Our parks are long, though. They kind of stretch end to end." A Bernal sphere, the interior of Messier Habitat resembled a long valley with curved walls. Jenny shared with Zack holoimages of Messier the last time he expressed curiosity about her home.

Together, they rode the elevator to Bariss's apartment on the fifth floor of Atalanta Arms, number 5B. His consort Zaaliah answered the door. The orange-spotted, white Devoran decorated her backward-swept frill with a net of red and yellow jewels. Her lips spread in a pointy-toothed grin. "Zack! Jenny! So good to see you both. Please, come in. Bariss is expecting you."

Decorated in typical Devoran fashion, their apartment featured flowing lines and sweeping curves. Zack noted wall-to-wall art and knickknacks reminiscent of vast seas and expansive beaches. Even their furniture, with its gentle curves and teal-trimmed white upholstery, reminded Zack of the ocean.

13

Zaaliah directed the two human youths to sit on a curved sofa facing the holoviewer as Bariss padded across the tile floor, his claws clicking with each step. "Thanks for stopping by. I know the beginning of the semester is busy, particularly for those of you who don't live here year round."

Bariss sat on the sofa and turned to face Zack and Jenny. "Jenny, how are your parents?"

"They're—" Jenny's voice caught in her throat. She swallowed her emotions. "They're going to be fine. It will be a long recovery, especially for my fath—" Her voice caught again, and she squeezed her eyes shut as she covered her mouth with her hand and stared at the floor.

"Anything you need, just let us know." Bariss turned his attention to Zack. "And you? Everything going all right?"

"I guess." Zack shrugged. "All my parents talked about this summer was moving to Vilicus. Mom isn't sure, but Dad's excited. He says she'll be able to get an even better teaching job there, and we shouldn't worry."

"What does your mother teach?"

"Um, life skills." Zack's mother insisted people needed to learn budgeting, basic cooking techniques, first aid, and the like. He figured if he ever wanted to know any of those things, he could just look them up on the Hypernet.

The Devoran nodded. Zaaliah sat alongside her consort. "A practical subject. Very valuable." Zack's expression must have belied his skepticism, because the female Devoran chuckled and patted his knee. "You'll appreciate it when you're older and living on your own."

Jenny cleared her throat. "Sorry, I'm better now."

"I know it's difficult." Bariss tapped his temple to activate one of his implants. The windows overlooking the park darkened, and soothing, light piano music started playing. "Look, I'm not supposed to be talking about this with you, but I wanted to make sure we were all on the same page before school started."

Zack furrowed his brow. "About the Athosians on Valtra?"

"Or the whole thing with Valtraxians being uplifted by them?" Jenny glanced at Zack, then at Bariss.

"Both." Bariss chuckled. "I'm sure you've noticed the increased number of Devorans on Cytherea, yes?"

They both nodded.

14

"There've been some... disagreements back home about whether the stratocracy has been performing satisfactorily and"—Bariss waved his hand—"Look, just try your best not to speak of either subject, all right? You never know who is listening, and I've heard that members of the former royal family might be coming."

"They're already here." Jenny eyebrows rose. "I saw one of them in Ishtar Plaza. I think she was about to give a speech."

"She?" Bariss snapped his mouth shut with a click of his teeth and eyed Zaaliah. "Princess Valianna?"

Their troop leader's consort crossed her arms over her chest and shook her head. "If she's here, then things are worse than we've been told."

Zack frowned and glanced at the female Devoran. "What's going on?"

"Politics. Devoran politics." Zaaliah forced a smile. "You probably should avoid Ishtar Plaza until they've gone. It has nothing to do with the EAC."

Bariss cast a sidelong glance at Zaaliah and sighed. "I moved here to get away from all that." He waved his hand. "It doesn't matter. Just keep quiet about all things Athosian, and it should be fine. I've already spoken to Dravs and Bob. We can talk more after you're settled, maybe after the Junior Ranger meeting next week."

The Devoran stood and ushered them out, reminding them once again to be careful to whom they spoke and to not speak of the events on Valtra related to Athosians.

Jenny and Zack stood in the hallway, staring at the closed door. Zack threw up his hands. "That's it? He could've just said that in his message."

"He didn't seem like he expected to hear about the Noble Devorans." Jenny tucked a lock of hair behind her ear. He noticed she didn't seem so much taller than he was anymore. They left the way they came, walking through the park rather than around it this time, before bidding each other good night and returning to their separate dorms. The travel pod proceeded to Anahita Dome and Jenny's dorm, en route to Hathor Dome, and Zack's dorm.

"I'll see you around, Zack."

"Yeah, I should finish unpacking." Zack rubbed the back of his neck. "Maybe my new roommate will be there now."

Although Steve lived in a different dorm, he hoped he would still get to see his friend from Alpha Centauri outside of any classes they attended together.

"New roommate? Who is it?"

Zack shrugged and related what Mickey told him. "I didn't even know Steve had a sister. I hope the new guy is easy to get along with."

Jenny squeezed his shoulder. "You'll be fine. Good night."

"Night!" He waved as she exited the travel pod. The doors hissed shut, and the pod whisked Zack away, exiting the dome and speeding along the exterior perimeter of Anahita Dome. The soft amber glow of the Venusian sky permeated the interior of the pod.

His C7 pinged with an incoming voice message. It was from Polly, the Alpha Centaurian student who seemed obsessed with him. "Zack Attack! Where are you? The girly-girls and me are meeting Dravs and Steve at the Neutron Café. Be there!"

Zack sent no reply. As much as he wanted to see Steve again, he'd rather finish getting settled before meeting up with Polly. Some days, Zack felt the universe couldn't lend him enough energy to interact with her.

~ * * * ~

Jenny kept her head tilted downward and avoided meeting anyone's eyes as she walked toward her dorm. It was rude to respond to her classmates' greetings with mere grunts and nods, so avoiding them seemed her best bet. As the evening dragged on, recurring thoughts of her parents worsened her mood. She dared not hope her roommates would be out socializing with other students, so she could slip into her room and her bed without interacting with any of them.

Her pessimism bore fruit; all of her roommates, as well as all the others who shared her dorm cluster, congregated in the common area. Crossing to her room reminded her of shoving her way through a crowded sale, and she forced herself to nod and smile at each person who greeted her. Jenny hurried past attempts to hug or convince her to linger and socialize, and when she reached sanctuary in her room, she shut the door behind her.

16

Her roommates, save for Cait Walsh, had yet to unpack. Arranged around their desks, Astrid and Gabrielle's packs and crates waited for the two cousins to sort through their belongings. Cait, on the other hand, had not gone home over the break, and her area lay in the telltale disarray of one who needed clutter to think and feel comfortable.

Jenny regarded her own bed. Hastily made up, floral pink sheets peeked out from under a solid black bedspread. Gifts from her parents, the sheet pattern featured a higher thread count than standard bed linens students ordered from the fabricators.

"Nothing but the best for our Genevieve," they'd say.

Jenny growled and leapt at the bed. She tore off the comforter and sheets, tossing her pillows across the room. The mattress shifted and nearly toppled off the frame when she yanked at the fitted bottom sheet in her attempt to remove it. The elastic finally gave way and sent her sprawling to the floor. She landed hard on her butt and bit her lip to avoid crying out in surprise. No matter how hard she fought, though, tears came unbidden, and she buried her face in her bedding to hide them.

The door hissed open, and the clamor of half-a-dozen conversations snapped her out of her frustration-fueled rage. Closing, it muffled the noise from the common area.

"Jenny?" She recognized the voice as that of Kim Hiriko, a fourth-year student hailing from Kaku Habitat—one of the EAC's Saturnian colonies—who shared one of the rooms in her dorm cluster.

Jenny concealed her face in the bedding she held. "What?"

"Are you all right? We heard a commotion. The others are worried."

Jenny wiped her face and stood, keeping her back toward Hiri as she nodded. "Fine. I'm fine. I just wanted to change my sheets."

Hiri stepped around Jenny and handed her one of the pillows. "I see that. How are your parents?" Long strands of dark hair escaped her ponytail, and sideswept bangs framed her warm, bronze face and large emerald eyes.

Jenny squeezed her eyes shut and bit her lip to keep it from trembling. Hiri touched her arm. "I'm sorry. I'm here if you want to talk. We all just want to help."

17

She nodded and sat down on the edge of her bed. News of her parents' accident traveled through the dorms like wildfire. Half her class walked on eggshells around her; the other half offered to help. Jenny wanted neither.

"For years, I just wanted my father to pay attention to me, to show me that he cared." Jenny hugged the pillow tight against her body as Hiri sat down next to her. "He"—she sucked in a ragged breath and sniffled—"he doesn't even know who I am now!"

As Jenny sobbed, Hiri put her arm around her shoulder. "He will remember."

She shook her head. "I don't know. It's like he's not even the same person."

"As the brain heals, his memories will return." Hiri gave Jenny a gentle shake before tapping the side of her own head. "I know."

"How..." Jenny regarded Hiri. "How do you know?"

Hiri brushed away her straight, black hair from where it had fallen around her face. "About five years ago, I was almost killed in an accident. My skull was crushed. They fixed me. I remember almost everything from before the accident now."

She took Jenny's hand and squeezed it. "There are a few memories that are missing, but all the people? I remember all of them from before the accident. It just takes time." Hiri chuckled. "I probably looked worse than your father does right now. They had to replace my eyes, most of my skull, my jaw, my teeth. My head is so hard now, I have to be careful, or I'll split the skin when I hit it on something. You've never heard anyone scream as loud as my little sister that time I knocked my head on a tree branch a couple of years ago and peeled away part of my scalp. It didn't really hurt that much, but there were about two-and-a-half centimeters of titanium-alloy skull catching the sun."

Jenny winced at Hiri's graphic description. Her mother told her the same thing about her father's memories, but with much less confidence. "I hope you're right."

18

Chapter 4

Upon his return, Zack found the common area of his dorm deserted. The furniture, in complete disarray, served as the only audience for the activated holoviewer. A news reporter stood in front of a digital representation of Saturn, illustrating the route for the upcoming regatta; a competition for solar sailing ships touring the Saturnian moons.

As he avoided cushions strewn about the room like rubble from a collapsed building, he hoped Susan and Victoria would decide on the correct arrangement for the furniture before he went to bed. He heard soft voices coming from inside his room and paused before opening the door. One voice belonged to Ix; the other, he assumed, belonged to the new student.

He opened the door. Ix, perched on its nest, gesticulated with four arms as it told the story of their trip to Bestic. Across the room, a student wearing little more than a pair of shorts over his head-to-toe black-spotted reddish-brown fur sat on what had been Steve's bed. A red bag sat next to him. The student's triangular ears swiveled to face Zack before he turned his dark-furred muzzle in the young human's direction.

Is he a Kerrolian? Maybe a Traxian? I can never keep them straight. He tried to remember what he learned about the two, closely related species. *Traxians have upright ears, or do Kerrolians? Traxians are vegetarians, I think. I wish I could see his teeth.*

Ix paused its story. "Kaneer, this is my friend, Zack Jackson."

"Um, hello?" Zack shut the door behind him and seated himself at his desk. The new student hopped off his bed and offered a fur-covered, clawed hand to Zack.

As Zack took it, the student bowed. Pressing his nose against the back of Zack's hand, he inhaled deeply several times before standing straight again. "You are Terran."

Zack glanced at Ix and then to Kaneer. "Yeah, I'm human."

"Yes, but you are from Terra."

"The human olfactory sense is not that keenly developed." Ix settled in so only his top two arms remained free. "They cannot distinguish by smell where each other are from.

19

Kaneer cocked his head as his black tongue protruded from between his lips. "Pity." He bowed again. "This one is Julani-Kaneer zin Fallah Hammurabi Al-Gehara. Zack Jackson may call this one Kaneer."

Zack's mind reeled at the rapid-fire introduction. *I'll never remember a name that complicated.* "Nice to meet you, Kaneer. Where are you from?" He didn't want to appear ignorant and ask the new student about his species.

Kaneer huffed. "Al-Gehara." His tone was that of one scolding a child for not listening.

Zack remembered hearing that in Kaneer's name. "Oh, I haven't heard of that planet."

The Valtraxian chittered for a moment. "It is the planet where the rebellion started."

"The rebel..." Zack stared at Ix before he remembered. "Oh! The one that replaced the Devoran Empire with the Confederation? Oh yeah, I remember that now from Confederation History." He scratched his head. "Sorry, a lot happened this summer. Sometimes I feel like whenever I learn something new, old stuff gets pushed out of my brain."

"It is fine." Kaneer returned to his seat on the edge of his bed. "I believe you were really asking what species this one is. This one is Kerrolian. We do not understand why humans have such trouble telling Kerrolians and Traxians apart." He stroked his fluffy tail. "They have pitiful tails, not this magnificence. And stupid ears."

Zack kicked off his shoes. He shoved them under his desk before swiveling his chair and laying his feet on his bed. "You're the first Kerrolian I've ever met. Are you the first one to come to Cytherean Academy?"

"First ever? This one does not think so." Kaneer rummaged through his bag and produced a file with which he smoothed the claws on his hands. "This one's parents are relocating to Vilicus, and they heard this is the best school in the EAC."

"Hey, my parents are thinking of doing that, too! Is everyone moving to Vilicus?" Zack pursed his lips. "Why don't you say 'I'?"

Kaneer dropped his hands into his lap and peered over his muzzle at Zack. "This one is too young to have earned the Right of Recognition. Even Father has not, though Mother, Julani, has. Father is very proud of her."

20

Zack shifted in his seat. "What do you have to do to earn the Right of Recognition?"

Kaneer shrugged, and his ears drooped a bit as he returned to filing his claws. "It varies. Great accomplishment, saving lives, being very, very old. It is a great honor. This one hopes something will come up over the next several years during school to allow Kaneer to be recognized."

"Ersidians talk about honor a lot." Zack fingered the braid of Mungus's hair at his waist.

"Yes. They talk."

"I was just telling Kaneer about our trip to Bestic where we received our honor braids." Ix clicked its mandibles together.

Zack turned to face the Valtraxian. "Yeah, when did you get yours? I don't remember you getting it on Bestic. Did Mungus send it to you later or something?"

"I was not present when you and Jenny received yours." Ix pressed one of its hands against its thorax. "Mungus gave me mine later, when you were sleeping. The painkillers you were given were quite strong."

"Oh, heh, yeah. I remember those." Mostly, Zack recalled how goofy he felt after leaving the hospital. He rubbed the tender spot on his arm where Xal bit him over the summer. "I hope I can avoid any serious injuries this year. It's getting old, getting hurt all the time."

Kaneer snorted. "If you keep getting hurt doing Junior Ranger activities, maybe you should quit doing them."

Frowning, Zack stared at his hands and sighed. "That's what my parents seem to think, too. I'm not quitting, though, even if they won't let me go on any more excursions."

He tried to change their mind after coming home from Valtra, but to no avail. His father's strenuous objection, shared by his mother, redoubled after seeing Zack's gnawed arm. He and Ix spent the next couple of hours telling Kaneer about their Junior Ranger expeditions. By the time the conversation wound down, Mickey returned. After introductions were made, they all decided to shut off their lights and at least pretend to go to bed, in case anyone tried to enlist them to rearrange the common area's furniture.

~   *   *   *   ~

21

Hiri helped Jenny obtain new sheets from the fabricator, then helped her clean up the mess before any of their dorm mates decided to turn in for the night. Jenny waited until her roommates were asleep before pulling on a track suit and slipping out to the common area. She sought to avoid questions from them, no matter how well intentioned they were.

The holoviewer bathed the common area with shifting light from news reports. Hiri and Verrak sat in easy chairs, watching the silent screen. Jenny assumed they had the sound directed into their implants. She noted the broadcast frequency in a display at the bottom corner of her vision, but she elected to just nod an acknowledgement of the two as she left the dorm.

The dim glow of the night cycle lights illuminated the corridor just enough to allow Jenny to see where she stepped. The students who arrived that day were in their rooms, either unpacking or sleeping. More would arrive the next day and the day after that. The third day started the term. She hoped focusing on schoolwork would distract her from her parents' situation enough that she'd finally be able to sleep through the night.

She spent the next several hours wandering the halls of Anahita Dome, first leaving the dorms of Skolio level and taking the stairs to Mytikas level where Anahita's shops and restaurants were located. Most were either closed or in the process of closing as she wandered, keeping her thoughts fixed on her classes.

Literature and Composition 305, Devoran III, Mathematics 313, Physical Education, Exobotany 301, Civics 301, and Life Skills II. To help her remember the names of the professors to whom she was assigned, she repeated her schedule to herself. Some were easy. She studied under Professor Hartnell for botany last year. Coach Dagon, of course. The ex-military Ersidian barked orders at his gym classes as if they were raw recruits, making him impossible to forget. She knew of her Devoran language professor, too, Professor Troughton, or Headmaster Troughton as he insisted students refer to him. The rest of the faculty under whom she'd study this term were unknown to her.

The top-level plaza of Anahita Dome contained shops spread throughout, unlike in Hathor Dome where across multiple levels, shops surrounded the central park. Few

22

students came here; the stores offered more expensive options intended for adult workers and military families living on Cytherea. Jenny stopped before the window of DeForest Outfitters, a manufacturer of top-quality outdoor gear, like the Junior Ranger uniform her parents purchased for her.

Shops like these sold patterns for use with home fabricators or fabricated garments to order and provided the patterns for future use. New fashions on display in the store window, appeared much like last year's but with slight changes.

"You'd probably insist I have all new clothes for this year, wouldn't you, Papa?" She confronted her reflection in the darkened window. An obvious symptom, dark circles under her eyes announced her insomnia. She paid no heed to the sound of approaching footsteps until a dark shape appeared behind her in the window.

"Are you a student here? It's late to be shopping, don't you think?"

She turned to face a hulking Ersidian security guard. His shirt strained to contain his bulging gut. The musky smell he exuded reminded her of Mungus. A thick white slash marred the black fur covering the Ersidian's face, drawing a vertical line from his scalp, over his left eye, and down his neck.

Jenny brushed her hair away from the honor braid Mungus had given her. After her first call with her parents upon arriving at her grandparents' home in Marseilles, she took Xal's suggestion and incorporated a bead into it to commemorate them. The stark white of the shell from which it was made contrasted her dark hair. "I couldn't sleep. My parents are... unwell."

The guard's dark, beady eyes focused on the braid, and he sniffed the air. She assumed he didn't possess implants; Ersidians only reluctantly altered their bodies with cybernetics when medically necessary. "You earned that?"

"I did. I helped save his life."

"We were told two humans had been given honor braids by a member of Clan Stonetalon. A Valtraxian, too."

Jenny nodded. "Zack Jackson and Ix. They're students here, too. Over in Hathor Dome."

"Well, you should be careful where you wander this late." The Ersidian gestured for Jenny to walk alongside him. "There are many transients here right now. Devorans, Kerrolians, humans from across the EAC, even some Ersidians, all looking for a better life on Vilicus. Maybe some of them are running from their old lives. We can't have eyes everywhere at once."

He led her toward the lift. His body radiated heat like an old furnace. "You should speak to the school nurse if you're really having trouble sleeping. He might be able to help."

A light flashed on the comm unit on his belt. He put a hand up to his ear. "Grodo here."

He paused to listen. Jenny's implants told her the guard's comm unit received an incoming transmission, but listening in would require her to possess military-grade implants, or illegal modifications.

"Yeah, all right. I'm on my way." He pressed the call button for the lift. He gestured inside as the doors opened.

Jenny stepped in as he held the door with his hand. "I'm not an expert on reading humans, but you look like you need rest. Try warm milk. Be safe, now."

"Thank you." Jenny waited for the door to close. Her hand hovered over the controls as she decided where to go next. She finally decided to return to Skolio level and proceed to her room.

She found Hiri still up when she returned, but Verrak had retired for the night. The young woman watched news footage of the Saturnian Regatta. Hiri patted the seat next to her. "If you can't sleep, sit with me a while. I'm sure I can tell you a story or two that'll put you out."

Jenny plopped down alongside her and nodded toward the screen. "Watching that might do it."

"Want to talk about it?" Hiri studied Jenny's face.

"No, not again. Not now. Not yet. Take your pick." Noticing her friend's hand moving in her direction, she folded her own in her lap and kept her eyes on the screen. The solar sailing ships glided in formation over Saturn's rings, diaphanous, insect-like wings catching the sunlight and propelling them in their parade prior to the start of the race.

"Fair enough. We'll just sit quietly, then." Hiri smiled, before reclining in the sofa and sighing.

Jenny didn't bother tuning her implants to the channel of the holoviewer broadcast. As they sat in silence watching the coverage of the regatta, she finally succumbed to fatigue and nodded off.

Chapter 5

The next two days passed swiftly for Zack. The chaotic nature of the start of the term almost overwhelmed him, but he took comfort in the fact that most of the time, he avoided both Dravs and Polly because of their busy schedules.

Once again, he appreciated having physical education at the end of the day. Coach Dagon wore him out without fail, and he couldn't imagine attending a class which required him to think after one of the Ersidian's workouts. The rest of his classes, EAC History, Literature and Composition 201, Astrosciences 201, Devoran Cultural Studies, Mathematics 201, and Ersidian II, were pretty much standard for a second-year student. Allowed some latitude, older students chose several electives and concentrations of study, such as which branch of science they wanted to specialize and which language to immerse themselves, but second-year students like Zack followed the standard core curriculum.

Dravs caught up with him on the last free day before classes started while he and his fellow Junior Ranger, Xal, examined an extracurricular activity listing. They sat in the rear corner of the Neutron Café, lucky enough to grab a table before Ishtar Plaza filled with Devoran admirers of Princess Valianna.

"Hey, Zack!" The blue Devoran bounded toward them. "You're rushing, rushing, rushing around so much it's been hard to catch up to you."

Zack snorted and shoved his hands in his pockets to keep the Devoran from grabbing them. "Yeah, I—"

"It's obvious he's avoiding you." Xal fixed his eyes on the listing. "Polly, too."

Zack felt his face grow hot, as it turned beet red. Dravs's jaw dropped open, but then he snapped it shut and grinned. "Give me some credit, Zack. You told me you're not interested, and I get that. Unlike a certain Alpha Centaurian, I can take a hint, especially when you're direct."

He thrust a clawed hand in Zack's direction. "We're still friends, though, right?"

Zack shook his hand and nodded. "Yeah, sorry. It's just... I've got a lot on my mind, you know?" He slumped and rested his arms on the table. Every time he found himself thinking of his parents' enthusiasm at leaving their home and friends behind to move to Vilicus and Jenny's parents undergoing reconstructive surgery, the weight of it all pressed down on him

"Anyway..." Dravs scooted around the table to share the screen Xal studied. "We all agreed to sign up for some sort of fighting class for Xal, right?"

The Ersidian snuffled. "You guys said you'd sign up for self-defense classes with me." He held a hand up to his mouth and coughed. "Krunk. Stupid allergies. You'd think they'd keep the filters in here clean."

"That's why we're here, Dravs." Zack tapped the screen. "What about this one? Judo? I hear it's all about throwing people around."

"Nah, we want Kova Kasi." Dravs pointed to another option. "I've been reading up on these since we got back from Valtra, and that's the one we want. It's been specially developed over the last couple of centuries so that most species in the Confederation can compete against each other."

Zack raised his eyebrow as he regarded the Devoran. "Humans, too? We're not part of the Confederation."

"Yeah, humans, too. If Xal didn't want you to throw him around in Judo, I doubt you'd get him to budge. It'd be like lifting a house."

Xal shoved Dravs. "I'm not that fat."

The Devoran laughed. "I didn't say you were. You're twice Zack's size, though. You'd smoosh him like a trogberry. That's why we should learn Kova Kasi."

"Sounds good to me." Zack eyed the young Ersidian.

Xal scrunched up his brow before nodding. "It makes sense, I guess." He tapped the screen a few times, then passed the tablet to Zack.

"Tuesday and Thursday evenings?" Zack waited for Xal's confirmation before signing up and passing the tablet to Dravs.

After adding his name to the Kova Kasi class roster, Dravs ordered a plate of Bornan cow knuckles for them to share. "Hey, have you two seen the princess?"

Zack shook his head. He tried to avoid the crowded park the last couple of days. Devorans gathered there were a bit too exuberant for Zack's taste. Xal also had not seen her.

Dravs slapped the table and grinned. "She's so gorgeous. Tall, stunning colors. I tell ya, I'd lick her feet clean if she walked a mile in slimy mud."

Xal curled his lip. "Ugh. That's gross."

A black-scaled Devoran with red eyes sidled up to Dravs. She patted the top of his head before taking the seat alongside him. "Aw, baby brother has his first crush."

Dravs smacked away her hand. "Shut up, Kat. She's not my first crush." He glanced at Zack and winked.

Zack choked on his beverage as Dravs grinned. Ducking his head, Zack coughed to conceal his blushing. Grateful for the dim lighting in this corner of the café, he kept his head down until he thought the color of his face had returned to normal.

"Well, don't get your hopes up, Stunt. She's too old for a hatchling like you, and you're too ordinary for a noble like her." Kat waved the waiter over and placed an order.

"Stop calling me Stunt. I grew three centimeters last year." Dravs glanced over his shoulder toward the center of the park. "I know I don't have a chance with her. It's just a fantasy, that's all."

Rubbing his snout for a moment, he faced his sister. "Why are you here, anyway? You never hang out with us."

"You're not the only one who wants a closer look at the princess, you know." Kat gestured toward Zack and Xal. "What about these two? Are they smitten with her as much as you?"

Zack reclined in his chair and regarded Xal. The Ersidian smiled a crooked grin before shaking his head. "No. I don't do scales. Zack?"

"Not me. Xal and I were just looking over the extracurricular activities when Dravs showed up. Besides, everyone's telling me to avoid Ishtar Plaza, but I can't give up eating here."

If he had enough system credits for it, he'd eat at The Neutron Café every day; it was his favorite place to eat on Cytherea. Most of his food allowance already went to them anyway. Eating in the school cafeterias was free, but they didn't serve Quantum Cola. While the pizza toppings tasted fine, the crust resembled warmed-over cardboard. Zack heard the academy upgraded all the cafeteria food fabricators over the break, so students could select whatever they wanted from a pre-determined list created by school dieticians.

A passing student caught Zack's eye. A French-blue dress complimented her sepia skin, and she wore her dark, red-highlighted hair pulled back in complex box braids.

He watched her as Kat and Dravs expounded on their admiration for Princess Valiana. Their adoration bordered on blind worship in Zack's opinion, so he just smiled and nodded from time to time and tried to enjoy his meal, probably the last from the Neutron Café for several days.

Zack sipped his drink. *Hard work starts tomorrow.*

~ * * * ~

It took Jenny the better part of the next day to work out the crick in her neck that resulted from falling asleep on the sofa next to Hiri. The nagging pain made even more irritating all the trivial, last-minute tasks required before the start of the term.

She avoided her roommates and rebuffed their attempts to engage her in conversation. Jenny wanted nothing more than to go down to the gym's hangar and reacquaint herself with her cloud glider, maybe take care of some maintenance tasks she must perform anyway before her first flight of the semester. The quickest route there would take her through Hathor Dome and into Ishtar Plaza, the hub of Cytherea's central dome. She didn't feel like encountering many strangers, so Jenny pulled up a map on her cortical implant and took an alternate route through various utility corridors and office sectors.

While occupants of the offices watched her with furrowed brows and expressions of confusion, no one questioned her as she passed. Compared with the chaos of Ishtar Plaza, the halls appeared deserted. The utility corridors even more so. She passed several Valtraxian maintenance engineers and other humans wearing utility jumpsuits, but they all kept to their business and left her to hers.

She observed a few students running laps in the gym when she arrived.

Coach Dagon sorted through gravball equipment near the hangar door. The Ersidian glanced up as she approached. "DuBois. What brings you down here today?"

Jenny gestured toward the maintenance bay doors. "I want to work on my cloud glider."

"They've all been checked out. Yesterday, I think. They don't need any work." He tossed a ball into a crate filled with similar ones.

"I need to check mine. It's important."

He put his hands on his hips. The tan-and-brown furred Ersidian stood at least a head taller than she did, his black nose twitching as he regarded her. "Why?"

"It keeps my mind off things."

"Things? What are you—fifteen? Sixteen? You're a cub!" He put a hand almost as big as her head on her shoulder. "What could possibly bother you so much you want to dig around in a greasy engine for fun?"

Jenny did not wish to discuss her problems with the Ersidian PE coach. "Maybe I find digging around in greasy engines fun."

"Maybe." Coach Dagon snorted and leaned closer. "But that's not been my observation."

Jenny sighed and then clenched her jaw. "My parents were nearly killed in a shuttle accident at Vilicus this summer. Working with my hands keeps me focused on everything but how horrible their injuries are. And the botany lab is closed to students right now."

"Oh." Dagon squeezed her shoulder. "All right." He walked her to the maintenance bay doors and opened them for her.

"Hey, Davis! You've got company."

Davis? Roger? Jenny swore under her breath. The sandy-haired boy scrubbed the engine intake on his cloud glider with a handheld wire brush, watching her with wide eyes as she entered. Jenny ignored him.

"Jenny?"

She spun on him. "After what you and your friends did to Zack, you do not get to speak to me. Ever."

His mouth dropped open, and he stepped backward. He nodded and stared at the floor. "Yeah, about that. I'm sorry. I—"

"It is Zack you need to apologize to, not me." She stepped toward him and poked him in the chest. "If he forgives you, I might. Maybe. For now, leave me alone."

"Yes, all right." He returned his attention to his engine.

Jenny called up her cloud glider on the console. She waited for it to be loaded into position from the docking racks at the top of the bay. Streaks marred its surface where water air-dried on the paint, but it otherwise appeared factory fresh. She ran her hands along the cold metal of the wing, feeling for imperfections, ultimately verifying Coach Dagon's assertion that the maintenance teams had been thorough. She glanced toward Roger, elbow deep in his engine. "Did you clean this one?"

He stopped and cleared his throat. "Yeah, maybe. I've spent all summer scrubbing these and touching up the paint." He chuckled. "Part of my punishment."

"It looks good."

"Thanks."

Jenny inspected her cloud glider's engine intakes. They were as clean as when they were new. She removed one of the filters and rotated it in her hands. It, too, was pristine. The fuel cells were fully charged. Both the backup power supply's capacity and engine-coolant-level indicators read full. Finally, she checked the restraint system. Visible wear marks on the straps indicated where the buckles fastened. Noticing the belts were no longer set to her specifications, she adjusted them. Performing the minor modification now would save preparation time before her next flight. She wanted to be out there right now, flying among the clouds.

The Venusian sky would have to wait.

Chapter 6

Polly caught up with Zack as he left his room and proceeded to his first class of the term. "Zack McAvoidin' Me!"

Her purple ponytail bounced as she jogged toward him. She took his arm, as they headed down the corridor toward the lift.

"Sorry, things have been busy." Zack kept his eyes fixed on the floor indicator above the door. "I feel like I'm being pulled in every direction at once."

They entered the lift, and he pressed the button to take them down to the classroom levels.

Another student approached the lift, but waved off Zack's attempt to hold the door for him. "I'll wait. I'm going up!"

Polly's grin widened as the doors shut. "Just you and me now."

Zack held his breath for the inevitable. Polly turned his head to face her and held his gaze for a moment before stepping backward.

"You're really not into me, are you?"

"I keep telling you, I'm not really into anybody right now."

Polly released his arm and huffed. "Barbara was right. I'm such an idiot."

"No, I don't think—"

The doors opened, and Polly left Zack mid-sentence. "See you around, Zackarooni."

He managed to gather himself and exit before the doors shut again. Polly disappeared into the crowd of students milling in the corridor. First-years, identifiable by their wide-eyed expressions of terror, appeared lost as they all tried to find their classrooms. Returning students moved with purpose, dodging slower students like obstacles on a training course.

Zack found his first period classroom, EAC History with Professor Maureen Stantion. The room, one of many large, tiered lecture halls, served as the setting for several of his classes. Dravs and Kat waved to him from the middle row of the middle tier of seats. Seeing no one else he recognized, he made his way to them and sat alongside them.

Kat ran a clawed finger around his ear. "You look a little lost."

"I think... Polly just broke up with me..."

31

"Huh. You always said you weren't together." Dravs cocked his head as he regarded Zack.

"I didn't think we were." Zack rubbed an itch on his nose, but he had little time to sort through the encounter before Professor Stantion took the lectern and began. A plump older woman with steel-grey hair falling around her shoulders, she cleared her throat and launched her introductory lecture.

Zack found the class more interesting than he expected. After reviewing the topics they would cover during the term and restating the same classroom rules every teacher in Cytherean Academy seemed to employ, she dismissed them.

The students wasted no time vacating the room. Dravs checked his chronometer as they climbed the steps toward the exit. "Huh. I think that's the fastest first period I've had. She finished in twenty minutes."

"I'll see you boys later." Kat put her arm around Zack and Dravs's shoulders before lowering her head level with theirs.

Zack wondered if he would ever catch up to the lanky Devoran in height.

"I'm going to waste some time in Ishtar Plaza and see if I can catch sight of her royal beauty."

"I'll go with you, Sis." Dravs and Kat left Zack to his own devices. He hesitated, considering following after them but instead sat on a nearby bench. His next class, Literature and Composition, would be held just a few rooms down from the one he just exited.

He read his history book while he waited. By the time first period officially ended, he finished the reading assignment. A familiar face caught his eye in the crowd of students. Two of them, in fact.

Roger and Lloyd. Roger stared straight at him, and Zack saw the recognition in his eyes. He shoved Lloyd away just as the other bully turned in Zack's direction and pointed down the hall. They laughed and quickened their pace.

Releasing a breath he hadn't realized he'd been holding, Zack gathered his things and joined the crowd. *Maybe without Barry, they'll leave me alone this year.*

~ * * * ~

32

Jenny's hopes her classes would distract her from thoughts of her parents proved unfounded. The longer the first day dragged on, the more she felt stuck in a time warp, moving at the pace of a sluggish snail, and the more her thoughts turned toward them.

She held herself together until the final class of the day: life skills. Her instructor, a fair-skinned, dark-haired woman who, based on her accent, clearly hailed from Messier Habitat, confirmed as much during her introduction.

"I am Corinne Marceau. If it is not obvious by the way I speak, I am from Messier Habitat, and you may all call me Cori. Or Corinne, if you prefer."

The teacher's voice and speech cadence reminded Jenny of her mother, Amélie. Stumbling out of her seat, Jenny banged her shin on a neighbor's desk as she fled the room. Cori continued speaking, undeterred by the interruption. Jenny heard the class giggle behind her, and she pushed her way through the door as it slid open at what seemed to be a glacial pace.

Only a pair of academy staff and a few cleaning robots occupied the corridor, so she sat on a bench near the room and covered her face with her hands as she tried to pull herself together. The nightmare image of her father's metallic, grinning skull flashed in her mind.

She heard the click of heels approaching. To her dismay, they stopped before her.

"I know not all students are fans of the life skills curriculum, but that was a reaction I've never seen before."

Jenny dropped her hands into her lap. "Your voice..." she spoke softly in French. "It sounds like my mother's."

Cori sat next to her. "You're a third-year student. Is being away from them really this traumatic?"

"No, you don't understand." Jenny shook her head. "They're on Vilicus, recovering from an accident. My father can't remember who I am. My mother—" The words caught in her throat.

"Ah, I see." Cori patted Jenny's shoulder. "There are others who teach this subject. I'll see to it they let you rearrange your schedule. Perhaps Winston..."

"That's not necessary." Jenny wiped her nose and met the professor's eyes. "I will be fine. I just wasn't expecting it, that's all."

"You must be very close to your parents." Crow's feet appeared at the corners of Cori's deep blue, almost violet, eyes as she offered Jenny a smile.

"It's complicated." Jenny sniffled again and straightened up. "I'm sorry for the disruption."

"It's quite all right, dear. Go back to your dorm. You can stay late tomorrow to make up for today."

It would cut into her cloud-gliding simulator time, but Jenny preferred returning to her dorm than reentering the classroom after making such a scene. She nodded and stood.

Cori touched Jenny's arm. "What is your name, dear?"

"Jenny DuBois."

"Feel better, Jenny. I will see you tomorrow."

Tempted to go to Ishtar Plaza for a bit before it became crowded after classes let out, Jenny decided to do so would be rude to Cori. She, instead, took solace in the silence of her dorm room. Bereft of roommates for at least another hour, she found it the perfect place to sit and relax.

She turned on the holoviewer and selected a period film to watch. She only half paid attention while her mind wandered. The plot seemed to cover a fictitious account of the early days of Earth's space colonization efforts, embellished for maximum drama, of course. She was pretty sure humans never encountered insect-like bipeds with acid for blood.

Midway through the film, half the cast had been horribly killed, and her roommates returned. With a crooked smile on her face, Hiri leaned over the back of the couch, watching the tension in the film grow. "Ditch class to watch documentaries?"

"Ha!" Jenny tilted her head to regard the other young woman. "These ships have magic gravity. I think this film is really old."

Hiri sat alongside Jenny. "Looks like it. I'm surprised any of these ancient things still exist. Was this filmed in only two dimensions?"

Jenny shut off the holoviewer. "Well, I made a fool of myself in life skills today, so I figured anything would be better. How was your day?"

"Lots of lectures, no content." Hiri shrugged. "Just like always on the first day. Feel like grabbing a bite to eat with me?"

Now that food entered the conversation, Jenny's stomach reminded her that she skipped lunch. She put her hand on her belly and smiled. "Food would be good. Going to the cafeteria?"

"I was thinking Bit Bytes, and then the Rampage Room."

An AR-enabled area occupying the rear parlor of Bit Bytes, the Rampage Room featured environments expressly designed for customers to skin themselves as towering monsters over hapless cities. Jenny heard of it, but never indulged. She did not often feel a desire to wreak havoc of that nature.

Today, however...

"That sounds like fun!"

~ * * * ~

Zack remembered how exhausted he felt at the end of the first day last term. This year, he felt tired, but not worn out. His newfound endurance pleased him, and he felt grateful all the hard work Coach Dagon put him through the previous year paid off.

The bounce in his step disappeared when he entered the dorm and heads turned. Barbara and Polly sat chatting with Susan and Ix. The twins watched him as he entered.

"Hi, everyone!" Zack waved and pretended their stares didn't bother him.

Ix cocked its head. "I do not believe you are being fair to Zack."

Polly wheeled on the Valtraxian. "I thought you were on my side!"

"I offered a sympathetic tympanic membrane to your plight." Ix skittered to Zack's side. "But I never said I agreed with your assessment."

Polly huffed and threw up her hands. "I should've known the boys would stick together."

Before Zack retorted, Ix drew himself up to stand on only four legs. "As I have repeatedly stated: I. Am. Not. A. Boy. I do

35

not possess gonads or reproductive organs of any sort. Please do not use gender-specific pronouns when referring to me. 'It' is acceptable."

Barbara tapped her sister's arm. "Drop it, Polly. I told you you were being too aggressive with the Earther."

Crossing her arms over her chest, Susan sat on the backrest of the sofa. "No, keep going. This is better than any of the shows I watch."

Dragging her sister into their room, Barbara glanced over her shoulder at Susan. "That's not helpful. Show's over. Sorry, Zack."

"Nuts." Susan dropped her arms and her smile and then turned her attention to Ix. "We're still on for tonight?"

The Valtraxian stroked Zack's arm and chittered. "Unless Zack needs me."

"Huh? No, I'm fine. Are you two going on a date or something?"

Susan laughed. "No! It's helping me with some math. I'm having trouble in geometry."

"Oh. No, go ahead, Ix." Zack sympathized with Susan. While he didn't personally find geometry all that difficult, he found many aspects of algebra challenging, especially at the beginning of the term after an entire summer of not utilizing it.

Ix followed Zack into their room. Kaneer lay on his bed, reading from his tablet.

He glanced up at them as they entered. "Is the drama over, Zack Jackson?"

"I guess." Zack tossed his pack on his bed before sitting at his desk. "I probably shouldn't have avoided her these last few days."

Kaneer rolled into a sitting position and set aside his tablet. "This one does not understand human courtship rituals. Could not Polly Wright determine by your scent you were unreceptive to her advances?"

"I don't smell that much. Do I?" Zack sniffed his armpit. He showered after PE and didn't detect any offensive odor.

Ix chittered and moved closer to Zack. "I detect nothing I determine offensive. Kaneer, humans do not consciously communicate with pheromones."

The Kerrolian's eyes widened. "How do you people understand each other?"

36

"A lot of people don't." Zack turned away and faced the wall. He picked up the orb from his desk and rolled the spherical lump of iron in his hands. He nodded goodbye to Ix as the Valtraxian left to meet with Susan. After several minutes of staring at the orb, he turned to Kaneer. "Want to go get something to eat?"

The Kerrolian jumped off the bed. "Yes, Zack Jackson. This one has great hunger!"

"Cafeteria? Or do you want to brave Ishtar Plaza?"

"Hm." Kaneer stroked his muzzle. "The smell of Devoran is very strong in the plaza right now. This one prefers the cafeteria."

"Suits me." Happy to oblige Kaneer's preference, Zack reflected on the excess of system credits he spent at the restaurants so far. The two students discussed their classes as they walked. Kaneer's complaints about how little actual instruction occurred during the first day sounded familiar to Zack. In the cafeteria, he recognized many of his classmates, though he did not see Steve. He assumed the other boy ate with his sister in the cafeteria in his dorm.

After getting their food, Kaneer regaled Zack about Al-Gehara and how his family sought a better life on Vilicus. Zack let the Kerrolian talk as he replayed the evening's events in his head. He couldn't decide if he felt glad or sad about the unexpected confrontation with Polly.

Chapter 7

The next few days passed in a blur. Coach Dagon's PE class and Tuesday evening's Kova Kasi class exhausted Zack before midweek. At least his fears about another confrontation with Polly proved unfounded, as she behaved as if they'd never been more than acquaintances. Barbara took him aside one morning as Polly bounded off to class. "Don't worry about her. She'll get over it soon."

Zack scratched his head. "So she is mad at me? Because I can't really tell."

Barbara laughed as they made their way toward the lift. "She's mostly disappointed you weren't ready for her and mad at herself for not listening to me. Look, I get it. I read up on you Earthers before we started here. Polly didn't want to listen, as usual. Like I said, she'll be chasing another guy before you know it." Barbara brushed her dark, purple-highlighted hair off her face.

Zack narrowed his eyes. "So, how are you two sisters again? I mean, she's so crazy and you're—"

"Not?" Barbara grinned. "Polly's trying too hard to be different from me, if you want my opinion. It's all an act. Believe me, when we're in our room and no one else is around, she's just as quiet and subdued as I am."

They entered the lift, and Zack pressed the button to take them down to the school level. "Well, between her and Kaneer, I think there's plenty of craziness to go around."

"No argument from me."

They went their separate ways once they exited the elevator. This term, they shared few classes, and Zack shared none with Polly. During his astrosciences class with Professor Bailey, he received a message from Steve inviting him to the VR pods that night. Zack readied a message in reply before he realized his friend's request conflicted with the first Junior Ranger meeting.

He deleted the message and declined, disappointed; their schedules didn't intersect at all this term. Zack still expected classes at Cytherean Academy to resemble schools on Earth, where one would see the same people year after year. Instead, hardly anyone he made friends with the past year shared his schedule this year.

The only class in which he encountered a few familiar faces was PE. He shared that class with the same Ersidians from the previous year, as well as Dravs and Kat. Before class began, Coach Dagon approached Zack. "Jackson!"

"Yes, Coach?" Zack had barely changed and exited the locker room when he heard the Ersidian calling.

"Hang back after class. I have a special task for you."

"Okay..."

Coach Dagon clapped him on the shoulder. "You're still interested in cloud gliding, right?"

Zack nodded, unable to even feign enthusiasm due to fatigue. He wanted only to rest and enjoy a leisurely dinner before the start of the Junior Ranger meeting.

"Good, this pertains to that." He pointed toward the rest of the class. "Now, get in line."

Like last year, PE started with laps, followed by calisthenics. At first, he jogged with Dravs during the early laps, but Zack found he moved at a faster pace, longer without tiring, and he soon left his friend behind. He discovered he almost kept pace with the Devoran's long-striding sister. Best of all, he didn't have to do extra laps for coming in last this time.

That punishment fell to Dravs.

After class, he waited for Coach Dagon while the others filtered into the locker room for showers and clean clothes.

"All right, Jackson. Come with me." Dagon gestured for Zack to follow him. The coach led him toward the cloud glider maintenance bay. "Have a good summer?"

"Not bad, I guess. Valtra was interesting. Jenny had some troubles..."

"I heard about that." Dagon pressed the button to open the door. An older boy crouched over a cloud glider's engine. The engine, partially disassembled, lay strewn about the area. He stood and faced Zack and the coach.

Roger.

Zack's heart dropped into his stomach.

"Davis here is going to get you started on learning cloud-glider maintenance."

He tugged at Coach Dagon's arm and shook his head. "But Coach..."

The Ersidian shook off Zack's hand. "You learn the basics or you don't fly. Ever. Those are the rules." He turned and left Zack alone with Roger.

The older boy dropped the spanner he held. With a clang, it bounced off the main engine housing. He approached Zack.

Zack locked his knees to keep his legs from trembling. Calls of "Filthy-Firsty" echoed in his thoughts.

Roger extended a hand.

Zack eyed the hand before meeting Roger's gaze.

The older boy wore a slight frown, but his brown eyes held no malice. "I owe you an apology."

"You... you do?" Zack stared at the proffered hand.

"I was wrong to go along with Barry last year. He went too far, and I didn't say anything, do anything to stop him. I'm sorry."

"He tried to kill me!" Although Zack expressed curiosity about a great many scientific topics, he had possessed no desire to endure unprotected exposure to the raw vacuum of space.

"I know. And I'm sorry for whatever part I played in not preventing it from getting that far. I mean, look, they held me back a year for hanging with Barry and not doing anything about his bullying. Coach says helping you with this will help make things right."

Zack regarded the debris field of engine parts that lay just beyond Roger. "I don't really want to learn how to take these apart. I just want to fly."

Roger lowered his hand and glanced over his shoulder at the disassembled engine. "Well, everyone has to learn the basics. Coach isn't going to let you fly without learning this."

He nodded at Zack. "So, what do you say we get started?"

~ * * * ~

Jenny hoped the Junior Ranger meeting would provide the diversion she needed and avert triggering another breakdown. If anyone had told her a year ago she'd be a wreck over an accident her parents survived, Jenny would have denied it.

The meeting convened in Isis Plaza. Jenny suspected Ishtar Plaza was Bariss's first choice, but he must have deemed it unsuitable since it was full of Devoran transients. Other members of her troop milled about the plaza where Bariss had erected several garden planters, each containing a variety of vegetation.

The label on each container indicated the planet of origin of its contents. One from Earth, another from Devorus, Ersid, Valtra, Kerrola, and others—a dozen in all. Jenny recognized some of the plants from her exobotany classes.

"Once everyone arrives, we'll get started." Bariss glanced up from the stool upon which he sat while he tinkered with a handheld machine. It resembled one of the scanners they had used while on Valtra to determine whether unfamiliar botanicals were edible.

Jenny scanned the area to see who had yet to arrive. Xal and Dravs stood near the box containing Devoran flora. Standing before the container from Valtra, Ix spoke with Ming. Bob stood staring at the Terran plants. Zack was...

Missing.

Her heart skipped a beat, and she glanced around the plaza a second time. *It's Cytherea—what trouble could he have possibly gotten into?*

Jenny fired off a quick message to him. "Where are you? The meeting is starting! Bariss is waiting on you."

Zack's reply arrived immediately. "On my way! Got held up after PE, and I still needed to eat!"

Jenny breathed a sigh of relief and approached Bariss. "Zack says he's on his way. He was detained in his last class and still needed dinner."

"Fine." Bariss shook the machine in his hands.

"He was probably trying to crash the city." Piotr snickered as he walked past.

"Hey!" The Devoran troop leader glared at Piotr. "We don't do that here. I'll never understand this human obsession with scapegoating."

"I'm here!" Panting, Zack ran into the plaza. The buttons of his shirt were crooked, and sweat plastered his hair to his head.

"Good." Bariss hopped off his stool and paced. "Let's get started."

The Devoran held up the device he'd been fiddling with. "You're all familiar with the toxicity tester we used on Valtra.

41

If you're on an excursion and everything has gone as planned and you're where you're supposed to be, you'll have access to one of these."

He tossed the tester toward the stool upon which he'd been sitting. It landed on the ground between the legs of the stool with the heavy thud indicative of hardened field gear. "What do you do when you don't have one of these?"

Ix raised one of its hands.

"Yes?"

"My gastric-implants negate ninety-nine point seven-five percent of known plant and animal-based ingested toxins."

Bariss nodded. "If you're not lucky enough to have a food taster with gastric implants, what do you do?" He pointed at Jenny. "What did you do when you crashed on Bestic?"

"We had access to the food packs in our escape pod, but we foraged a bit."

"Foraging is good." Bariss clasped his hands behind his back. "How did you know what was safe?"

Jenny nodded in Zack's direction. "Zack had the *Junior Ranger's Guide to Bestic* on his PDA."

"As hilariously out of date as that guide is, it must have been a valuable resource. Plants catalogued in it won't suddenly become toxic."

Jenny approached Zack and helped him straighten his shirt. They stood near the Kerrolian planter. Bob lumbered over as they listened to Bariss.

"What we're going to learn tonight is a quick-and-dirty way to forage when you don't have access to those resources. Just you and your wits against the wilderness." He gestured toward the plants, mostly broad-leafed flora featuring a variety of leaf shapes and textures. Some bloomed with colorful, if unremarkable, flowers. Several, particularly those from Valtra and Kerrola, possessed red leaves. "There is an elaborate test you can use to determine for certain if a plant is toxic. It requires you to fast at least eight hours and take things slowly. You can read up on it; we're not going to cover that tonight."

He pointed at a thorny bush in the Terran planter. "I'm going to teach you what to avoid. These rules may encompass some edible plants, but better safe than sorry, yes?

"See this? A rose plant from Earth. Avoid plants with thorns. Now, rose water is used in various Earth recipes, and roses themselves are generally edible. Still, better safe than sorry."

He approached the Devoran vegetation. "If the plant has shiny leaves, like this astrochaunus, avoid it." He snapped the stalk of the flower. Bariss held up the broken stem to show everyone the milky fluid oozing at the end. "Likewise, if the plant's sap is milky or discolored."

The Devoran tossed the flower into the planter. He stroked a yellow-spotted purple flower with his claw. "Avoid umbrella-shaped flowers or anything with white or yellow berries. In fact, you should avoid plants with seeds inside pods."

Several students raised their hands. Bariss held up both of his and nodded. "I know, I know. There are many varieties of plants on Earth that grow beans or seeds in pods that are perfectly nutritious. The chances of you running into one of those plants on Uninhabited Wilderness Planet Alpha Two are astronomically small."

Jenny remembered from her exobotany class that attempts to transplant indigenous foliage from one planet onto another required more care and personalized attention than random chance provided. Generally speaking, what made a planet's biome suitable to plants native to that planet rendered it unremittingly hostile to alien fruits and vegetables.

"Don't eat mushrooms or anything else that looks like a fungus. Again, this is a better safe than sorry rule. If anything you eat tastes bitter or soapy, spit it out immediately. If it smells like almonds—that's a nut from Earth for you off-worlders—it's off limits."

Dravs raised his hand. "How are we supposed to know what an almond smells like?"

Bariss retrieved a small bowl from the Terran planter. "If you're not familiar with the smell of almonds, we have some here." He rattled the bowl. "These are the non-toxic ones, of course."

He returned the bowl to the planter before gesturing for everyone to gather around him. "There's a cheesy old saying, but it has a basis in truth: 'Leaves of three, let it be.'"

One of the older Junior Rangers, a girl from Voyager squad, giggled. "Leaves of four, smoke some more!"

Even Bariss laughed. "I don't recommend that. If it's toxic to eat, breathing the smoke isn't going to do you much good." Starting with the planter full of Terran plants, he reviewed them one by one, explaining how they resembled plants from other worlds.

They spent the evening examining the flora in the boxes, reciting the rules over and over in different ways until the assembled Junior Rangers convinced Bariss they understood. Certain others did so as well, Jenny used her implants to record several iterations.

During a brief period where Bariss took a break from lecturing, he sent Jenny a message. "Can't meet tonight. I'll contact you and Zack later. Things are well, something came up at home."

Jenny replied with an acknowledgement.

"I'll forward you several recommendations for books you can read on edible plants. They're useful guides. Have a good evening, everyone. See you next time." Bariss stood and gestured toward the door.

As the Junior Rangers went their separate ways, Jenny caught up to Zack to let him know about Bariss's message and then returned to her dorm.

She walked into a heated discussion among Gabrielle and Astrid, cousins from Norway, and Cait, Verrak, and Daniel about the Saturnian Regatta and their favored competitors. Jenny stayed just long enough to wave hello before retiring for the evening.

Finally, for the first time since she returned to Cytherea, she drifted off to sleep.

Chapter 8

Within weeks, Zack felt as if his head would explode from all the new knowledge his professors crammed in it. From literary classics to geometric formulae to planetary types and basic astronomy, even Junior Ranger meetings taught Zack more than he believed his brain could hold.

Time flew, and before Zack knew it, an event he dreaded crept up on him.

His birthday.

Last year, a call from his parents woke him at an unholy hour, and later, some of his roommates surprised him with an impromptu party. The party he didn't mind; the ill-timed call from his parents, however, he could have lived without. Nothing jump-started one's heart like a middle-of-the-night call from millions of miles away. At any other time of the year, such a call would portend doom.

This year, the call didn't come. Instead, Zack awoke to a message from his parents. "Didn't want to wake you up like we did last year. Happy birthday, Zack! We love you and are proud of you. P.S. Check your account."

He checked his system credit account and located a deposit from his parents. All through cleaning up, breakfast, and his first several classes, he daydreamed about how he'd spend the money.

I could throw a big pizza party! Invite all my friends! Or, I could take my best friends to Bit Bytes and go to the Rampage Room. Oh wait, I don't have implants; that won't be much fun.

Oh! Extra time in the VR pods... I wonder if I return it, if Mom and Dad would let me go on the next Junior Ranger excursion. As yet, Bariss had not announced its location. If he wasn't going to be allowed to participate, he hoped the destination selected would be someplace boring, like Earth.

Shortly before lunch, he received a text message from Steve. "HAPPY BIRTHDAY, MATE."

He sent a quick thank-you and asked whether Steve was free that evening. Right after he sent it, Zack remembered he had Kova Kasi with Dravs and Xal.

As Zack tried to figure out how to recall the message, Steve's reply arrived. "Sure. What time?"

Nuts. I can't back out now. Zack double-checked his schedule. He could meet Steve after class. He decided eight o'clock would work and suggested they meet at the Neutron Café.

After receiving Steve's acknowledgement, Zack sent an invite to Dravs, Xal, Ix, and Jenny asking if they would like to meet Steve and him at eight. Their positive responses put a spring in his step that carried him through the rest of the day.

When he returned to the dorm to change before Kova Kasi, he found Polly and Barbara waiting for him. Kaneer and Ix huddled around one of the side tables and played a game.

Polly held a thick, round cake with bright yellowish-green icing. "Happy birthday, Zackarooni. Fourteen today, eh?"

Barbara leaned over the cake and lit the candles. As the sisters sang to him, Zack felt his face grow hot, and he shuffled his feet until the singing stopped. Then he blew out the candles.

"Erm, thanks. I haven't had cake on my birthday since I left home."

"Well, we had a little help." Polly glanced at Ix. "Bug-not-a-boy contacted your parents to give us a few hints."

Ix drew itself up and chittered.

"Polly!" Barbara glared at her sister before producing plates and forks she'd hidden on the sofa, and they cut into the cake. Polly distributed them, and everyone waited for Zack to take the first bite.

The cake, spongy and moist, hit Zack with a burst of flavor—citrus chiffon with lemon icing. Zack's eyes widened, and his smile broadened as he savored each bite of his absolute, most favorite dessert in the galaxy. It reminded him of summer days and lying on warm rocks after swimming in the local pond with Tom and his cousins.

"Wow, this is great." Zack tried not to spew flecks of cake as he spoke. "You two made this?"

Polly giggled and eyed Barbara. A slow smile spread across Barb's face. Polly hummed. "Ah, well, when your favorite Zack-attack is having a birthday..."

"No, we did not." Barbara nudged her sister. "We ordered it from a bakery over in Freyja Dome."

Kaneer and Ix finished their cake. The Kerrolian held out his plate for more. "Tell me of this celebration, Zack Jackson. What did you do to earn this birth-day?"

Polly huffed. "Earn? It's a birthday, you goof. Don't Kerrolians celebrate the day they were born?"

"No, Polly Wright, we do not. A child does nothing to be born. It is brought into the world entirely without choice."

Ix chittered and cocked its head. "Humans seem to place special importance on celebrating the relative position of their home world on the day they were born. When their planet returns to that location, they mark it with gifts, confections, and fellowship. Many do, at any rate."

"Yeah, we just do, that's all. It's a birthday!" Zack watched the Kerrolian's ears twitch and tried to figure out if Kaneer was joking with him or not.

"Although"—Ix tapped a finger on its torso— "due to the inherent inaccuracies in the Terran calendar, the planet is not technically in the exact same location of its orbit—"

"It's close enough!" Polly shoved another piece of cake at Kaneer. "Shut up, eat your cake, and stop ruining McZacken's birthday!"

Zack laughed and put his plate in the recycler. "Thanks for the cake. It was great. I need to get to Kova Kasi."

"Don't let that great furry beast throw you around too much," Polly called after him as he ducked into his room to change. His Kova Kasi uniform closely resembled a karate gi; the loose fit rendered it suitable for many martial arts. He found Polly, Barbara, and Ix still trying to explain birthdays to Kaneer when he emerged.

"Lookit the Kung Fu Master!" Polly whistled.

Zack put his hands on his hips. "So, you're not mad at me, anymore, huh?"

Polly shrugged and brushed a lock of purple hair away from her eyes. "I was more mad at myself and disappointed. It's all cool now."

"Good. Come to the Neutron Café at eight. You too, Kaneer. I want to have pizza with all my friends."

"Uh... Pizza?" Mickey entered the room, lugging his guitar case.

Zack nodded. "Neutron Café, eight o'clock. It's my birthday!"

"Oh yeah. Happy birthday." Mickey patted Zack on the shoulder. "If I don't fall asleep, I'll be there." He covered his mouth as he yawned. "Been a long day."

47

"See you then!" Zack waved and made his way to the auxiliary gym. He wasn't sure what Polly had heard, but as yet, Xal had not yet thrown him around. Thus far, he'd been able to avoid sparring with his massive friend.

~ * * * ~

The notification blinked in the periphery of Jenny's vision, a dreaded reminder of what she should do before going to meet Zack and their friends.

"Call us tonight, please." The message from her parents contained nothing more.

Her heart raced when she first read it, and it took the better part of ten minutes to calm herself. *If something bad happened to them, it wouldn't say "us" and would want a response immediately.*

On the one occasion she wanted her classes to drag on, they seemed to fly by, and before she knew it, the time to return to her dorm and make the call had come. On her way back, she placed a call to Hiri.

An avatar of her friend popped up in the bottom corner of her sight, confirming that, like Jenny, Hiri had communication implants, just as Jenny suspected.

"Oh, hi, Jenny!" The avatar looked exactly like Hiri, except with shorter blue hair, instead of the long, black tresses she possessed in reality. Jenny's own avatar pretty much exactly resembled how she appeared in person.

"Are you busy? I need a favor." Jenny entered the transport pod. Several other students bound for Anahita Dome boarded, then the pod whisked them away.

The avatar bobbed up and down. "Nah, just hanging out in Ishtar Plaza trying to see that Devoran princess. What do you need?"

"I have to call my parents. Can you meet me in my room? I want someone there with me. Not on the call, but nearby, you know?"

"Oh sure. I'll head that way now."

"Thanks, Hiri. I'll be waiting for you."

"Okay, bye!"

"Bye." Jenny closed the channel and shut her eyes as she relaxed in her seat. *At least I'm finally sleeping again. I hope this call doesn't mess that up.*

When she arrived at Anahita Dome, Jenny rushed to her dorm. Verrak, seated alone in the common area while watching the news on the holoviewer, ignored her when she entered.

A snippet of the broadcast caught her attention.

"...Archaeologists on Valtra claim the site is of special historical significance and have demanded the Confederation allow them access."

Verrak changed the channel and snorted. "Busybodies always sticking their noses in dusty old things no one needs to know about."

Jenny shook her head and entered her room, grateful for the private communications terminal Cytherean administration granted her since her parents' accident. She filed a formal petition via her counselor explaining her trepidation and discomfort with the spectacle of potentially emotional conversations with her parents on the public terminal in the common area.

She didn't wait long for Hiri to arrive. She pulled over a chair from Astrid's desk and sat just out of sight of the terminal camera. Jenny took a deep breath and connected to her parents' communications address. After a moment, her mother appeared on the screen.

Dark circles underlined Amélie's bloodshot eyes. She smiled. "Genevieve! I'm so happy you called. We've so much to tell you." She launched into a jargon-filled explanation of their current conditions, much of which went over Jenny's head.

Jenny nodded and waited for her mother to finish speaking. She knew from experience her mother forgot about the communication lag between Cytherea and Vilicus. "I'm glad you're doing better, Mother. How is Papa? Has he remembered anything yet?"

She awaited her mother's response.

"Not much, but you should speak to him yourself." She swiveled the terminal before Jenny protested.

Her father's metallic visage popped into view. A single, glowing red eye peered into the monitor. Bandages obscured what flesh remained on his head. "You are Genevieve. The one they say is my daughter."

Jenny closed her eyes and swallowed. She felt Hiri squeeze her leg in support.

"Yes, Papa. What have they done to your face?" She pointed at the screen, but then slapped her hand into her lap when she realized he couldn't see what she pointed at.

A skeletal metal hand reached up and stroked the bandages. "They are... grafting... no... growing skin now. Within forty-five days, I will regain my former appearance. Though"—his hand reached up and rubbed his short hair—"it may take a while for my hair to regrow to its previous length."

"I'm"—Jenny composed herself—"glad you're doing better. I hope you start remembering things soon."

Her father perked up and tilted his head. "My name. I remember my name. I am François Florian DuBois."

"That's good, Papa." She reached up to the disconnect button with a trembling hand. "I must go. It is a friend's birthday today."

"Good-bye."

"Au Revoir." Jenny ended the call. "Did you see him? He's not even human anymore." She buried her face in her hands. "He's a monster!"

"Don't say that." Hiri pried Jenny's hands away from her face. "Would you think that of me if I were different than I am?"

"But you're not."

Hiri chuckled. "I wasn't always Hiriko. My parents named me Hiroki."

Jenny glowered at the screen as if her anger would make it disappear. "That's not that different." She turned and regarded Hiri. Jenny stared into her dorm mate's emerald eyes and squinted. "Oh. *Oh!*" Jenny's eyes widened, and she felt her face grow hot. "I'm sorry. I'm such an idiot."

Hiri squeezed her hand. "Don't worry about it. You see what I mean, though? I know you didn't know me before, but I'm fundamentally the same person. I just feel more like me now." She laughed. "My family will tell you I behaved differently early in my therapy, but that settled down eventually, especially once I got my hormonal implants."

Jenny glanced over her shoulder at the terminal screen. "You really think he'll remember? That he'll even look the same when they're finished?"

"I know it." Hiri placed a hand on Jenny's cheek and turned her head toward her. "The accident I had? It was caused by other children. They didn't understand why I was different. My parents didn't care how I dressed, of course. They were always supportive and kind."

"The other children almost killed you?" *Do all my friends get bullied almost to death?* Jenny hoped she misinterpreted Hiri's statement.

Hiri closed her eyes. "Like I said, it was an accident. They were being mean, and things got out of hand. Anyway, my memories returned, and so will your father's. I promise."

Jenny felt tears well up in her eyes. "How can you forgive them so easily?"

"It's not easy." The corners of Hiri's mouth curved upward. "But if you carry that bitter seed in your heart your whole life, it poisons you. I didn't want to be unhappy all the time."

Jenny sighed and slumped in her chair. "Sometimes, I hate being patient." Taking Hiri's hand, she exhaled and then sat up. "My friend Zack has invited a bunch of us to the Neutron Café for pizza for his birthday. Please come with me?"

The young woman nodded and smiled. "I'd be happy to." She flicked her hair. "Let me do something with this real quick."

Jenny watched her leave before she shut down the terminal. *At least I'm not a complete wreck right now. I knew she'd help.*

Chapter 9

When Zack arrived at the Neutron Café with Ix, Kaneer, and the Wright sisters in tow, they had to wait for a table. The increased number of Devoran migrants in Ishtar Plaza meant spaces were scarce, especially for large groups, and more of Zack's friends were on the way. The café, more than happy to accommodate the students, rearranged furniture as diners finished their meals and vacated their tables. They knew student business had greater longevity than the Al-Geharan transients.

Steve arrived while they were waiting. His curly hair hung longer, and he stood taller than Zack remembered.

"Hey, mate! Have a good summer?" Steve wrapped Zack in a bear hug and lifted him off the ground.

"Yeah," Zack rubbed his arm. "No one tried to space me, and I got to explore some ruins on Valtra with Ix."

"Right on. How are you, Ix?" Steve offered his hand to the Valtraxian.

Ix shook it and chittered. "I am well, thank you."

Zack introduced Steve to Kaneer. The Kerrolian bowed and sniffed Steve's hand as he had done with Zack. "Ah, like Polly and Barbara Wright, you are from Tereshkova Colony. Welcome to this one's acquaintance, Steve Taylor."

Steve grinned at Zack. "Yeah, right. You could smell that? I wash my hands. Sometimes more than once a day, yeah?"

Kaneer laughed and shook his head. "Truly, you humans have pathetic olfactory senses."

Just as they learned their table was ready, Jenny arrived with a friend. She sat next to Zack and introduced him to Hiri.

"Jenny's told me some stories about the trouble you all get into on Junior Ranger trips." Hiri smiled and then nodded across the table at Ix. "She's lucky to have friends like you."

Ix cocked its head. "And we are fortunate to know Jenny. We work well together."

Zack followed through on his earlier thought, instructing the waiter to put their pizzas and drinks on his bill. He shared with his friends the gift of funds from his parents. After devouring a half dozen pizzas and too many pitchers of

Quantum Cola, they parted for the evening. Everyone had early classes the next day, and no one enjoyed attending classes in a sleep-deprived state.

Lingering until almost all his friends departed, Zack found himself alone with Ix and Kaneer.

Ix stroked Zack's arm. "Happy birthday again, my friend. I will see you at the room; I have to check something in the engineering lab."

"See you, Ix."

As Ix left, Zack seized an impulse. He gestured to Kaneer. "Let's see if there's anything cool going on with these Devorans." He felt a twinge of guilt as he ignored Bariss's warning, but after how well dinner proceeded, he decided no harm could come from a walk in the park.

Resembling abstract representations of seashells, Devoran tents transformed the otherwise orderly plaza paths into a maze. Sticking close to Zack, Kaneer bumped into him every time the human boy stopped to look at pieces of Devoran art.

Prolific Devoran sculptures dotted the grass between their tents and the paths like lawn ornaments. In the areas devoid of sculpture, Devorans sat, chatting, playing musical instruments, and otherwise ignoring the human and Kerrolian in their midst.

A sinuous dancer skipped and twirled to music strummed on a long-necked stringed instrument. Zack's eyes followed her until he tripped over a golden, braided rope and found himself staring down the barrels of half-a-dozen military rifles.

Someone clapped their hands. "Come, come. This was clearly an accident, and he is obviously a student of this fine school, not an assassin."

One of the Devorans covering Zack with a rifle curled his lips. "The Kerrolian, perhaps. Do you not recognize this human, Your Highness?"

Highness? Zack craned his neck to see the speaker. A brilliant blue Noble Devoran, standing a head-and-a-half taller than the rest, peered down at him. The frills on her head were covered with an ivory-colored shell-and-feathered headdress.

"Hm. Perhaps." She pushed past the soldiers and offered Zack a hand.

"Highness!"

She pulled Zack to his feet and spun on the soldier, poking him in the chest with a clawed finger. "Do not presume to command me."

The soldier bowed and backed away. "That was not my intention. Please forgive me."

"Return to your duties."

The soldiers snapped to attention, saluted by crossing their fists over their chests, and spun in place before retreating.

Kaneer dropped to one knee. "This one is privileged to meet a Noble Devoran. From their address, may this one presume you are Princess Valianna?"

"Oh, how nice. Please, stand." She gestured for Kaneer to rise. "Yes, I am Valianna Hallox. The princess... is a formality. What is your name? My soldiers seem to think I should know you."

"Zack Jackson."

"Ah, yes. I've been briefed on you. And your friend?"

The Kerrolian bowed. "Julani-Kaneer zin Fallah Hammurabi Al-Gehara."

Valiana smiled. "Tell me, have you studied Confederation History yet?"

"A little." Zack rubbed the back of his neck. "There was a lot to cover, and I don't remember some of it." A quiet voice in his head reminded him Bariss forbade him from interacting with these people. *Well, he's not my father, and he's not a teacher. I'm probably not going to get to go on any more Junior Ranger trips anyway.*

"Ah." She gestured for the two to follow her. "Well, when my family abdicated and the Devoran Empire dissolved, our titles were forfeit. But there are still those, at least on Devorus, who believe they were better off before the stratocracy took over. The rest of the Confederation doesn't seem to care much one way or another."

Zack remembered snippets from last year's class of the coup to which Valianna referred. The Devoran Empire had been the central power behind the Confederation until a civil war deposed the royal family and replaced it with a government run by the military. The rest of the Confederation accepted with few reservations the new government of the former Devoran Empire.

She led them into a tent easily three times larger than the others. Curtains divided the structure into several distinct spaces. Typical, deep-seated Devoran chairs surrounded a fire pit in the central room. Valianna sat in one and invited the two students to join her.

Zack shifted his weight until he found a comfortable spot. Unless he positioned himself in a certain way, he felt as if he would fall through the tail hole in the chair made for Devorans.

She faced the two students, hands on her knees. Even seated, the Noble Devoran towered above Zack and Kaneer. Princess Valianna leaned forward. "You've made ripples in the upper echelons of the Devoran stratocracy."

Zack chuckled as his eyes darted around the tent. "I didn't mean to."

Her toothy smile reminded Zack of a shark about to feed. "Now, Zack, tell me—I want to know everything about your encounters with the Athosians."

A lump stuck in Zack's throat, and cold sweat ran down his spine. He recalled the threats Devoran Ambassador Sleesix made before they left Valtra. Despite Ambassador Crocker's reassurances the Devorans couldn't actually throw him in the Arkadian prison for talking, he pondered the possibility that Valianna planned to set him up. *That's crazy. You're Zack Jackson, not some intergalactic super-spy.*

He started with the story about the cult of Athos on Bestic.

~ * * * ~

"So, he's cute."

Jenny only half heard Hiri as they headed to their dorm. Eating with her friends proved a nice diversion, but once she parted from them, her thoughts returned to her parents—specifically, her father's lack of recognition.

He certainly seems proud that he remembers his own name, though.

"Hmm?" Hiri's voice broke through Jenny's ruminations.

"Zack. He's cute. How long have you two—"

"Oh! No." Jenny laughed. "He's my friend, but I'm not interested in him in that way. He's more like a brother."

"Ah, well, I'm glad we clarified that."

Jenny stifled a yawn as they reached the door to their dorm cluster. "It needs to be the weekend."

"Still not sleeping well?" Hiri touched Jenny's arm.

"Better than I was, but not great." She yawned again. "I have a test tomorrow, too."

"Ugh, me too, in Basic Engineering. Professor Vale just loves to throw in questions he didn't cover in class, too." Hiri laughed. "I guess he expects us to read the materials in addition to doing all the classwork."

"Crazy, right?"

Hiri smiled and then hugged her. "See you tomorrow."

The next day arrived far too early for Jenny. When she awoke, she felt as if she had just gone to bed. When she finally activated her communications implant after taking her shower, the dreaded flash of a waiting message popped up.

From Ariana, a young woman whom she befriended on their Junior Ranger trip over the summer, Jenny played it:

"Dearest Jenny, I'm sorry I haven't written before now. Things got out of hand. When I returned to San Angeles from Valtra, my uncle was very upset. He said I tricked him into signing the permissions form, and he wasn't happy when I pointed out he didn't stop me from going.

"He yelled. A lot."

Jenny paused playback, clenching her teeth while she donned her clothes and passed through the common area. Hiri was either not up or gone already, so Jenny headed for the cafeteria and resumed the message.

"Then he got into a fight with the neighbors over it, and he was arrested for disturbing the peace. When they released him, he apologized and asked what I wanted to do. It was like he was a different person. I heard he received counseling during the few days he was away. So, I told him what I wanted: to attend one of the science academies. I'm living with a sponsor family on Vilicus now. They're very nice, and I like it here very much. They're an older couple from Toronto, and they are also hosting a Devoran student who attends school here.

"The school is much nicer. There's a strange old man who teaches Basic Astrosciences. He reminds me of a crazy grandfather. His class is never boring. He says the school here is just as good as Cytherean Academy; it just hasn't been around long enough to get a reputation.

56

"I should go. I just wanted to let you know I'm all right and I'm not living with my uncle on Earth anymore. Vilicus is close to Venus, right? Close enough for vid-calls? Ariana."

Jenny set a reminder to send a reply after classes. Though mixed with bitter undertones, the general optimism of Ariana's message brightened Jenny's day, mellowing the storm cloud of her impending test. Not even a temporary power outage dampened her spirits. It helped that the outage didn't affect her literature class; their tablets didn't require city power to operate.

In mathematics, the test itself was not as difficult as Jenny expected. Professor Baker didn't believe in "gotcha" questions, and she spent much of her free time studying for it, having reviewed not only the problems assigned for homework, but also the optional ones at the end of each section. A dark part of Jenny's mind nagged her. *What if it was easy because I didn't understand it at all and just thought I did?* She bludgeoned away those baseless doubts with daydreams about the upcoming weekend.

After classes ended for the day, Jenny secured one of the quiet rooms in which to compose her reply to Ariana. With others around her, she felt self-conscious using her implants for communication. Even though her implants picked up and transcribed sub-vocal speech, Jenny was not yet practiced enough to do it without moving her lips. Though most passersby seemed to understand implant communication appeared as if she whispered to herself, some still stared as if they had never witnessed a seemingly single-sided conversation.

"Dear Ariana, I'm sorry to hear your uncle was upset, but I'm pleased to hear everything worked out for the best. If you ever need anything, don't hesitate to ask.

"Things are going well here. I'm still having trouble dealing with my parents' injuries. That I can't be with them is probably making it more difficult, but I can't be there and go to school here at the same time.

"I don't have anything terribly exciting to report. Classes, Junior Ranger meetings, trying not to cry myself to sleep every night. It wouldn't be so bad if my father recognized me. I think that's what makes it so difficult. Ever since I can remember, I've tried to win his affection, and now, he doesn't even know who I am.

"Anyway, I think Bariss is going to tell us about the next JR excursion at the next meeting. I hope you can go. Zack, Dravs, and Xal are all right, but we need more girls there!

"Thanks for writing. Vid calls should work if Venus is on the same side of the sun as your place on Vilicus. I'll have to look it up. Anyway, I know you'll do well there. Jenny."

She listened to the message once more before she sent it. She signed out of the quiet room and returned to her dorm. Hiri and Verrak sat alongside Cait and Gabrielle, playing a game on the main holoviewer. The scoreboard indicated Hiri would obliterate all of them.

"Jenny!" Verrak waved for her to join them. "Take Hiri's place so some of us can have a chance."

"You just need to get more in tune with popular culture, Verrak." Hiri giggled.

"We watch more holofilms than you." Astrid pointed to herself and her cousin. "Are you sure you're not keeping the answers in that bionic brain of yours?"

"It doesn't work that way."

Jenny neared Hiri. "Hey, want to grab dinner together?"

"Sure." Hiri signed out of the game before sticking out her tongue at the other players. "You all get what you want, anyway. Good luck!"

Jenny tossed her bag onto her bed before joining Hiri in the hallway. "Thanks. I didn't want to eat alone tonight."

"No problem. Where do you want to go?"

"Cafeteria okay? I don't want to use up all my system credits this early." Jenny pressed the call button for the lift.

"Sounds good." Hiri rocked on her heels and shoved her hands in her pockets. "Doing anything after?"

Jenny shook her head. The lift arrived with a ding. They boarded it, and Hiri pressed the button for the level containing Anahita Dome's cafeteria.

"There's new film at the theater: *Sky Above Honor's Peak*. It's an Ersidian film about a warrior who returns home and finds love with one of the nomadic Uurts." Hiri raised her eyebrows and smiled as she regarded Jenny.

Closing her eyes, Jenny leaned against the rear wall of the lift and chuckled. "They should have called it *The Coach Dagon Story*."

"Maybe it is!" Hiri laughed.

Jenny had not enjoyed a night out purely for fun since before she left for Valtra last summer. "All right then, it's a girl's night out!"

Chapter 10

Kaneer chased Zack en route to class. "Zack Jackson! We must speak!"

Zack held the lift until the Kerrolian entered. "What about?"

"That Noble Devoran. You ran off so fast last night."

The lift hummed as it sped them toward the school levels. "She kept us too late." He stifled a yawn. "I feel like I didn't sleep at all."

"But was it not an amazing experience? She is a princess!"

The human shrugged. "I guess. Was she even hatched yet when the Empire dissolved?"

The lift jerked to a stop, and the lights flickered before extinguishing. Zack's heart pounded in his chest.

Emergency lights snapped on, bathing the lift in a red glow. Zack reached across Kaneer and pressed the button for their floor.

Nothing.

"Krunk."

Kaneer's ears flicked forward. "There is a power outage in this sector."

Zack glanced at the Kerrolian. "How do you know that?"

"They are broadcasting the message over the city's public communications channel."

Zack almost said, "I don't hear anything," before remembering Kaneer had implants just like almost everyone sixteen and older from Earth. He pulled out his C_7 and saw the broadcast message, confirming Kaneer's report.

"Well, nuts. We're going to be late for class." Zack slumped against the wall and sat on the floor.

"Surely they will not hold that against us. We cannot control power outages."

"Probably not." In truth, Zack wouldn't mourn missing part of his EAC History class. Although he found Professor Stantion likable, she was not the most engaging speaker, and he feared he would struggle to remain awake and focused in her class. He felt equally unenthused about Literature and Composition, but Professor Wade-Smyth's energetic teaching style made nodding off difficult.

60

Kaneer hummed a tune Zack assumed was a Kerrolian song. As he did so, the Kerrolian squatted and pulled his tail around, stroking it and winding it around his neck.

After two repetitions of the song, Kaneer stopped and stared directly at Zack. He held out a hand toward his human friend. "Will you take my hand, Zack Jackson?"

"Why?" Zack narrowed his eyes. The Kerrolian's yellow eyes bored into him.

"Please, it is important."

Sighing, Zack took Kaneer's hand. The Kerrolian brought it up to his muzzle and sniffed it before dragging his tongue along the back of Zack's hand. "Mmm. Yes. Good."

"Eww!" Zack snatched back his hand and wiped it on his pants. "Why did you do that?"

"This one wanted to know if you would be good to eat if we are trapped in here so long that we begin to starve. Survival is this one's number-one priority."

His eyes widening, Zack pushed himself away from Kaneer. The Kerrolian grinned at him, licking his pointed teeth, and laughed.

"It is a joke, Zack Jackson! You believe Kaneer's lies too easily!"

"Lies? What else have you lied about?" Zack crossed his arms over his chest, keeping his hands safely tucked under his armpits.

"Lies. Jokes. There is little difference, no? What is a lie but a joke intended to be taken seriously?"

Zack looked away and snorted. "I don't think they're the same thing at all."

~ * * * ~

Kaneer apologized to Zack many times over the course of the next several days, but he always left the interaction snickering. The Kerrolian clearly considered joking about eating Zack the height of humor.

Finally, Zack could stand it no more and gripped his friend by the shoulders before leaving for his Junior Ranger meeting. "Look, it's fine, okay? Stop apologizing! I'm more upset by that now than I was by you tasting me!"

61

The Kerrolian held up his hands. "Yes, yes! This one understands. Kaneer will speak of it no more."

"Good."

Zack met his friends in Hathor Dome's VR Lounge. Ryll Bob droned on and on, relating a joke to Xal and Dravs. As he tried to listen in, Bariss shouted for everyone's attention.

"All right, we have a few things to go over tonight before we get started." He gestured for the Junior Rangers to gather around. "First, by now you all have no doubt heard that the Halloween celebration is cancelled due to excessive squatters in Ishtar Plaza."

The official city announcement Zack heard was worded in a more diplomatic fashion.

"However, Princess Valianna has invited all the students to the Festival of Starlight instead. It's a Devoran festival that takes place in the spring—"

Several hands shot up.

"Devoran spring, which it is now on the continent where that holiday originated." The hands lowered. "I am aware that Cytherea considers this autumn. How they decided to go by only half of Earth's season-keeping, I'll never know..."

"All right, the feastival!" Dravs pumped his fist. "I am going to eat everything. Every. Thing."

Xal snickered and elbowed the Devoran in the ribs.

"If you are interested in Devoran culture at all, I recommend you attend. Secondly"—Bariss held up two fingers—"the destination for our next excursion is Ersid."

Zack's heart leapt until he remembered his parents' decree. Slumping his shoulders, he steadied himself on a nearby VR pod to keep from falling to the floor.

"We've been invited to travel with an Uurt tribe on one of their migrations across the Plains of Black Blood. It should be quite the educational experience."

Concentrating on keeping his legs locked in place so they'd hold him up, Zack tuned out the rest of Bariss's lecture on the upcoming excursion. He wished Bariss had delayed the announcement until later in the term; he didn't want to stew about it all year.

Maybe since it's Ersid, and they know Mungus, they'll make an exception.

"All right, get into your pods. If this is your first time, hang back so I can show you the ropes. The rest of you, head for the marshalling area."

The excitement of controlling a remote probe on the surface of Venus accomplished little to lessen Zack's angst over the excursion he likely wouldn't experience. He climbed into the pod, strapped himself in, and closed his eyes as he waited for the interface to load.

Meanwhile, his mind reeled with schemes to convince his parents to permit him to travel with the Junior Rangers to Ersid.

~ * * * ~

Using VR to inhabit the body of a robotic probe was not high on Jenny's list of fun activities. Driving it around proved easy enough, even though the thick atmosphere of Venus made it feel like she walked through soup.

Atmospheric refraction created a sort of fishbowl effect, distorting the periphery of her vision. She found if she slowly turned her head from side to side, she became accustomed to the perspective. The hazy, brownish-yellow scenery reminded her of burnt egg yolk.

"Take a moment to get your bearings." Bariss's voice crackled over the comm system. "These probes are in a different location than the last ones we used. We're in a valley between Thetis and Ouda Regio. Those are the two landmasses on either side of you."

The incredible density of the atmosphere muffled the whirr and grinding of probe motors and tracks on the scorching surface. Jenny checked her heads-up-display, or HUD; the current surface temperature read 1167 Kelvin or 894 degrees Celsius. She admired the engineering skills of the Devorans who designed these probes; they were built to last.

She steered her probe toward the marshalling area indicated on her inset map. Tiny green dots on the map represented probes controlled by the other Junior Rangers. She turned toward Bob, his probe just to her left.

"Query: is everything all right, Jenny?" Bob's translator spoke in a perfect monotone through her comm system.

"Yes, why?"

"Statement: one of your manipulator arms is dragging."

Jenny checked her status display. The arm in question did not respond to her commands. "I can't move it. It's stuck. Or broken."

"Statement: one moment, I will assist you." Bob rolled his probe toward Jenny. He lifted the inoperative arm out of the dirt, and tucked it under one of the other manipulator arms.

"Hopeful statement: that should do it. The arm should stay in place if you use one of the other ones to hold it down."

"Thanks, Bob." Jenny locked the arm in place, so she wouldn't accidentally use it. The rest of the Junior Rangers were well on their way to the marshalling area, so she and Bob engaged their motors on full speed to catch up. Plumes of viscous sludge arced from their treads as they rambled over the uneven surface.

"Despite the high temperature and crushing pressure"—Bariss's voice crackled as lightning flashed across a bank of clouds in the distance—"there's some really fascinating evidence of volcanism over in this area."

Jenny's HUD indicated Zack lagged behind the main group. She sent a tight-beam message directly to his probe. "Everything all right?"

"Fine. Just upset my parents aren't going to let me go to Ersid."

Despite all her personal drama, she remembered him complaining on Valtra that his parents decided Junior Ranger excursions were too dangerous for their only son.

"Well, I probably can't go, either. At least you can ask your parents. My father barely knows his own name right now."

Zack didn't respond. Jenny nestled her probe between Bob's and Xal's as Bariss continued his lecture on the basaltic flow at the location in which they were parked. She decided she wouldn't go to Ersid if Zack couldn't go. As much as she wanted to see Mungus's home world, obtaining permission from her parents in their current state presented a challenge she didn't wish to undertake.

~ * * * ~

Zack understood Jenny's attempt to console him by saying she couldn't go to Ersid either, but he didn't care. He spun his probe and moved away from the group gathered at the base of the lava flow. Ahead of him, a mound of ochre ground jutted like a blister from the side of the plateau.

The brown sediment, streaked with dull yellow grit, resembled wax that had flowed from a diseased candle and covered whatever lay underneath. He reached forward with a manipulator arm and scratched at the dirt.

Expecting to find nothing more than another layer of dirt under the current layer, Zack excavated aimlessly. No prior civilizations existed on Venus, and surface conditions were far too harsh for any extensive exploration to have occurred before his arrival.

Bariss's voice crackled over his comm system. Zack paid no attention to it until an alarm blared in his ears and his HUD flashed with red lights.

"Back to the marshalling area. Everyone, back, Now!" Zack recognized Bariss's even, but stern, tone.

"What's going on?" As Zack turned around to face the group, he caught a flash of light coming from the area he had scratched with his probe.

"That storm changed course. It's coming straight for us. The electrical discharges are going to disrupt communication from Cytherea. Such a forced disconnect could cause catastrophic neural feedback if the safeties don't engage in time, and I'll not have anyone in my troop fall prey to dumpshock. Not on my watch. Now, move it!"

Zack spun in place to see if he could determine quickly the source of the light he thought he saw.

His scraping revealed a flat bit of steel-colored metal with a flashing green light embedded in it. Sludge-like dirt oozed over it, concealing it. He scraped it away once more.

That can't be.

The green light flickered.

"Is your probe broken, Jackson? *Get moving!*"

Zack backed away from the light as the sludge flowed down over it. He turned and headed in the direction of the main group, pausing to arrange some loose stones into a makeshift landmark so he could resume his exploration when he returned.

As lightning flashed across the sky, his probe jerked and lurched as though stuck in glue. Bariss shouted for everyone to disconnect as soon as they returned to the marshalling yard.

Normally, if communications disconnected while operating a probe, the pod's safeties protected the operator. However, if static discharge overloaded the system and forcibly disconnected someone from the VR system before the safeties engaged, it could leave the probe operator susceptible to all manner of neurological trauma.

Of course, Zack had no implants, so forcible disconnection posed somewhat less peril to him. At worst, he might experience nausea and headache for a few hours. Someone like Jenny, though, whose VR interface fed images and data directly into her brain, would be subjected to considerably higher risk. Zack had read stories on the Hypernet about people experiencing temporary paralysis, brain damage, even death.

Ahead, he observed the probes lurching to a stop before settling into Wait Mode as the Junior Rangers logged off. He sped toward the marshalling area as his vision cut out. He felt the tracks of his probe grind to a halt still a dozen or more meters from the main body of the group. His HUD still displayed his position, albeit against a background of pitch black.

His unit disconnected.

With a flash of white, the real world reappeared, and the VR pod hissed open. Other Junior Rangers hopped out of their pods. Zack unstrapped himself and rolled out.

Bariss walked toward him, a scowl cutting his face. "What was that? Did you even hear anything about the lava flow?"

"Sorry, Bariss. I thought I saw something odd on that mound behind it." In that moment, Zack decided to keep what he saw to himself. "I was stupid. It was just a thing on my HUD. I got confused and thought I was seeing something on the ground." He chuckled and regarded his feet. "It's been so long since I've been in one of these things, I forgot what it's like."

"Right." Bariss huffed and turned to the group. "All right, well, everyone seems to have gotten out okay. We'll call it an early night. See you next week. Think about the Festival of Starlight. I think you'd all enjoy it."

Bariss approached Zack, but a call interrupted him. After a few grunts, the Devoran turned and left the VR pod lounge.

"So, want to go do something tonight?" Dravs put his arm around Zack. "I have a ton of VR credits. We could play a game or something."

Zack pulled out his C7 and checked the time. He had a couple of hours. "Sure."

"Jenny? Xal? Bob? Ix?" Dravs nodded at them in turn. "Want to solve the "Mystery of Megas-tu" with me?

Chapter 11

Jenny considered telling Dravs she'd already solved the "Mystery of Megas-Tu." She spent a lot of time playing games in VR between her return from Valtra and the start of the term on Cytherea. Ix did not hesitate to beg off, saying it already knew all the secrets. The Valtraxian wished them luck and returned to the dorms.

In the end, she decided not to spoil their fun and climbed into the pod. She logged in, and after the usual flash of white, found herself in a space station lounge. Dressed in a neatly pressed yellow skirt and matching blouse, both hung straight in defiance of physical laws. Her biggest objection to these interactive mysteries was how they didn't model reality. All their space stations and ships seemed to possess magic gravity. A petty objection, to be sure; these stories took place in entirely fictional universes, where everyone communicated with each other across light-years with no delay.

Zack approached her, still attired in his Junior Ranger uniform. "Hey, how'd you change clothes?

Jenny laughed. "Just go into your settings. You can wear whatever you want."

Dravs came up behind Zack and slapped him on the back. The Devoran wore a leather kilt with a strap crossing from his right shoulder to the opposite side on his waist.

"This is going to be great, you guys." His teeth flashed in the harsh white light of the space station as he glanced at his surroundings and grinned. "These Seven Galaxy stories are so cool."

"Wry observation: the ambient temperature is twenty-three degrees Celsius." Bob's avatar, a lanky, ebony-skinned biped with pointed ears and short-cropped, shaggy blue hair, stretched as he acclimated to a body without an envirosuit.

"Aw, Bob. Why are you an Aelfar? They're the hated oppressors." Dravs scowled at the Ryll.

"Factual statement: I find this form aesthetically pleasing. With sincerity: I have no intention of oppressing you."

"Where's Xal?" Jenny searched for the Ersidian. A grey-skinned, four-armed humanoid waved at her.

"Here." Xal's avatar stood twice as tall in this program as his Ersidian form.

68

"Cool, a Kroze!" Dravs nodded in appreciation. "If we need a door knocked down, you're our guy."

"I'll bet he'd be great at opening jars of pickles." Zack grinned as he admired Xal's hulking virtual form.

Dravs led them into a nightclub. A pounding techno rhythm assaulted Jenny's ears, and the strobing, wheeling rainbows of light became a headache-inducing kaleidoscope. Females of several different species writhed on the dance floor. Some of the dancer's proportions were distorted, arms and legs elongated, flopping like noodles as they danced. She recognized one dancer gyrating past as a character from popular children's fiction.

She pulled Dravs aside. "What did you do?"

When Jenny experienced the "Mystery of Megas-Tu" and she entered this club—it was required to kick off the story—the club's music contained far less pounding rhythms and reminded her more of jazz than an auditory weapon.

The Devoran grinned. "I hacked the graphics engine and added some mods to make it more fun. Seven Galaxies stories are so grim." He admired the room, his tongue dangling from between his pointed teeth as he snickered. "The noodle arms crack me up."

Jenny snorted and approached Zack. He stood, slack-jawed. She closed his mouth. "Everything okay? We can leave. He's not supposed to be hacking the program like this."

"Leave? Isn't this where the story starts?"

"Unbelievable." Jenny gave in and followed Dravs as he approached the club manager.

Dravs buried himself in the part of master investigator. Meanwhile, Xal stood watch over Bob, the target of withering looks by every character in the club, especially the humans. From what Jenny remembered, Aelfar, like Bob's character, were universally despised because of their wanton cruelty. The fact they kept human slave colonies didn't help their reputation. Were it not for a warbot-size Kroze staring down every scowling patron, a conflict certainly would have ensued.

As it was, Dravs spent so much time pumping the club manager for information that by the time they gained the first clue about the mystery, the one-hour alert chimed.

Jenny waved her hand to gain her friends' attention. "I have to go. It's getting late, and I have a cloud-gliding trial tomorrow. I need to get some rest."

"Aw, we were just getting started." Dravs crossed his arms and frowned.

"You spent too much time talking to that guy." Zack scratched his head. "Does his favorite color matter?"

"It might!"

Jenny knew it didn't. She bade farewell to her friends and signed out. The rest of the group soon followed, but she didn't wait around for them to exit their pods. Only the hiss of releasing latches told her they followed her lead and exited the program.

Jenny found Hiri watching a historical drama when she arrived at the dorm.

"Have a good night?" Hiri paused the program and peered over the back of the couch at her. The man on the holoviewer, dressed in the garb of a late-twenty-first-century physician, froze in a half-sneer, half-laugh.

"Not bad. I don't care much for piloting remote probes during some of these meetings, but the other activities usually make up for it."

Hiri followed Jenny into her room. Astrid and Gabrielle, seated and reading on their respective beds, greeted Jenny before returning to their studies.

"Hey, can I ask you something?"

Jenny turned down her bed and nodded. "Of course."

"Want to get dinner tomorrow? Just you and me?"

"Where did you have in mind?" *Ugh, tomorrow. My parents are scheduled to call again. I hope Papa has more skin.*

"Bit Bytes."

"Sounds good."

"Great, it's a date!" Hiri leaned forward and pecked Jenny on the cheek, then turn and left the room. She rubbed the spot the other girl kissed.

Astrid eyed Jenny over the top edge of her tablet. "Aw, isn't that sweet?"

"What?" Jenny eyed her roommate's raised eyebrow. Astrid lowered her head and snickered.

A date? I'm going on a date?

~ * * * ~

When Zack returned to his room, he found Ix in the common area with Polly and Barbara watching the news on the holoviewer.

"EAC archaeologists on Valtra have been ejected from a site they claim proves Valtraxians are a species uplifted by the Athosians." The screen displayed a picture all too familiar to Zack—the site of their last camp on Valtra over the summer. "Devoran officials have declined to comment on the archaeologists' claims and maintain the EAC team failed to present proper authorization to commence digging in a protected area on a Confederation planet. EAC officials say the Devorans revoked the archaeologists' access after their arrest. The investigation is ongoing."

Ix chittered. "The dig site shown appears to be identical to where you and Jenny fell through the floor." Ix moved around the sofa, cocking its head as it regarded Zack.

It sure looks like it. He remembered his promise, although he didn't want to lie to his friend. "I think it might have been."

"That man said Valtraxians were uplifted?" Ix glanced at the screen and then again at Zack.

"Did he? I just got here, I wasn't paying attention."

"Curious."

"Pipe down, you two." Polly tossed a crisp at Zack. It missed him and bounced off Ix's carapace. "Some of us are trying to keep up on current events."

"Sorry."

Ix retrieved the crisp and tossed it toward Polly. It landed on her head. Zack snickered at her shouts of protest and alarm. He ducked into the room he shared with Ix before she retaliated.

He noticed something odd about his desk. His tablet rested where he left it, but neither the iron star nor the bust of his head remained.

"Ix? Has anyone been in here?"

"No, Zack."

71

A glint on the floor caught Zack's eye. He crouched and found the bust lying upon the floor between the bed and the desk. He discovered half the iron star there, too.

Half?

He resumed his examination of the desk. An oil stain ran down its side. Farther back, near the wall, he found the other half of the iron star, as well as both halves of the sphere in which it had been encased.

"What the...?" He inspected the fragments. The cool metal felt rough to his touch, and its concave interior was empty.

"How is this hollow? Ix? Look at this."

He held up the pieces toward the Valtraxian. Ix chittered as it examined the parts.

"There is an organic residue inside."

"Organic?" Zack ran a finger along the inside of one of the halves. Gooey slime coated the tip of his finger. He recoiled and placed the pieces on his desk.

"Gross." Zack wiped his finger on his pants. "Wait, what's that on the floor?"

He pointed to a dark smudge leading away from his work area. Ix chittered and followed the trail. It led to Mickey's bed, disappearing under it. Zack dropped to the floor and lifted the dangling blanket. Lack of light under the bed made it difficult for Zack to detect any difference in the carpet's color.

"I need a flashlight." He fumbled at his belt for his C7.

Ix lowered itself and flicked on a flashlight it pulled from its myriad pouches. "The trail appears to lead to that vent."

Sure enough, when Zack followed the beam of Ix's flashlight, he noticed the dark smudge led directly to the vent where several of the louvers lay bent, as if something had forced itself through.

"Does this... there was something *inside* that iron star?"

Ix turned off its flashlight and took one of the fragments off Zack's desk. "It would appear so."

"Hey, what's going on?" Mickey entered and tossed his guitar case on the bed before he sat down.

Zack and Ix explained what they discovered. When they reached the part about the iron star's inhabitant crawling under Mickey's bed and into the vent behind it, the young man pulled his feet up off the floor and scooted to the edge farthest away from the vent.

"Uh, that's freaky. Do you think Kaneer will switch beds with me?" Mickey hugged his knees.

Ix tugged at the foot of the bed. "Perhaps if we move the bed away from the vent, I can examine more closely and determine if the creature lingers."

Mickey slid off the bed and gripped one end, while Zack grasped the other. They grunted as they pulled it away from the wall. Ix scrambled over the bed and inspected the grate.

"Zack, may I borrow your multi-tool?"

"Sure." Zack removed the device from its holster and tossed it to Ix. The Valtraxian steadied itself against the wall with one hand, aimed the flashlight at the grate with another, and used two more to open the multi-tool before working to open the vent cover.

Sniffing the air, Kaneer entered. "Are we reconfiguring the room? Kaneer should have been made aware of this beforehand. This one would have been willing to assist."

"Not quite." Zack reiterated his discovery a third time.

"This is most disturbing. We are not allowed to keep pets." Kaneer wagged his finger at Zack. "Very sneaky, Zack Jackson!"

"It isn't a pet!" Zack picked up half the iron star from his desk and tossed it at the Kerrolian.

Kaneer caught and sniffed it, his nose crinkling as he recoiled. He tossed it onto Zack's desk where it clattered across the top and came to rest against Zack's tablet. "Vile."

"I thought it was just a piece of metal."

"I do not see the creature, Zack." Ix turned around and perched on the edge of Mickey's bed, facing the three other students.

"Well, where did it go?" Zack craned his neck to see around Ix. The vent cover lay on the floor, but he could see only a few inches into the vent itself. Far too small for any of them to crawl into, the space remained a mystery.

"I do not know. The vent system for Cytherea is extensive. Through the ducts, it can access any room on this level and possibly move throughout the city." Ix cocked its head. "It will likely run into trouble at the junction fans."

Zack opened his mouth to respond when the lights switched off. The room plunged into pitch darkness. Only the light from Ix's flashlight cut through the inky blackness.

The Valtraxian held up the flashlight to illuminate its face. "Perhaps it eats power cables."

73

Chapter 12

"Hey, did you hear about the power outage in Hathor Dome's dorms last night?" Astrid plopped her tray on the table and seated herself alongside Jenny. Anahita's cafeteria bustled with an unusual amount of activity, which Jenny suspected was due to closure of Ishtar Plaza's park for Festival of Starlight preparations.

"I read something about it on the city news net. Did they find the cause yet?" Jenny stirred another scoop of sugar into her coffee. She needed it extra sweet.

Astrid tied her platinum-blond hair into a ponytail, running her fingers through it and frowning. "Ugh. Takes forever to dry." She picked up a sweet roll and bit into it before answering. "They're being coy about it. I've heard rumors..."

Jenny understood student gossip regarding city operations bore little resemblance to the truth. "I'm sure all those conflicting stories are all correct in every way." *I hope Zack didn't have anything to do with it.*

Astrid snorted. "No doubt!" Her head turned to watch a passing pair of Devoran athletes. Jenny didn't remember their names, but she recognized them from the school's gravball team.

Sipping from her cup, Jenny winced at the scalding, bitter brew. She added another scoop of sugar.

Jenny's other roommates, Gabrielle and Cait, joined them.

Cait snorted as she sat down. "You're daft, Gabby. Absolutely bonkers."

"Says you." She snatched a muffin from Cait's tray.

"What's going on?" Astrid tried to take the muffin from Gabrielle, but the auburn-haired student took a bite out of it first.

In retaliation, Cait stole Gabrielle's bacon. "Gabby thinks Duncan's got the hots for Bradley. Any fool can see Duncan's been making moon eyes at Zoe."

Jenny didn't know Duncan, Bradley, or Zoe well enough to understand the dynamics of that triangle. Who dated whom did not interest her in the least.

Gabrielle shook her head. "Nope. Besides, it doesn't matter. Hey, Jenny. Did you take Baker's test yet?"

74

"Yes. We're supposed to receive the results today." Jenny watched the cafeteria entrance for Hiri. Before she realized what she'd done, she added three more scoops of sugar to her coffee.

"That essay question at the end was the worst!" Gabrielle furrowed her brow. "If a train leaving Vancouver carrying fifty passengers travels east at two hundred kilometers per hour, meets a train in Calgary traveling west at two hundred and ten kilometers per hour and fifteen passengers transfer, what airspeed velocity would a swallow have to travel carrying two coconuts to meet one at Kamloops then overtake the other one in Medicine Hat?"

"You remembered that from the test?" Jenny sipped her now too-sweet coffee. *Eh, it's close enough.* "You know that was an optional question, yes?"

Gabrielle dropped the lone slice of bacon she saved from Cait's thieving fingers. "What? I spent so much time trying to get that one first I didn't finish the test!"

"It was even labeled! 'Joke question: five extra points.'" Jenny laughed.

Astrid gripped her cousin's shoulders and hugged her. "Aw, maybe you got it right?"

The only reason Jenny knew the answer was because her father was inordinately fond of the joke. "The answer is 'African or European?' in regard to the swallow. It's an ancient Earth joke. The train has nothing to do with it."

Gabrielle groaned and buried her head in her hands. "That shouldn't even be allowed. It's maths! It's not a joking matter!"

Astrid laughed. "Trick questions suck." She snatched Gabrielle's forgotten bacon, winked at Cait, and ate it. "I'm glad I got Davidson for maths. Even if he does think it's serious business, that might 'save our lives one day.'"

"It wasn't a trick question, though." Jenny sipped her coffee. "It was clearly labeled as a gag. You weren't penalized for answering it incorrectly or just skipping it."

Astrid's cousin scoffed. "Jokes in maths.... how is that going to save my life or even help with my career?" She searched her tray for her bacon, then narrowed her eyes and glared at Cait.

"Professor Baker wanted to be a comedian, I think." Jenny checked the time. She downed the rest of her coffee, shoved the remainder of her buttered croissant into her mouth, and gathered up her dishes.

"Off to class?" Astrid caught Jenny's knife as it slid off her plate and placed it on top, under her thumb.

Jenny grunted and nodded. She mumbled something resembling "good-bye" and dumped her dishes in the recycler before leaving the cafeteria. She rushed down the hallway to the transit station, and boarded the travel pod to Hathor Dome with no time to spare. It promised to be a busy day that wouldn't end when her classes were over.

~ * * * ~

Sleeping on the sofa with Kaneer and Mickey was not the ideal situation, but Zack made do. Since the city switched to night-cycle, even their window remained opaque. Without lights of any kind, they decided the utter darkness in their dorm room made it too dangerous to remain in it. Even Ix's ocular implants did not penetrate the blackness; they required some ambient light to process visual information, albeit much less than human eyes. The Valtraxian pulled its blankets into the common area. It made a temporary nest beneath the holoviewer.

Fortunately, the power outage did not affect the common area. From what Zack overheard discussed among the techs sent to assess and repair the damage, only their room was affected. Before the techs arrived, Zack stashed the broken iron orb in his desk.

The rest of their dorm mates gave them no end of grief for breaking their room. Zack explained first to Alastair, then Polly and Ian, that blame did not lie with them, but he finally gave up and ignored their jibes.

After cleaning up and getting dressed, Zack approached Ix. "Want to go to Breaking Fast this morning? I don't feel like the cafeteria." A restaurant that served only breakfast in Ishtar Plaza, many students ate at there as an alternative to the various dorm cafes.

"Ishtar Plaza is closed." Ix strapped on its harness.

76

"Closed?" Zack thought a moment. "Oh, that's right. The Starlight Feastival."

"I believe it is called the Festival of Starlight. Dravs seems to misunderstand the name."

"I think he gets it wrong on purpose."

Zack's C7 pinged. He opened it as they headed toward the cafeteria. A video message from Ersid awaited him. "Hey, it's Mungus!"

He pulled up the message. Ix moved to leave, but Zack gestured for the Valtraxian to remain while he played it.

"Hey Zack." The Ersidian sounded exhausted. His braids hung bedraggled and frayed, heavy with perspiration. "The Royal Citadel is tough. I've just completed the first of ten trials. I'm a First Circle Cadet now. Whoo." Mungus spun a finger. "My sire thinks this is going to be the greatest thing ever for me. I don't know that I agree, but I don't have much of a choice. How are things going on Cytherea? Rap that bug on its hard head for me, will you? Give Jenny a hug for me, unless you're not into that, then just tell her I said 'Hey.'"

Zack grinned and tapped Ix on the head with a single finger. The Valtraxian cocked its head and chittered before it returned its attention to the message.

"Once I'm finished, I'll be required to serve a tour in the Confederation Defense Force. The upside is I can request a duty station; I'm not obligated to be in the Royal Guard or stay on Ersid. I might request duty on Vilicus just to annoy my sire and get back at him for making me quit the Junior Rangers and all that. Maybe by then, your parents will have moved there and we can see each other over your summers.

"Let Jenny know I lit some incense in the Temple of the Ancestors for her parents. It doesn't do much more than stink up the room, but some people think it helps."

The Ersidian grinned. "See you around, Zack. Don't forget to send me a reply in a timely fashion this time."

Mungus referred to a message he sent the previous year when, for the better part of the school term, Zack continually forgot to send him pictures from their trip to Bestic.

"Skip? Remind me to reply to Mungus tonight." *That should do the trick.*

"Acknowledged, Zack. Reminder set."

77

"Thank you for not rapping my head as hard as Mungus would have, Zack." Ix touched the human's arm.

Zack laughed. "No problem."

"When we were on Valtra, did you see anything Athosian? In the arena perhaps?"

Zack felt as if he'd been hit in the gut with a club. "Uh, buh, we... umm. What?"

"I have been thinking about that news report. You seemed to have stumbled into something in the ruins, but no one will say what. You have been unusually reticent to speak of what you saw under there."

All thoughts of breakfast evaporated. Zack stumbled to a bench outside the cafeteria and sat down. The Valtraxian regarded him with its two large, compound eyes. It stroked Zack's upper arm. "You are uncomfortable. If you cannot speak about it, I understand."

"I can't, Ix. I'm sorry." Zack hated keeping something from his friend, but he didn't want to lie to the Valtraxian, either. *I already blabbed to the princess, but that was different. She's an important person.*

"Do you think it is possible? That Valtraxians were uplifted from ignorant animals by the Athosians?"

Mention of Athosians turned the heads of a few passing students, but they didn't linger. Zack couldn't fill even a tiny teacup with what he knew about uplifting animals. He had never heard the term prior to encountering the lab on Valtra. "I don't know. Is something like that even possible?"

"In theory. We are all implanted with cybernetics from an early age. No Valtraxian is exempt. It is possible without them we are simply, as so many humans are fond of observing, big bugs."

Zack did not and would never believe that. He put his hand on top of Ix's. "You're more than just a big bug, Ix. You're my friend."

"Yes, Zack. I am yours, as well. I would not have friends such as you had I not asserted my individuality and left the hive. I feel fortunate." The Valtraxian tapped Zack's C7. "We should eat, or we'll be late for class."

"Go ahead." Zack gestured toward the cafeteria. "I'm not hungry anymore."

"Very well." The Valtraxian skittered into the cafeteria. Zack heard a chorus of greetings for his friend and smiled. He returned his attention his C7.

"Skip, send a message to Mr. McPheely. I need to talk to him soon."

"Acknowledged, Zack. I can make an appointment for you through the school's scheduling system. Will tonight after dinner be convenient?"

"That'd be great, Skip. Thanks."

"You're welcome, Zack."

He wanted to respect Bariss's wishes, but he wrestled with having to lie to his friend. Zack believed Ix deserved to know what they found there. His counselor would know what to do. Attired in a green-striped black skirt and matching jacket over a white shirt, a girl sitting on a nearby bench raised her hand in a half wave. After a moment, he recognized her as the girl in the blue dress from the other day. He looked away when he felt his face flush and hurried to his class.

Indecision weighed on him all day, and that heavy feeling increased when Coach Dagon called him off the track while they ran laps at the beginning of class.

"Jackson! A moment, please."

Zack veered off the course and jogged toward the big Ersidian. "What do you need, Coach?" He panted the words, working to catch his breath during his brief respite.

"Stay after class. Roger wants to take you out in a glider."

Of all the times... "Today? I can't."

Coach Dagon put his hands on his hips and eyed his human student. "You can't?"

"I have an appointment with Mr. McPheely."

"Regarding?"

Zack regarded the artificial turf and shuffled his feet. "I can't say."

"Oh." Coach Dagon huffed. "One of *those* things. Fine. I'll tell Roger to can it tonight. Got any appointments tomorrow?"

"Isn't tomorrow night the Festival of Starlight?"

"Yeah, tomorrow night. You don't have any classes during the day, do you?" He poked Zack in the chest, causing the human to stumble backward to keep his footing. "Put it in your schedule."

"I will."

79

"Now, go." Dagon gestured toward the track. "Finish your lap."

As Zack jogged away, he heard the Ersidian call after him. "Don't be last!"

Being last meant having to jog an extra lap. Zack didn't believe Coach Dagon would make him run that extra lap since he would be the reason Zack finished last, but he raced to catch up so he wouldn't have to find out.

Chapter 13

Zack, his tray laden with spaghetti and meat sauce, garlic bread, and a glass of water, sat next to Kaneer. Bob sat across from them.

"Are those worms, Zack Jackson? They look like worms."

Bob extended a pseudopod through his open faceplate to probe at the plate of food before him. "Wry observation: maybe it's vermicelli."

"Ew, gross. No!" Zack picked up a clump of spaghetti with his fork and showed it to his friends. "It's just pasta."

"What is it made of?" Kaneer leaned forward and sniffed the noodles dangling from Zack's fork.

Zack retracted the laden utensil. He stuffed its contents in his mouth before the Kerrolian moved too close. "Um, wheat?" He swallowed the half-chewed pasta. "I think."

"Bah! Plants are what food eats!" Kaneer held up what resembled a barely cooked sausage. "Why do you humans insist on burning all your meats and filling your bellies with plants?"

"Factual observation: humans are omnivorous." The speaker on Bob's translator unit flashed in rhythm with the words. His pseudopod squirmed on the plate, enveloping all the food on it.

"My mother says talking with your mouth full is rude, Bob." Zack snickered as he tore into his garlic bread.

"With mocking laughter: ha, ha, ha. I don't have a mouth."

Fat spurted across the table, splattering on Bob's environmental suit as Kaneer bit into the sausage. "Is there anything Ryll won't eat?"

"Thoughtful reply: rocks." Bob extended a second pseudopod, and cleaned the meat juice off the front of his suit. A drop of gooey liquid spattered on the top of his helmet.

"Sprinklers must be leaking again." Kaneer poked a grey hunk on his plate. "This one does not believe this sausage is meat."

Zack glanced above them. Another dollop of goo dangled in a long string before falling and splattering on Bob's helmet. "That's not water."

The ceiling panel gave way, and an object fell, smacking into Bob's helmet with a wet plop. It pulled itself up to the top of the Ryll's helmet, an octopod-type creature with translucent, pearl-colored skin ringed with eyes. Its tentacles splayed beneath it as it wobbled. Bob poked his helmet with a pseudopod.

"With barely restrained panic: that is definitely not water."

Zack stared, mouth agape. "An Athosian?"

The student passing behind Bob screeched as the creature extended a tentacle toward him. The sound caused other nearby students to gasp and shriek.

More students turned and stared. The small blob on Bob's head wiggled its tentacles. It leapt off the Ryll's helmet toward a passing student.

Pandemonium erupted.

"Grab it! Don't let it get away." Zack dumped his bowl of half-eaten spaghetti onto his tray and dove over the table. Cafeteria monitors shouted for order.

Bob spread his arms and legs to block the other students from running up the aisle in the direction the little blob leapt. Another student waved her arms in the air as she fled.

"Get it off! Get it off." She disentangled it from her hair and tossed it across the room.

"Over there." A dark-skinned student with red streaks in her braids pointed Zack toward the creature's location. It ambled along the floor as it headed for a vent.

Clutching his bowl, Zack sped toward it. "Out of the way! Out of the way."

Panicked students crossed his path, and he dodged to avoid stumbling into them. He caught sight of the creature as it wrangled with the louvres on the vent grate.

Zack raised the bowl with which he intended to trap the creature.

His foot caught on a Devoran's tail.

The bowl flew from his grasp, and he pitched forward, crashing into a chair before bouncing to the ground and onto his back.

"What's all this then?" A man attired in a suit sneered at Zack and glanced at the vent grate. Zack knew Professor Chapman, one of the school's exobiology teachers, by reputation but had yet to take one of his classes.

"I tried to catch it, but it got away."

"A pet?" Chapman's moustache twitched. "Pets are not allowed in Cytherean Academy."

Zack groaned as he tried to sit up. "Not my pet." He pointed above the area near where he'd been eating. "It fell out of the ceiling."

"Nonsense."

Several of the students milling about chimed in and corroborated Zack's story. Bob lumbered over and pointed at the slime trail on his helmet.

"Emphatic statement: it landed on my head."

Chapman peered at Bob's helmet and scoffed. "Ryll don't have heads. Nevertheless, your point is taken."

"I think it's an Athosian." Zack grabbed his knees.

"Nonsense. It was likely just some slimy vermin brought in with the Devoran transients." He glanced at the students and clapped his hands. "Everyone, go about your business now!"

As Zack scowled at the professor and opened his mouth to protest, someone offered her hand to Zack and pulled him to his feet. He recognized the girl in the blue dress who caught his eye a few days earlier. She smiled as his hand lingered in hers.

"You almost had it."

"Uh, yeah..." He couldn't pull his gaze away from hers. *My butt hurts.*

"You're Zack, right?" She withdrew from his grasp and clasped both hands behind her back.

Chapman pushed the two aside as he spoke aloud to the air, obviously conversing on a communications implant. "Yes, get the scrubbots in here and a maintenance bot. There's something in the vents... I don't know. A *thing*. I didn't see it."

They walked toward Zack's table. Bob stood, pseudopod extended from his helmet, slurping up all the spilled food on the table, including Zack's discarded spaghetti.

"We're in a couple of classes together." The girl pushed one of her braids off her shoulder. "I'm Rio."

"Rio..." Zack tried to remember which classes of his she attended. *An Athosian... where did it come from?*

"EAC History. You sit in the back with those two Devorans, the blue one and the black one."

"Oh yeah, Dravs and Kat." Zack's stomach grumbled as he watched Bob finish eating their food. *I need to do something...*

"Also, Devoran Cultural Studies."

Bob's faceplate clicked shut. "Tentative query: you were finished with your food, weren't you, Zack?"

"Not really." Zack waved his hand in dismissal. "I wasn't going to eat it off the table, though." He glanced at the service lines and hesitated. *Ugh. I'm hungry. I guess there's nothing I can do, but I need to tell Jenny and Bariss right after I eat. Maybe Mister McPheely, too.* He checked the chronometer on his C7; there was still time before his appointment.

One corner of her mouth upturned, Rio stood alongside him, head cocked as she regarded Bob.

Zack coughed and pointed to the line. "Um, I'm going to get more food."

"I'll go with you. I haven't had dessert yet."

Rio waited in the queue alongside Zack. She stood only slightly taller than he, and he wondered why he hadn't seen her last year.

"Are you a first-year?" He regretted his question as soon as he asked it; if she were a first-year, they wouldn't be sharing EAC History and Devoran Cultural Studies.

"It's my first year here, but I transferred." Her voice possessed a soft, almost lyrical quality.

"Oh, where are you from? Earth?"

Her light blue eyes appeared almost silver, sparkling in the light from overhead. "We... move around a lot. I was... born... on a ship."

"I'm going to be moving soon, too." They reached the front of the line, and Zack scanned the dinner options. After watching Bob envelop his spaghetti, it no longer appealed to him as a meal. "I mean, I'll still be going to school here, but we're moving to Vilicus. That whole Earth Reclamation Project thing."

Rio nodded and smiled. "I'm familiar with it. I spend most of my time on Vilicus, it seems. I think you'll like it there."

Zack selected fish and chips from the menu. The dispenser dinged as it delivered his freshly fabricated meal. Dinner violated his mother's rule against foods all having the same color, especially golden brown, but it sounded good.

"What are you going to have for dessert?"

Rio studied the menu. "Peach pie sounds good. I don't know what a peach is, but I've heard 'peachy' used as an adjective."

"You've never had a peach?" Zack punched up an order for two slices of peach pie. When they arrived, he piled them on his tray and proceeded to the now-clean table. Bob still lingered.

"I don't plan on spilling this for you, Bob." Zack raised his eyebrows as he regarded the Ryll.

"In mock offense: I wasn't going to eat your food. Again." Bob placed his hand over his chest. "Lighthearted statement: have a good night. I must go study."

Rio watched him lumber away as her fork hovered above the slice of pie. "Are all Ryll as funny as him?"

Zack swallowed his half-chewed mouthful of steaming, hot fish. "Beats me. He's the only one I know."

~ * * * ~

Jenny rushed to freshen up after classes. *It's just two friends going out to dinner... I think? Hiri called it a date.* The prospect both thrilled and frightened her. While she brushed her hair, her parents called.

"Mother? Papa?"

The screen crackled before coming into focus. Her father's eyes glowed red, the only visible part of his face almost completely covered in bandages. Her mother smiled, her hair freshly styled in a feathered pixie cut. "Genevieve! We've so much to tell you!"

Jenny tugged at a knot in her hair. *I just washed this. How does this happen?* "You have good news then?"

"Oh yes." Amélie nodded at François. "Would you like to tell her, dear?"

His head turned like a stiff, unlubricated machine breaking loose for the first time in ages. "Yes. I will tell her." His cadence resembled that of a dispassionate machine. It reminded Jenny of Bob, minus the Ryll's sense of humor. "Gen... Jenny. I remember you prefer to be called Jenny. I was... proud to hold you in my arms the day you were born."

The brush slid out of Jenny's hand. It dangled as it remained attached to her hair before dropping to the floor. "You remember? Everything?"

He lowered his head. "No. Not everything. But some. The rest will... return in time I am told."

A tear ran down Jenny's cheek. Hearing her father reveal his pride at her birth hit her in a way she didn't expect. She wiped her eyes. "That's good. That's so good, Papa."

"Yes. Good."

Her mother panned the camera away from her father and focused it on herself. "Tell us something, Genevieve. About school? Good news?"

Jenny's mind went blank. She considered what to share, momentarily at a loss since her parents so rarely asked about her life.

"I... um... I have a date tonight." As soon as she blurted it, she cringed. She had not intended to share that kind of personal detail of her life with her parents just yet.

"That's wonderful!" Her mother beamed. "I hope he's a nice boy."

She was. Jenny bit her cheek, attempting to maintain a neutral expression. "She is one of the girls in my dorm. A year ahead of me, but very nice. I think she wants to be an engineer—I'm not sure what kind—and she likes the same kind of old films I do."

"Oh! Well, that sounds lovely." Amélie's smile dimmed a bit. "I hope you enjoy yourself, dear, but don't let it interfere with your studies."

"I won't, Mother."

François turned his head toward his wife. "She is a good girl, Amélie. Responsible. An attentive student. She never disappoints us."

Jenny found herself staring at the out-of-focus image of her father over her mother's shoulder. She couldn't remember the last time she'd heard unvarnished praise like that from him. Tears rolled down her cheeks as she sat, weeping, unable to speak.

"Well, we'll let you get ready for your date. Adieu, petite chou." Amélie waved and disconnected.

Jenny dried her eyes and finished getting ready. Crying made her eyes puffy and red, and the remedies she tried seemed ineffective. She tried rinsing with cool water, but it didn't seem to help.

To her credit, when she met with Hiri, she asked only if Jenny was all right.

86

"Parental call. Things are improving. You were right about my father's memory."

"I'm glad." Hiri took Jenny's hand. "Anytime you want to talk, okay?"

"Thanks."

Bit Bytes bustled with off-duty workers, including a smattering of Devoran personnel. Jenny received a request from Hiri to link their augmented reality implants, so they'd see the same alterations.

After approving the request, the French café overlay flickered, instantly replaced by a Tuscan veranda overlooking a vineyard.

"I hope this is okay. I spent hours trying to find the right setting."

"It's lovely." Jenny glanced at her surroundings. "Not what I expected, but it's very nice."

Jenny took in the Tuscan setting, which featured the sun hanging low in the sky, casting pastel colors across scattered clouds. A copse of evergreen Cyprus stood like a grove of pillars in the distance, and workers tended rows of grapes in a vineyard between the veranda and the trees.

Hiri led Jenny to a table for two, and the two sat opposite each other. "Have you ever been to Italy?"

"No, just France."

Hiri squeezed her hands together and smiled. "Oh, I love autumn in Tuscany. My parents took us there a few times. They tried to divide our holidays between Earth and Titan. We even climbed Olympus Mons on Mars once. I'm sure you've done that a dozen times." One of the largest mountains in the solar system, Olympus Mons sprawled, covering an area nearly as large as France itself.

Jenny pursed her lips. "I'm from Messier Habitat, not Mars. I've never been to Olympus Mons, only the Ocampo-Friedmann Memorial in Aresville."

"I know. I just figured since you were so close…"

"My parents hardly ever took me on holiday with them. That's why they had me join the Junior Rangers." She pulled up the menu on the table's ordering screen. The menu at Bit Bytes changed depending on the environment overlay chosen. Jenny ordered pumpkin and radicchio risotto and flipped the ordering screen toward Hiri so she could order.

"I bet you've seen some really interesting things with them."

A couple of years ago, Jenny would have denied being at all interested in Junior Rangers outings or activities. Now, however, she admitted, Zack, Ix, and Mungus ignited something within her. She took a breath and met Hiri's green eyes.

"I have, but first"—she smiled—"I want to hear about you."

Chapter 14

Learning Rio lived in Hathor Dome, albeit in a different wing of the dormitory than him, put a spring in Zack's step. He walked her to her room before heading to Mister McPheely's apartment.

"Thank you, Zack. You're quite the gentleman." Rio squeezed his hand.

"Well, I... it's..." He felt himself blush. "You're welcome."

"Maybe you'll notice me in your classes now." Smiling, she lowered her head and raised an eyebrow.

He chuckled and studied the pattern in the carpet. "Yeah, I will."

"Good night."

"Night!" He continued staring at the carpet until the door closed. Passing students paid him no mind, and once the door shut, he hurried away.

Zack pulled himself together and rushed to his appointment. Although he now ran late, he somehow managed to meet all the lifts as they arrived. Proximity of his counselor's apartment just a few levels below the dorm, more than made up for any delays. He arrived at the McPheely residence five minutes early, time enough to catch his breath.

Using his C7, he left Jenny a voice message when she didn't answer his call. He checked the hallway twice before recording it.

"Jenny, you'll never believe what happened at dinner. An Athosian fell out of the ceiling on Bob. It was tiny and tentacle-y, and I chased it when it ran out. I tried to catch it in my spaghetti bowl, but it was too fast, and too many other kids got in my way. Everyone saw it"—he scowled—"except Professor Chapman. He didn't see anything. Call me back right away."

He waited for a minute, staring at the sign on the McPheelys' door. The placard read: *I hope you're having a great day. Please knock and await my response.*

Zack called her again. "Jenny! I know you're getting this. You gotta call me back. It's important! Really, really important!"

It was almost time for his appointment, and he didn't understand why she did not answer his calls. Almost sure she wasn't cloud gliding that night, he knew for certain she didn't have classes this late. He called her a third time before giving up.

As he raised his hand to knock on the door, his C7 alerted him to an incoming message.

Jenny.

~ * * * ~

Halfway through dinner, a message notifying her of an incoming call flashed in the periphery of Jenny's vision. She checked the caller's identity—Zack. She filed it to review later and refocused on Hiri's story about the time she and her family went hiking on Titan.

"So, my brother is lying there sprawled out, all of Xanadu before us..."

Another call from Zack arrived. Jenny dismissed the notification.

"My parents just look at him. I'm laughing my butt off—"

A third message from Zack. Jenny couldn't help herself and huffed in annoyance.

"Is something wrong?" Hiri's smile faded.

"Zack keeps calling. He normally isn't this persistent." Jenny pulled up the first voice message. Zack babbled rapidly about an Athosian in the cafeteria. She initially assumed it was some sort of joke and listened to increasingly frantic pleas in his second and third messages.

An Athosian? Here... that's not possible.

Hiri reached across the table and took Jenny's hand. "What is it? What's wrong?"

"He's really upset, but it can't be what he says... it's just not possible." Jenny sighed. Reluctant to carry on a long, sub-vocal conversation with Zack while Hiri sat across from her, she sent a short reply. "Zack. An Athosian? Are you sure? How do you know? Where is it now?"

"Maybe you should call him." Hiri squeezed her hand. "It's okay."

Zack's reply came before she called him. "I've seen one before, remember? It's a baby, smaller than the ones I saw on Bestic. It's loose in the city."

90

If any other student told Jenny a baby from a supposedly extinct species ran loose on Cytherea, she wouldn't believe them. She remembered Zack had seen a live one, though, and their experiences on Valtra taught them the traces the species left behind could still be deadly to the unsuspecting.

Jenny held up her hand. "Give me a minute. I'm so sorry."

"It's fine, really."

As the call connected, Jenny stared at her risotto. She pushed it around the plate with her fork until Zack's avatar appeared.

"Jenny! What are we going to do? We have to do something!"

She rubbed her temple with one hand while the other stirred her food. Jenny concentrated to keep from speaking aloud so her conversation with Zack would not be overheard. "What can we do? I mean, you said it's in the vents, right?"

"I need to find it!" Zack's unanimated avatar stared at her. True to form, he never bothered to update it as he seldom took advantage of the technology he possessed. Since he rarely made video calls from his C7, Jenny assumed he felt it was unnecessary. Or he forgot.

"You do? Aren't there CDF soldiers here? They can take care of it."

"That's just the problem! They'll blame me! I need to get rid of it before anyone else finds it."

Jenny groaned and shut her eyes. "No, no, no. Zack..."

"I think it might be my fault it's loose."

She dropped her fork in shock. "What?"

"I think it came out of that iron star thing Professor Gladstone gave me last year. It broke open the other day. There was goo in it, just like the goo it left on anything it touched."

She shook her head in disbelief, even though he couldn't see her. "So, what do you want to do?"

"I'm going to go look for it. In the maintenance corridors."

"That's crazy. You can't get in there." Jenny glanced up at Hiri. Jenny read concern in her friend's furrowed brow.

"Dravs says he can get me in."

Of course he can. "Bad idea. It's bad. Don't do it, Zack. Just don't. Promise me? Talk to an adult first. Bariss, or maybe Mister McPheely."

"I... I have an appointment with him in a few minutes."

"Just... wait until tomorrow. We can meet up and talk then, okay? Please?" Jenny did not want to discuss forbidden subjects during a clandestine meeting with Zack the next day, but if it was the only way to keep him from charging into the maintenance corridors looking for an Athosian, then she would do it.

"Okay, I'll wait."

"Good. I have to go. I'm on a date." She disconnected the call before he said anything more, sighed, and stirred her risotto a bit more before meeting Hiri's gaze. "Boys!"

~ * * * ~

Zack considered Jenny's words as he raised his hand once again to knock on the McPheelys' door. An idea struck him.

I should contact Professor Gladstone. He gave me that thing.

"Skip, cancel my appointment with Mister McPheely. Find a listing for Professor Gladstone on Vilicus instead."

"Acknowledged, Zack. Your appointment was to begin two minutes ago. What would you like to send as your reason for cancelling?"

He started toward the lift. "Oh, um... The problem I wanted to talk about isn't a problem anymore, and everything is just fine now."

"Acknowledged. Message sent. Accessing Hypernet to connect to Vilicus public directory. Stand by."

He entered the lift and pressed the button to take him to Ishtar Plaza. By the time he arrived, Skip returned the listing for Professor Gladstone.

Zack found a bench near a pair of Devoran drummers. Not wanting to be overheard, he composed a quick, text-only message to the professor.

"Professor Gladstone, that iron star thing you gave me last year broke in half the other day. It was hollow and had some kind of goo inside. I think there was something living in it. I thought you said it was just a solid sphere of iron. Do you know anything about it? Zack Jackson."

He listened to the beat for a moment before sending a message to Dravs telling him where to find him. To his surprise, Dravs showed up just a few minutes later with Xal in tow.

"Hey, I thought you had an appointment with your counselor?" Dravs eyed Zack as he spoke, but he moved his head in time with the rhythm.

"I changed my mind."

"You know"—Xal slapped his hands against his side in time with the cadence—"if something's bothering you, they can really help."

"Are you still in, Dravs?"

"Yes! I missed out on all the fun on Valtra." The Devoran grinned and slapped Zack on the shoulder. "Do you want to do it now?"

"Jenny thinks I should wait, but I think waiting will just make it worse." He hopped up and headed in the direction of the lift. "Let's go."

"Do what?" Xal followed them. "What are you two up to?"

Dravs stopped and faced the Ersidian. "You heard about that thing that attacked Bob in the cafeteria, right?"

Xal nodded.

"Zack and I are going into the maintenance corridors to try to find it."

"Oh." Xal frowned and looked away as they resumed their walk. "Aren't the maintenance corridors restricted and locked? You can't get in there."

Dravs laughed. "Sure I can. My father showed me how to pop those locks. They're not that secure."

They found a few clusters of students dining when they arrived, but fortunately, the secluded location of the maintenance corridor access hatch, which sat behind the recycler units, kept their activities out of sight of the diners.

Dravs crouched down by the status panel. "Keep an eye out, will you?"

Zack shoved his hands in his pockets and stood with his back to Dravs, watching the entrance to the nook in which the Devoran worked. He heard Dravs's thick tail swish against the carpet. Xal shifted his weight with nervous energy and glanced around them, his eyes darting to and fro, as if keeping watch for a predator.

93

As he and Xal guarded the area, Zack recalled the infant Athosian the cultists used to threaten him with on Bestic. If there was any chance the one running loose on Cytherea could indoctrinate and influence people the way the cultists on Bestic seemed to have been affected, he needed to stop it before it gained control over anyone. While he waited, he withdrew his C7 from his pocket and found a detailed map of the city that included its maintenance corridors.

"There! See? Nothing to it!" Dravs dusted off his hands and stood. "If they really wanted to keep people out, they'd use better locks."

Zack inspected Dravs's handiwork. The Devoran pressed three buttons on the panel. The hatch slid open.

Zack clapped Dravs on the shoulder. "Good work! Let's go."

Zack ducked inside the hatch. Unlike those seldom-used, publicly accessible hallways he and Steve explored the previous year, the corridor featured exposed conduits and pipes running along the ceiling and beneath the floor grates. Wires and tubes ran the length of the walls.

"Are you coming?" Dravs clicked his tongue and huffed at Xal.

Zack poked his head out of the hatch. Xal shook his head and backed away.

"I can't, guys. If we get caught, we'll be in so much trouble. I'm having a hard time keeping my grades up as it is."

"Come on, you wimp." Dravs motioned for the Ersidian to join them.

Zack put his hand on the Devoran's arm. "No, it's okay. You don't have to come with us, Xal. Thanks for helping me keep watch. Don't tell anyone, okay?"

"No, I won't. Good luck, you guys."

Dravs snorted and shut the hatch. Dim emergency lights provided scant, but sufficient, illumination for the two to see where they traveled. Zack consulted the map on his C7 and pointed ahead.

"If we take the first right, then go to the end of the hallway, we should be close to the vent." He kept his voice low in case it carried through nearby ducts.

"Hey..." Dravs gripped Zack's arm. "What are we going to do if we find it? I mean, we don't have guns or anything."

Nuts. I hadn't thought of that. Zack shrugged and pursed his lips. "I don't know. I'm making this up as I go."

Chapter 15

Jenny conversed over dinner with Hiri for longer than she expected. As they finished dessert, Hiri frowned and squinted before she burst out laughing.

"What?" *Is there something on me?* Jenny wiped her mouth with her napkin. *Maybe someone is sending her messages.*

Upon stifling her laughter, Hiri shook her head. "Oh, Nicole is asking me inappropriate questions. Andrea isn't helping." Jenny didn't see Hiri's roommates much, and consequently, she didn't know them that well.

"What did you tell them we were doing?"

Hiri waved her hand. "The usual—dinner, maybe the Rampage Room afterward."

Jenny patted her stomach. "I don't know if I'm up for stomping around."

"Me neither. That cake was too good. I'm absolutely stuffed, but I have no regrets." As if to punctuate her sentence, Hiri stifled a belch. "Excuse me."

"Shall we take a walk? Go back to the dorm?" Jenny waved off the waiter when he tried to refill her glass of water.

"I'm not ready to go back yet, but a walk sounds nice. Ishtar Plaza?"

Jenny looked over her shoulder. The sounds of Devoran festival preparations in the park carried into the restaurant. "The park is still closed. I was thinking the arboretum in Aphrodite Dome."

Hiri chuckled. "You know, I've been here four years, and I still haven't been there."

"Well, let's go then." Jenny rose from her seat and followed Hiri. The older girl's hand found Jenny's as they walked, a tentative touch. When Jenny didn't pull away, her grip firmed.

As they strolled, Jenny described the arboretum and the plants within to Hiri. Although she hadn't gone there yet this semester, she expected it to appear much the same as before the break. Filled with various plants from Earth, Rigel Kent, and Wolf 359, the garden also featured some small sections containing plants native to Devorus, Valtra, and Ersid. Jenny became quite familiar with the area during some exobotany class projects during the past year.

95

Delays at the transit pod station detained them the better part of an hour before the pair finally arrived at their destination. De Jussieu Arboretum occupied the part of Aphrodite Dome analogous to Ishtar Plaza in Hathor Dome—the large, central area directly beneath the dome itself. Special filters installed on the dome allowed entering light to appear as Earthlike as possible. The hazy Venusian atmosphere normally made all daylight a shade of amber, which did not complement the natural coloration of most of the plants and flowers.

The lights were dimmed for the night cycle, and currently few plants bloomed. It didn't matter to Jenny, though. The babble of a stream winding through the grassy area lent a pastoral feel to the conservatory. The air-circulation system rustled the leaves of the trees, carrying with it a hint of fresh greens.

Jenny closed her eyes and inhaled. For a moment, she imagined she was outside.

Hiri took in their surroundings in wide-eyed delight. "If you couldn't see the dome, you'd swear you were on Earth."

Jenny led her to a secluded spot near the brook. Several large boulders lay scattered about, and nearby a flower bed sat covered in ornamental grasses. The last time Jenny visited this area, daffodils bloomed in that same flower bed, yellow-and-white trumpets standing proudly in the meadow of the arboretum.

She sat on one of the smaller boulders. "I like to come here and just sit. When school became too stressful last year, I would just come and forget about everything for a little while."

Hiri sat next to her, intertwining her arm with Jenny's. "I can see that." She rested her head on Jenny's shoulder.

The two sat silently until Jenny lost track of time. The illusion of being on a planet faded when Jenny's unconscious mind noticed the absence of birds. Insects still buzzed about, necessary for pollination of many plants in the arboretum.

I wonder how they keep them from getting into the rest of the city. She admonished herself for letting her mind wander to such mundane subjects and glanced at Hiri.

The other girl studied Jenny's face, the corners of her mouth upturned. She leaned closer, a twinkle in her eye.

Jenny felt warm, like someone cranked the heat up in her room, despite the light breeze.

Hiri's lips parted slightly, and she reached up to caress Jenny's cheek.

Their lips met, and time stood still.

~ * * * ~

"Ow! Watch it!" For the third time, Dravs bumped into Zack, sending him stumbling into the wall.

"Sorry."

Zack shone his flashlight along the floor and walls. They were close to the ductwork connecting to the cafeteria vent according to Zack's estimate. He saw no sign of the Athosian. Of course, Zack didn't think it was capable of passing through metal walls. Shining his flashlight up and down its length, he found no exits.

Behind them, the duct followed the wall to the corner, before going straight up and exiting through the ceiling. Zack led Dravs along the duct that ran the length of the cafeteria wall.

"Zack!" Dravs hissed. "Check it out."

The Devoran crouched and pointed at a small hatch door hanging ajar. They were at least a dozen meters away from the cafeteria vent now. Zack knelt and opened the hatch fully. The tattered remains of an air filter dangled from its frame. A dark stain coated the edge of the hatch, trailing away from the ductwork and down the corridor.

"Looks like it got out through here."

"Pralkt." Dravs clicked his teeth together as he swore. "I owe Xal a glommy bird dinner."

"What? Why?" Zack gestured with his flashlight at the Devoran.

Dravs shielded his eyes from the glare. "I bet him we wouldn't find anything. Sometimes, I think he goes along with anything you tell him 'cause he still feels bad about mauling your arm."

Zack rubbed the spot Xal had bitten over the summer. "Yeah, well, let's keep moving."

The slime trail in the utility corridor led them away from the cafeteria. The sounds of the air-circulation system grew louder. Soon, the air became thick with moisture.

97

"Heh, it's like a sauna in here."

Wiping sweat from his brow, Zack glanced at Dravs. The Devoran didn't seem bothered by the heat or the humidity. The trail continued past the air-scrubbing system and led straight to a ladder well.

Checking his C7, Zack noted their position relative to the cafeteria. Another maintenance access hatch lay ahead, but he expected it, like the one by the cafeteria, would be locked.

Zack shone his flashlight in the ladder well, first up, then down. The slime trail hugged the wall and headed downward.

"Hey, it can walk on the walls." Dravs nudged Zack. "Cool!"

Steadying himself with one hand on the wall, he jammed the flashlight through his belt so the light pointed down. Zack reached across the well and seized the ladder to begin his descent.

"I know I'm just along for the ride, Zack, but maybe I should go first?"

"Why?" Zack backed away from the ladder well.

Dravs swished his tail. "Because if I'm above you, this is going to be dangling in your face the whole way."

"Good thinking. You go first. Do you want my flashlight?"

The Devoran shook his head. "Nah, I'll just try not to look up and blind myself. How far down does this go?"

"According to the plans I have, at least one level. It's hard to read."

"Fantastic." Dravs jumped across, grabbed the ladder, and began his descent. Zack followed. Hand over hand, he moved downward, pausing at times to allow Dravs to move his hands out of the way. The Devoran moved slower than Zack and complained about his tail getting in the way.

"These ladders were obviously not designed by Devorans."

"Well, this is an EAC facility." Zack looked down before taking the next rung. His C7 buzzed with the reminder to respond to Mungus's message. As he placed his foot, his hand reflexively reached to silence the notification, and he slipped.

Zack howled as he slammed into Dravs. The Devoran's grip failed as well. Together, they tumbled down the shaft, swearing and hollering until they landed in a heap at the bottom. A wave of nausea swept over Zack as a foul odor assaulted his nose.

"Get off!" Dravs yelped and shoved Zack aside. Zack winced and sat up, yanking his flashlight from his belt.

"Grazzt! That smarts."

Zack shone the light on Dravs, whose arm dangled from his shoulder at an unnatural angle. A fresh wave of nausea hit him.

"I think it's broken." Dravs whimpered and grimaced as he pulled his arm close to his body.

Holding his nose, Zack glanced around them. "We must be near one of the waste treatment facilities."

"Or a garbage dump."

As his flashlight passed over a pile of refuse, some bit of rubbish reflected the light. He swung his flashlight.

The Athosian sat perched on half a melon shell. It wiggled its tentacles and shrank back, flipping the melon shell on top of itself.

"Did you see it?"

"See what?" Dravs cracked open an eye and regarded Zack. "I'm pretending I can't see my arm. It doesn't hurt as much."

"I'm really sorry. We need to get you out of here." Zack pointed at the upturned melon. "The Athosian is under there."

"Well, get it."

Zack crawled toward the refuse, noting the odor didn't improve as he approached. He searched for a stick or a length of metal to use as a probe, but he found nothing. He set down the flashlight and withdrew his multi-tool from its holster.

Using the screwdriver attachment, Zack flipped the melon off the Athosian. The creature, in the process of digging through the refuse, froze when its cover disappeared. It shrank into the hole it dug.

Zack felt around for his flashlight. He lifted it to bash the Athosian. It raised its tentacles over its head and flattened itself even more.

"Get it, Zack. It'll grow up. It'll kill us all, especially since it knows what's in our garbage."

The Athosian trembled before Zack. He lowered his flashlight and put down the multitool. "It's afraid."

"Good."

Zack sat and studied the frightened infant. It lowered its tentacles to pull some of the trash closer around itself.

"What. Are. You. Doing?"

Zack regarded his friend. "I can't just smoosh it, Dravs. It's a baby!"

99

Dravs groaned and scooted forward, curling his lip as he stared at it. "Well then, what are we going to do with it?"

"I don't know. I didn't bring anything to carry it in." Zack searched through the refuse. Since it consisted of mostly miscellaneous junk and uneaten food, he did not locate an object that could double as a container.

Accompanied by a beep, a light glimmered farther down the corridor. Zack turned his flashlight toward it and observed a scrubbot, cleaning the floor. The Athosian saw it and leapt toward Zack.

He backpedaled but not fast enough. The Athosian latched on to his shoulder. Dravs cursed and shoved Zack when the human bumped into him.

"Watch it!"

The Athosian trembled on Zack's shoulder, and instead of flinging it off, he hesitated. Before resuming its course, the bot beeped rapidly as it paused by the refuse pile.

"Do you think you can get the access hatch down there open?"

Dravs nodded. "Are you going to take that thing?"

Its tentacle brushed Zack's neck. It felt leathery and coarse instead of slimy.

"Huh, it's drier than I expected."

The Devoran peered at the Athosian. "I heard they're mostly aquatic. It's warm and humid, but not really wet in here."

Zack had an idea. "Let's go. I think I know where I can stash this guy."

Dravs shook his head as he pushed past Zack and proceeded toward the access hatch. "Oh, good grief. We are going to be in so much trouble if anyone sees you with that thing."

Chapter 16

"You know what would be nice?" Hiri sighed as she and Jenny, lying on their backs, gazed upward.

"If the sky was real?"

"I was just thinking that!" Hiri's light lavender scent mingled with that of the grasses and other foliage.

The arboretum's sky was, of course, nothing more than the top of the dome. With the night filters fully engaged, the lighting simulated that of dusk on Earth, including the faint pinpoints of distant stars. The projection simulated what a night sky would look like from the city's current location on Venus, though for both Jenny and Hiri, born in extraterrestrial habitats, none of it looked familiar. For a moment, Jenny envied Zack and his stories of the night sky in Wyoming.

Hiri nuzzled Jenny's neck, planting soft kisses. "Got anything going on tomorrow?"

Jenny thought a moment. Cloud gliding was the only thing on her schedule for Saturday. "Just—"

Jenny heard a branch snap, then a splash in the nearby water. She sat bolt upright.

"Krunk!"

She recognized the voice—Zack. Her communications implant didn't show any pending messages.

"Zack?" she called out to the darkness.

"Jenny? Is that you?" Zack emerged from around a nearby tree. His pants were soaked through, and a strange growth dangled near his neck.

"Me and Hiri."

Hiri sat up and waved to Zack from alongside Jenny.

"Oh, hi. Oh!" Zack seemed to realize he'd interrupted something. "I'm sorry."

He wrestled with the lump on his shoulder. Jenny adjusted her ocular implants for better low-light vision. It was no growth; instead, he bore a translucent, tentacled creature. As Zack moved closer, eyes, surrounding the creature's body, came into focus.

Jenny's every muscle tensed. "Zack. What is that?"

"Oh, this?" It squirmed in his grip. "This is that Athosian I told you about."

Jenny scooted backward, grasping Hiri's hand.

101

"An Athosian?" The other student's tone revealed her disbelief. "That's... that's just a plushie or something, right?"

"Ugh, stop squirming." Zack stumbled and fell to his knees. He set down the creature on the edge of the stream. "He was getting all dried out, so I thought this would be a good place to hide him for now."

"Are you insane?" It was the only reason Jenny considered to explain why he would harbor an Athosian. "How did you get it here without being seen?"

"It wasn't easy." Zack rinsed his hands in the water. "Dravs broke his arm while we were chasing after him, so once we got out of the utility corridors, Dravs made a big fuss and caused a distraction. I hid Squishy there under my shirt."

He pulled his shirt away from his chest, fanning it. "It's all sticky and gross under there now."

Jenny narrowed her eyes as she regarded him. "Are you indoctrinated?" She remembered him saying something about indoctrination regarding the juvenile Athosians he saw on Bestic.

"No." He blinked and cocked his head. "I don't think so. I mean, I don't think they're all superior to us and we deserve to be ruled by them or anything."

"This is too weird." Hiri rested her head on Jenny's shoulder as she hugged her arm.

"You can't hide that thing here." Jenny shifted and pulled her legs under her. Running away might be in her immediate future, and she wanted to be ready.

"I couldn't kill him, and I couldn't just leave him down by all the garbage and sewage." Zack dried his hands on his shirt. "You said this stream is pretty deserted. He should be able to hide here for a few days until I figure out what to do with him."

One of the reasons Jenny brought Hiri here was because people who visited the arboretum tended to stay near the flowerbeds. There wasn't much to see at this end of the stream, and with none of the plants in bloom, weeks could pass before this area received any visitors. Jenny closed her eyes and counted to five. "I take it you didn't talk to Counselor McPheely or anyone else about this?"

"Umm..." Zack looked away. "Well, not exactly..."

"Mon dieu." Jenny rubbed her temples.

Zack pushed himself up. "I need to run. I should go to the nurse's office and see Dravs. His broken arm is kind of my fault."

"Your fault?" Jenny rose and helped Hiri to her feet.

"I fell when we were climbing down a ladder and landed on top of him." He waved, as he jogged away. "Sorry for interrupting your night."

Jenny cast a sidelong glance at the Athosian splashing in the water. It seemed harmless enough. She pulled Hiri away from it. "We should go."

"But what about—"

"You don't want to get involved, believe me."

~ * * * ~

Zack arrived at the nurse's office panting and dripping with sweat. Dravs sat just outside the door, waiting for Zack. He cradled his arm and leaned against the wall with his eyes closed.

"I'm here; I'm here."

The Devoran cracked open one eye. "Did you get rid of it?"

"Yeah, I—"

Dravs held a clawed hand in Zack's face. "I don't want to know. Do you know how hard it is to look nonchalant and pretend everything's fine when people pass by and ask if you're okay?"

"Let's get you fixed." Zack pressed the door chime. Students were required to check in at the nurse's office, rather than going to the hospital proper; at least, if they brought themselves. After the final dinner period, however, the nurse's office closed for the evening. It was possible Nurse Carentan wasn't in and would have to travel from home to attend Dravs.

A voice crackled over the speaker. "Yes? What is it?" Nurse Carentan's clipped tone conveyed his annoyance at this late interruption.

"Dravs Sallaron. I think my arm is broken."

"Is bone sticking out?" the nurse inquired as though protruding bone were no more serious than a paper cut.

"Um, no. But it really hurts."

His reply met with an annoyed growl. "Fine. I'll be there shortly." The speaker crackled and clicked off.

"Great." Dravs bashed his fist against the panel. "If I'd known I was going to have to wait longer, I would've pressed the button as soon as I got here."

"I'm sorry, Dravs. I hurried back as soon as I could." Zack examined the Devoran's arm as best as possible without touching it or asking Dravs to move it. His normally shiny blue scales appeared discolored and dull around his shoulder and upper arm.

Dravs grunted before exhaling a long breath. "It's not really your fault. I know it was an accident. It just really hurts, Zack."

No words of comfort came to Zack's mind. He felt bad for losing his grip on the rungs of the ladder, but as Dravs said, it was just an accident. For the better part of an hour, he stood with his Devoran friend outside the office awaiting the nurse's arrival.

Nurse Carentan, an Uurt and native of Ersid, shuffled down the hall toward them. Uurts shared their world with Ersidians and shared a common ancestor. However, Uurts resembled both Ersidians and centaurs from Earth mythology. He wore a wrinkled, blue scrubs top over his ruffled, greying black fur.

"So much for an enjoyable evening at home." Nurse Carentan looked down his snout at Zack. "Why am I not surprised to see you here, Jackson?"

He tapped the control pad, and the door slid open. As they entered the office, the lights sprang to life. Cytherean Academy's head nurse pointed to an exam table at the far side of the room as he pulled on a white lab coat.

With Zack's help, Dravs climbed onto the exam table.

"All right, let's have a look at you." He ran his hand along Dravs's wounded arm. The Devoran whimpered at the Uurt's touch.

"How did this happen?"

"I fell." Dravs winced as the nurse took his arm and straightened it.

"Then I fell on top of him."

"Do I even want to know what you were doing?"

Dravs and Zack answered at the same time.

"No."

"Probably not."

The Uurt chuckled and palpated Dravs's arm some more, humming as he did so. He then pulled a small scanner out of his lab coat pocket and waved it over the Devoran's arm and shoulder.

"Well, I have bad news and good news. The good news: your shoulder is dislocated, but no bones are broken."

"Oh. That's good?" Dravs slumped.

"The bad news: I need help popping it back into place." Nurse Carentan turned to Zack. "Go on back to your dorm now. Your work here is done."

Zack first glanced at Dravs and then the nurse. "But I want to help. I can help him get to his dorm after you're finished."

"Nope. It's against regulations, and it'll be a few hours before he's in any state to go home." The Uurt pointed behind Zack. "The door's over there."

Nurse Carentan stepped over to the dispenser. He ordered some medication before tapping the comm panel. "Hey, darling. I'm going be a while. Got a dislocated shoulder to deal with."

Coach Dagon's gruff voice distorted through the tinny speaker. "Fantastic. Should I wait up?"

"If you want."

Zack squeezed Dravs's arm. "I guess I'll see you tomorrow?"

"Maybe, if I feel up to it." Dravs offered Zack a week smile. "Definitely at class on Monday. I'm going to try to milk this with Kat all weekend."

"Okay, I'll see you around, then. I'm sorry, Dravs."

Zack left his friend to the Uurt's ministrations. Part of him wanted to go check on Squishy, as he'd dubbed the Athosian, but he knew the more he hung around the arboretum, especially in the later hours, the more attention he would draw to himself. Instead, he returned to his dorm.

He retrieved his C7 as he waited for the lift. The reminder to respond to Mungus still displayed prominently on the screen. He cleared it. *I'll deal with that tomorrow. I have to figure out what to do with Squishy first. Maybe Ix can suggest something.*

~ * * * ~

105

Obvious from the noise escaping into the corridor, Hiri and Jenny's roommates gathered in the common area of their dorm. Rather than enter and endure an uncomfortable interrogation, they lingered in the hallway.

Hiri fretted over what happened in the arboretum. "Should we tell someone?"

"No." Jenny shook her head. "I think that would be a bad idea. I'm sure Zack has a plan." *I hope he has a plan. He'd better have a plan.*

"Okay, if you're sure." Hiri took Jenny's hands and pressed her lips to them. "I had a really nice time tonight."

"I did too. Hopefully next time, we can find a place where crazy boys won't interrupt us with their schemes."

Hiri laughed. "I know, right?"

"Tomorrow's the Festival of Starlight." Jenny had not intended to go, but if Hiri was willing... "Going?"

"With you I might." Hiri smiled. They kissed one last time before entering their dorm. Austin, Wes, Verrak, and Andrea whooped and hollered at the gravball game displayed on the holoviewer. Jenny and Hiri lingered long enough to acknowledge their roommates' greetings, then turned in for the evening.

The next morning, Jenny awoke to a message from Zack requesting she meet him in the arboretum as soon as she finished eating breakfast. She considered telling him no. If that really was an Athosian he found and carried up there, she didn't want anything to do with it.

On her way to breakfast, Jenny met up with Hiri. Of all the meals to eat in the dorm cafeterias, she liked breakfast by far the best. Decent coffee, pastries as good as any Jenny got on Messier Habitat, and best of all, the eggs were real. Messier didn't have chickens, but Cytherean Academy kept some as part of its agricultural program. They were housed on a farm in Isis Dome. Jenny hadn't visited it, but she heard it was as realistic a pastoral farming environment as one could experience without setting foot on a planet.

"Zack wants to meet with me this morning, probably to discuss... the thing." Jenny nibbled on a cinnamon roll as Hiri dug into an omelet. "Can you come with me?"

"Mmm..." Hiri swallowed. "I can't this morning. I have to work on an engineering class project with that Valtraxian student."

"Ix?" Jenny hadn't realized Hiri knew Ix.

"Yeah, how do you... oh yeah, you're both Junior Rangers. I can't believe he's only a second-year and he's in fourth-year engineering classes."

"It." In her mind, Jenny heard Ix's lecture on Valtraxian genders.

"Hmm?"

"It. Ix is a drone. Valtraxians have four genders, remember?"

"Oh yeah." Hiri guzzled her double-sweet mocha. "It's so hard to get that right. You'd think I, of all people, would be an expert at it."

"Nobody's perfect."

"Ha! Have you seen Ix's test scores?" Hiri finished her meal. "Gotta run. I'll see you tonight?"

"Definitely, for the Festival of Starlight."

Hiri gave Jenny a quick peck on the cheek and dashed out of the cafeteria. Jenny sighed before finishing her breakfast, preparing herself for whatever trouble awaited her.

Chapter 17

When Zack returned to his room, Ix was not in it. Despite his best efforts, he didn't stay awake until the Valtraxian returned, and when he woke in the morning, Ix had already left. A quick message to the Valtraxian revealed it was busy helping another student with a class project, so Zack pulled on clean clothes and wandered toward breakfast.

During his morning meal, he received messages from Roger asking when he expected to arrive at the hangar. As much as Zack wanted to check on Squishy beforehand, he decided too much delay might appear suspicious, so he headed directly for the cloud-glider area.

Coach Dagon stood near an equipment locker, inventorying gravball equipment. Zack wondered if the coach engaged in other activities when he wasn't teaching.

"Everything all right, Jackson? How'd your meeting with McPheely go?"

"Yeah, Coach, everything's fine. I ended up not having to meet with him. Are you going to the festival tonight?" Zack hoped his query would be enough to change the subject.

"Maybe. If my mate wants to go. Our quiet evening at home last night got interrupted by an injured student." The Ersidian pointed to the area in which the environmental suits were stored. "You'll have to get scanned before you get a suit. It looks like you might have grown a bit since your last fitting."

Grown? Finally! Zack sped to the enviro-suit storage area. The thought he might have grown enough to rate a new suit pushed all other thoughts out of his head. He pulled up the menu and activated the scanning function.

As he stood as still as possible, waiting for the scan to complete, his mind wandered, returning to Athosians and exploration. *I wonder what that thing was down on the surface? That was the night the iron star broke open.* He made a mental note to ask Bariss when he saw him at the festival tonight if he planned any additional exploration in the probes.

"Scan complete." The voice of the machine reminded him of Skip. According to the display, his measurements had indeed changed enough to require construction of a new environmental suit. The fabricator unit made short work of it, and by the time Coach Dagon completed his inventory, Zack had suited up.

"All right, Jackson. Looks good. I think Davis is waiting for you. Have a good flight." Coach clapped Zack on the shoulder. The weight of the Ersidian's meaty hand felt like getting smacked with one of his mother's roasts, and it sent him stumbling toward the door.

Zack found Roger leaning against his cloud glider when he entered the hangar. When he saw Zack, the lanky older boy patted the side of the vehicle.

"Ever flown one of these before?"

Zack nodded. It looked just like Jenny's glider, albeit colored with a different paint scheme. "I went out with Jenny during class last year."

"Oh yeah, that's right. I got stuck with that Devoran." Roger laughed. "I thought he was going to yack in his helmet during the flight."

"That's the only time I've been out in one. Dravs is fine on big ships, though. He just gets really anxious if he feels the motion of the vehicle or turbulence."

"How did you do? Get airsick?"

Zack shook his head. "No, just during my first translation. Flying is fine."

"Good. Most of your training will be in the VR simulator, of course." Roger motioned for Zack to come closer as he circled the glider. "But there's no substitute for hands-on experience, especially when it comes to pre-flight inspections."

Zack moved closer. During the pre-flight check, he kept an arm's length between himself and Roger, despite the older boy's urging that he should lean in close to see some of the components he pointed out.

"Look, I get that you don't like me." Roger held out his hand to Zack. "And I don't blame you. But I'm not going to do anything to jeopardize my flight status. Besides, Coach will rip my head off if anything happens to you. We're going to go out, do a quick couple of laps around the city, then come in. All I ask is that you give me a chance. Please?"

Zack met Roger's eyes as he considered his words. *I guess Coach wouldn't ask him to do this if he didn't think it was safe.* He nodded and shook Roger's hand.

"All right. Let me get strapped in. Then back in toward me. Like you did with Jenny last year, right?" Roger approached the cloud glider and attached his harness. The glider hummed to life, and the automatic linkage system secured him to it.

After Zack latched his restraints, Roger initiated the launch sequence. His voice crackled over Zack's comm system. "Make sure you tune your comm system to channel seventy-seven point five—Cytherea Flight Control."

He did as Roger directed. The flight controller's voice came in clear over the speakers in their helmets. "Glider Romeo-Delta-Seven, you are cleared for launch."

"Roger."

It took Zack a moment to realize Roger gave a confirmation, rather than uttered his own name. The jolt of launch was a stark contrast to Jenny's smooth take-off last term.

"Sorry about that; the launch rails must not be lubricated properly." Roger grunted as he leaned into a sharp turn that pressed the breath out of Zack's lungs.

Roger straightened and leveled the glider before banking into a gentle turn that put Cytherea on their left. Zack's heart pounded in his chest, and he made the mistake of looking down into a particularly dark and ominous cloud flashing with lightning.

"You okay down there?"

Zack nodded.

"Zack? Are you okay?"

Zack smacked his helmet. *Idiot. He can't see you nodding.* "Yes, fine. Sorry."

"Okay, good. Sorry about that sharp turn. One of the flaps felt like it was sticking, and I just wanted to make sure it was working properly."

"Is it?" Zack hoped nothing was wrong with their glider. Cytherea had several safety systems in place to recover pilots before they plummeted to their deaths. Nevertheless, he didn't want to put them to the test.

"Yeah, yeah. Everything's cool. Sometimes, you gotta put these things through the wringer to make sure everything you thought was working is."

They continued their gentle turn, keeping the city to their left. Zack took the opportunity to enjoy the scenery. Fifty miles up, they were far above any landmarks, not that they would have been visible through the thick, cloud-choked carbon-dioxide atmosphere. Viewing the clouds over Venus reminded Zack of looking through cotton gauze the color of wet sand.

Far off in the distance, he saw signal lights blinking in a regular pattern. Cytherea was the only major city on Venus, but there were other small aerostat mining outposts and the like. According to the HUD in his environmental suit's helmet, the settlement in the distance was Plass Colony, a carbon-dioxide mining facility.

"Check that out!" Roger pointed to a ship approaching in the distance.

Zack recognized the EAC design, a military shuttle of some sort. His HUD identified it. "Looks like Shuttle *Aramus* from the *EACS Denali*."

"*Denali*, huh? That's a long-range cruiser, if I recall. What the heck are they doing here?"

Zack wished he could see the ship. It either hovered in orbit, too far away to be more than a glint of light passing overhead if it were visible, or it had departed already after sending its VIPs to Cytherea.

"It wouldn't be for the Festival of Starlight, would it?" Zack's breath caught in his throat as a horrible thought crossed his mind. *What if they know about Squishy? Maybe they know I found that thing on the surface!*

"I doubt it. That's just a courtesy to us for jamming up Ishtar Plaza because we can't have Halloween. It really stinks. I always liked Halloween."

"Me too."

"Yeah, hey, what the heck were you dressed up as last year, anyway?" Roger decreased their airspeed to allow the shuttle time to pass and dock without crossing too close to their flight path.

"You mean that costume you, Barry, and that other guy wrecked?"

"Yeah, it was pretty cool, actually. I'm sorry about that."

Zack detected regret in Roger's voice and decided to accept it at face value. "It was an Athosian."

"Athosian, huh? Those guys the Devorans wiped out? I guess you can't get any more ghostly than that without being something out of those old horror stories."

Too large to land in a docking bay, the shuttle docked with one of the extendable egress tubes. Roger piloted the glider, climbing to a higher altitude, and flew over the ship, before banking again to turn them toward the city.

"Attention, Glider Romeo-Delta-Seven, you are required to return to dock three-two-seven immediately by order of the Cytherean Garrison Commander."

"What? Why? Did we do something wrong?" Zack's pulse raced. *They did find Squishy. I'll bet Dravs spilled his guts—*

"Acknowledged, Control. Glider Romeo-Delta-Seven proceeding to docking station three-two-seven." Roger accelerated and altered their flight path to a more direct approach vector. "Don't worry about it, Zack. The EAC always gets weird if cloud gliders are out when one of their shuttles shows up."

Landing went smoother than launch. Once they freed themselves of the cloud glider, Roger showed Zack the post-flight checklist, and they secured the vehicle for storage.

"Next time, I'll let you do pre- and post-flight on your own. I'll send you files to read up on the procedures, so you won't have to do it by memory from today. Sound good?"

"Yeah, fine."

"Great." Roger slapped Zack on the back. "Have fun at the Festival of Starlight tonight. Tell Jenny I said 'hello.'"

"You're not going?" Zack loosened the closures on his suit, breaking the seals that kept it airtight.

"Can't." Roger smirked. "Part of my punishment. It lasts all term. Too bad, too. Halloweens come and go, but I doubt they'll have this one again once all these Devorans leave."

"Yeah…" Zack glanced around the hangar bay, avoiding Roger's eyes. He waved and jogged away to change out of his suit before the air became thick with awkwardness. Although he found it difficult to sympathize with one of the students who bullied him and Xal last year, Roger seemed like a decent person away from Barry's influence.

Still, Zack felt Roger's punishment was just. He checked the time after donning his regular clothes. Although he missed lunch in the cafeteria, there were still several hours before the Festival of Starlight began. He decided to go check on Squishy before searching for something to eat.

~ * * * ~

Since she had nothing on her schedule until the Festival of Starlight that evening, Jenny took advantage of her free time and returned to bed for a quick snooze. She did not normally indulge in naps, of course, but she welcomed the opportunity when earlier in the term, she couldn't sleep much at all.

After a leisurely shower, Jenny treated herself to a cinnamon roll and coffee from the cafeteria. Just as she finished it, she saw the notification for an incoming call.

Her parents.

She stuffed the remainder of the cinnamon roll into her mouth, washed it down with coffee, and sped to the nearest quiet room. She had no desire for her friends to witness a one-sided conversation with her parents over her implants.

Why now? Mother knows the address of the comm terminal in my room. She answered the call as she dashed inside and closed the door.

"Why are you calling my personal number? Do you want everyone nearby to see me breakdown if you have bad news again?"

Her mother appeared, dominating her vision. Her dark hair was pulled back, and she wore a light blue jogging suit. "Oh, Genevieve, I am sorry. I tried your terminal, and I was worried when you didn't answer."

"I was eating." *Or I was in the shower.* She hadn't bothered to check the terminal for missed calls before she left for her snack.

"Of course." Her mother tucked a stray lock of hair behind her ear. "I have news of your father."

Jenny's heart caught in her chest. "What's happened?"

"Oh, Nothing bad. He's gone in for the last of the skin grafts today, and they're going to put in proper ocular implants, too. He should look like his old self the next time you see him."

Jenny breathed a sigh of relief. "I'm happy to hear that."

"He was asking about you." Amélie took a breath and leaned in closer to the camera. "He still does not remember everything, but it is getting better. Everything will return to normal soon, Genevieve."

113

Normal? If what we had before was normal, I'd rather leave it. "That's good, Mother."

"I won't keep you." Amélie blew her daughter a kiss. "I'm sorry if I interrupted your breakfast."

"I'll call tomorrow after classes to check on Papa, all right?" Jenny hoped if she put the onus on herself, her mother wouldn't call her in the middle of the festival this evening.

"Talk to you then! We love you very much, Genevieve."

"Je vous aime aussi." Jenny disconnected the call, leaned back in her chair, and rubbed her eyes. *Well, at least that's over with for today.* She checked the time. The festival was hours away yet. *I guess I'll go to the arboretum to make sure Zack's little monster hasn't destroyed the place.*

Chapter 18

"Squishy?" Zack hissed between clenched teeth. He searched up and down the banks of the stream near where he last saw the little Athosian, but to no avail. Reluctant to shout, Zack kept his calls for the creature subdued. Not only did he doubt the Athosian knew the name Zack had given him, but he also didn't want to draw attention to himself.

A flicker of motion in the water caught his eye, but when he approached to get a closer look, it disappeared. The arboretum dome had brightened to approximate full daylight, and the foliage cast soft, dappled shadows across the babbling brook. The air smelled musty and moist; a heady, earthy scent of loam wafted from the freshly watered grassy areas and fertilized flower beds.

He found the rocks where he'd interrupted Jenny and her friend and the location where he had placed Squishy in the water. He recognized his footprints on the banks of the stream. Zack heard rustling in some nearby shrubs and darted behind a tree.

When footsteps sounded in the grass near the rocks, he dared peer from behind his hiding place.

"Jenny!"

She jumped.

"Zack! What are you doing here?"

"Looking for Squishy." He glanced around for Jenny's friend, Hiri. It appeared Jenny came alone.

Jenny pursed her lips. "That's what I was doing, too."

Together, they searched the area around the rocks, in every bush, and behind every tree. Zack didn't want to go to the other side of the stream yet; crossing here would soak him. He preferred crossing at the rock-filled ford upstream, near the center of the dome.

"It could be anywhere, Zack." Jenny wiped her brow as she rested against a boulder. The air in the arboretum felt heavy with humidity during morning hours, causing them to perspire at the slightest exertion.

"Dravs said they were aquatic, and he looked pretty dried out when I found him in the utility corridors." He kept his eyes fixed on the water. "Does anything live in that stream? Fish, maybe?"

"No, I think the only fish in the city are in the aquariums." Jenny rose and crouched next to Zack at the edge of the stream. "Did you see something?"

"I don't know, maybe." His eyes scanned the length of the stream. "Maybe we should search up and down the banks."

Jenny pointed upstream. "The crossing is up that way."

They proceeded along the bank in single file, watching the stream for movement and only averting their eyes to take care with their footing to climb over obstacles. When they reached the crossing, Jenny paused. "I think instead of us each taking a bank, one of us should go upstream and the other downstream on the other side. Otherwise, we could be here all day, and we're going to both need to shower again before the festival tonight."

Zack almost protested; he hadn't showered at all yet, but he decided that detail didn't invalidate her point. "Well, okay. I've already searched most of the area downstream, so why don't I go up, and you take the opposite bank downstream? Maybe you'll see something I missed."

"Sounds good." Jenny tapped her temple. "Call or send a message if you find anything."

Zack moved slowly upstream, careful to avoid tree roots and rocks that choked the bank. Zack estimated he spent more time climbing and crawling over treacherous obstacles than searching the stream. He forced himself to stop now and then to inspect the water. When he reached the stream's source, one of Cytherea's systems that pumped water up from under-floor pipes, he climbed over the collection of stones and rocks that concealed it and worked his way down the opposite bank.

He had nearly returned to the crossing when he noticed movement in the water. His toe caught a protruding root. Just as he stumbled forward and splashed into the flow, the creature lurched forward. It was then Zack saw him clearly.

Squishy! The Athosian's tentacles latched onto Zack's shoe and enveloped his foot. He flailed his arms, falling backward as he tried not to crush the infant creature.

Zack held his foot in the air. Squishy squirmed as he kneaded Zack's foot. Growing up with dogs familiarized Zack with the sensation of being bitten, but he felt no pressure or jaws clamping down on his toes. Writhing on the ground, he reached into his pocket, withdrew, and activated his C7.

"Skip, send a message to Jenny: Found him!"

"Acknowledged, Zack."

He heard footsteps race toward him. She must have been nearby when she received his message. She stopped short when she saw him lying on his back, foot in the air, with an Athosian crawling and squirming around his shoe.

"What are you doing?"

"I think he's playing. Do you think Athosian babies play?"

Jenny shook her head as she stepped around him. "I think you might be crazy."

Zack felt the strain in his spine as he lowered his leg and shook it to dislodge Squishy. The creature dangled by one tentacle before falling into the water with a splash. Jenny offered him a hand and helped him to his feet.

"Now that I found him again, I don't know what to do with him." Zack wanted to bring the Athosian to his room, but he believed neither Mickey nor Kaneer would understand or approve.

"Honestly, I think it seems happy here." Jenny crouched down and watched it swim against the stream's current. "This should be okay for a few more days at least."

"You think so?" Zack had doubts. He heard a lot of students talk about visiting the arboretum last year. Granted, it was later in the term, when the plants from exobotany classes bloomed, but the prospect the infant Athosian could be discovered still worried him.

"Yes, I do." Jenny tapped his shoulder. "I'm going back now to get cleaned up, maybe have a snack before the festival. I'll see you there?"

"Yeah, Dravs won't let me miss it. He says he's going to show me all the good things to eat."

She left him to observe the Athosian swim and splash. On a whim, he took out his C7 and recorded several minutes of the creature playing before following Jenny's lead and heading to his dorm. He wanted to have enough time to get cleaned up and put on fresh clothes for the festival that night. Zack's mind wandered to thoughts of the probe he left on the surface of Venus. Despite his best efforts, he couldn't help but wonder if what he found there related to Squishy.

117

~ * * * ~

Hiri returned about the time Jenny finished showering and dressing. She attached the honor braid Mungus gifted her as Hiri watched.

"Your hair is already so long and beautiful, what do you need that for? It looks coarse."

Jenny smoothed the honor braid. "It's from an Ersidian, an honor braid for saving his life. I don't wear it all the time, but tonight seems like a good occasion."

"From your Junior Ranger friend? Xal?"

"No, Mungus, on the Bestic trip."

"I'd like to hear about that sometime." Hiri took Jenny's hand as they left the dorm and made their way toward Ishtar Plaza.

"You're working with Ix on a project, right?" Jenny preferred to hear about Hiri's activities than recount the Bestic trip yet again.

"See, it uses a tirdium dynamo to create a magnetic field strong enough to repel superheated plasma." Hiri waved her hands to illustrate as she described the project. "In theory, the field will be strong enough to protect a probe long enough to penetrate the star's corona, allowing it to enter the upper levels of the star's atmosphere... so to speak."

Stellar physics was not a subject Jenny studied, but seeing Hiri so excited brought a smile to her face. "So, this probe is going to be shot into a star?"

They boarded the travel pod with a group of other students, all bound for Ishtar Plaza and the Festival of Starlight.

"Well, that's the plan." Hiri tucked a lock of hair behind her ear. Sometime since Jenny saw her last, she had refreshed the sapphire highlights in her dark hair. "The corona is so hot, though. Designing a probe to withstand temperatures high enough to ionize pretty much any alloy we can create is challenging."

"It seems like that would be a job left to professionals, not students." Jenny thought the whole project seemed too advanced for even Cytherean Academy's brightest students.

"I thought so, too. But Ix is convinced he can get this magnetic shielding thing to work. Really, I don't get why he is even a student here."

"It."

"Oh yeah."

Jenny chuckled. "Ix is mostly here to learn customs and social skills. I think the science and engineering is for fun, since it would have learned all that at its hive before it emancipated itself."

"Only a Valtraxian would tackle such a complicated project for fun."

They disembarked from the travel pod. Even from the transit station, they heard the party in Ishtar Plaza. As they traveled up the corridor, more and more people crowded the halls. Multicolored streamers hung from ceiling fixtures, and they were forced to slow their pace until they reached Ishtar Plaza and the crowds parted to follow the street to either side of the park.

"Wow, look at that!" Hiri stared at the kaleidoscopic array of Devorans dancers twirling around the plaza. Their bodies were painted in brilliant colors, and they wore sheer black fabrics that sparkled in the light. Staccato drumming provided the beat behind the music, a mixture of chimes, blown shells, and horns, to accompany their movements.

"Excuse me, ladies." Leading a group of armed soldiers, a human attired in an EAC fleet officer's dress uniform pushed his way past Jenny. The group paused before the two students.

"Try not to look too uptight, squad." The officer gestured toward the crowd. "This is a celebration. Enjoy yourselves a bit, but don't forget we're on duty." He pointed toward the pavilion at the center of the plaza. "I'll be over there if you need me."

The soldiers nodded and disbursed. The officer ducked through the crowd until he reached the path leading into the park. While the EAC maintained a military presence on Cytherea, Jenny noticed the officer's uniform insignia did not belong to the Cytherea garrison.

"What do you think that's about?" She gestured toward the soldiers and officer.

"Beats me." Hiri shrugged. "Maybe they're here to keep an eye on all the extra Devoran soldiers who are here protecting that princess or whatever she is."

Jenny nodded. Technically allies, Confederation and EAC forces still experienced tension when a group of either set up shop in the other's territory. Neither Cytherea nor the EAC belonged to the Confederation, and Jenny pondered whether that increased tensions.

The aroma of roasting meat wafted past their noses, causing their stomachs to grumble. The young women followed the scent to an area of the park where they found a whole animal roasting over an open pit, tended by a pair of green-scaled Devorans wearing long knives in sheaths slung across their backs. Jenny observed Dravs, one arm in a sling, pacing to and fro on the other side of the spit. She found herself mesmerized by the sight of the beast rotating over the hot coals, and she noted the scene, in an age of vat-grown meat and fabricator-dispensed food, served as a curious callback to a more primitive, departed era.

Jenny waved at Dravs from across the roasting pit. The young blue Devoran raced around the spit, slipping on grass that due to its proximity to the fire had been wet down to prevent it from igniting. He narrowly avoided barreling into Jenny and Hiri as he skidded to a stop.

"Isn't this great?" Dravs balanced on one foot as he wiped mud off his sole.

Hiri regarded the Devoran revelers with wonderment, her eyes widening and a grin overtaking her face. "It's something, all right. What happened to your arm?"

Dravs rubbed his shoulder and looked away. "Zack and I were fooling around, and he kind of fell on top of me. Dislocated my shoulder."

Hiri winced. "Ouch. Are you going to be okay?"

The Devoran giggled. "Yeah, the nurse gave me something to relax the muscles; they were spasming after they popped my shoulder back in. It makes me kind of hungry, though."

"You're always hungry. Have you seen Zack?" Jenny glanced at the crowd, but dozens of dancers, tents, and other students blocked her view.

Dravs cleaned the other foot and shook his head. "I haven't seen him yet, but I got a message from him about ten minutes ago."

One of the Devorans tending the spit drew his blade and sliced off a sizzling piece of meat. "Hey, Blue-scale! Catch!" He flung the meat toward Dravs.

Dravs jumped into the air and snatched the meat as it sailed toward him. He laughed, juggling it with one hand. "Ouch! Ha, thanks."

He tore off a hunk with his teeth. Then he presented it to Jenny and Hiri.

"No thanks." Jenny shook her head and grimaced.

Hiri, however, gripped the end with two fingers and pulled off a small strip, wincing as hot juices streamed down her hand. She popped it in her mouth, and her eyes bulged as she chewed. She swallowed the half-chewed morsel. "What is that thing?" She wiped her mouth on her sleeve and stepped away from the roasting pit, eyeing the spit as if it might come alive and attack her.

"Grund cow."

Jenny pursed her lips and glared at Dravs. "You know we're humans, right?" Grund cow, a Devoran delicacy, was known throughout the galaxy as being unpalatable to humans.

He shrugged and tore another piece. "It would've been rude not to offer it to you. Besides, some humans like it."

Hiri suppressed a gag. "This one didn't."

Jenny took Hiri's arm. "Let's get something edible."

"There's a table full of other food." Dravs pointed, the meat he held flapping as he gesticulated. "It's on the other side of the princess's pavilion."

She struggled to keep up as Hiri dashed in the direction Dravs indicated. As much hunger as gnawed at Jenny's stomach, it was no match for Hiri's desire to eradicate the flavor of grund cow.

Chapter 19

"Are you almost ready?" Zack ran his fingers along the honor braid tied at his waist as he shouted toward the bathroom from his seat on the sofa. He promised to go with Kaneer to the festival, but when he made that promise, he didn't know the Kerrolian would take so long to get ready.

Kaneer shouted an unintelligible reply. Polly, seated on the sofa next to Zack, flipped through programs on the holoviewer and laughed. "Want me to go see what's keeping Fuzz-butt?"

"I'm tempted." Zack looked over his shoulder toward the closed bathroom door, as if staring at it would make the Kerrolian clean himself faster.

"Let's go!" Shutting the door to the bedroom behind her, Barbara approached her sister and tugged at the back of her shirt.

"Watch the silk, Grabby McHandy!" Polly batted away Barbara's hand. Standing, she smacked Zack on the knee. "You should come with us to the Rampage Room and leave Fuzz-butt behind."

"As much as I'd like to stomp Berlin with you, I don't have implants, remember?"

"Too bad, Earther!" Polly clucked her tongue. On the way out, she stopped by the bathroom Kaneer occupied and banged on the door. "Move your fuzzy behind, Furface! The Zack Attack awaits!"

She grinned and saluted Zack as they left. It was then Zack noticed she left the holoviewer set to a program that discussed in graphic detail Devoran mating and courtship rituals. He fumbled for the controller and switched off the screen.

A few minutes later, Kaneer finally emerged. Fluffier than Zack had ever seen it, the Kerrolian's fur made him look a bit like a puffball with legs.

"Apologies, Zack Jackson. As you can see, this one had... trouble."

Stifling a giggle at Kaneer's ridiculous appearance, Zack doubled over and coughed to conceal his mirth. "You can hardly tell."

"You lie, Zack Jackson, but not as well as Kaneer." He padded toward Zack and crossed his arms over his chest. "Let us go, yes? This one is hungry and grumpy. Grungry? Hungpy?"

Zack snorted. "I think people say hangry. Hungry and angry."

"Ah yes, a portman toe."

"Sure, if you say so." Zack snickered as he led Kaneer out. A steady stream of students waited for the lifts, and when they reached Mytikas level where Ishtar Plaza was located, the line grew more congested, exactly the situation Zack hoped to avoid by leaving early. Plans thwarted by Kaneer and whatever fur-care disaster his Kerrolian friend suffered.

"Hey, can you smell Dravs in this crowd?"

Kaneer stared down the length of his muzzle at him. "There are many, many scents in this plaza now, Zack Jackson. One Devoran among thousands is beyond this one's ability. Perhaps Zack Jackson should have brought a blood-dog."

"Bloodhound." Zack doubted even DD, his parent's genetically engineered dog, could pick out Dravs's scent. Of course, DD was mostly Labrador retriever, not bloodhound. "Come on, we'll find him the old-fashioned way. He'll probably be hanging around the food."

While it took them better than fifteen minutes to navigate the crowd, they did, indeed, find Dravs near food. He milled about a roasting pit set up in the park. Zack noticed drool dripping from the Devoran's mouth as he salivated over the rotating, roasting meat.

"Zack! You made it and—" Dravs burst out laughing. "Is that Kaneer? What kind of electrical storm did you two run into?"

Kaneer curled his lips and growled. "It is not funny. This one ran into difficulties while bathing."

"I'll say!" Dravs tapped the shoulder of one of the green-scaled Devorans tending the spit. He turned, shaved off a foot-long strip of meat and dropped it as his eyes landed on the puffy Kerrolian. Dravs snatched it out of the air.

"Ow! It's hot, hot, hot!" He bit off a chunk and offered it to Zack. "Grund cow?"

"Grund cow?" Kaneer pushed Zack out of the way and grabbed one end of the hunk of meat, tearing into it with aplomb.

"Hey!" Zack stumbled backward, bumping into something hard. He recoiled. After catching his right foot on his left foot, he fell forward. A hand grasped his collar and kept him from tumbling to the ground.

123

"Easy, kid."

An EAC Fleet officer righted Zack and straightened his shirt. He noticed the man held an almost spherical bottle of brown liquid in his other hand. Zack's eyes widened when he recognized the insignia on the man's uniform as the rank of major. He stood up straight and swallowed.

"Oh, I'm sorry. Sir!"

The major put his free hand on Zack's shoulder. "At ease, there, kid. Sir's not necessary when you're not in the service. Having a good time here?"

Dravs approached them, chewing and slurping the grund cow. "Sorry about that." He held out the meat. "Grund cow?"

"Oh, no thanks." The major held up his free hand and shook his head. "That stuff disagrees with me something fierce." He nodded to Zack and smirked. "You should try it, though."

"Yeah?" Zack pulled off a strip of meat from the hunk Dravs held. It peeled away like string cheese the color of medium-rare beef brisket. He sniffed it but smelled mostly smoke from the fire pit.

He popped it in his mouth. The meat tasted sour, like it had been soaked in vinegar. It required careful chewing, but it did not feel tough or dry. "Mmm, kind of reminds me of sauerbraten."

His mother often tried new recipes. One winter, before Zack enrolled in Cytherean Academy, she decided to cook a different cultural dish each night. His family enjoyed a culinary tour of Europe, then East Asia, South America, and Africa before spring arrived.

Dravs narrowed his eyes. "You don't hate it?"

"It's not bad. It's not the best thing ever, but it's not bad. How do they get it to taste like that when it's roasting on a spit? It doesn't taste smoky at all."

"So much for getting revenge for my shoulder. Figures you'd like it." Dravs scowled.

The major laughed. "How about that? Kid, you're better off not knowing, believe me." He pointed at Dravs. "Don't you tell him why grund cow tastes like that. Let him look it up if he really wants to know."

Zack pulled out his C7. The officer pushed down his hand and shook his head. "Later, enjoy the night. Then ruin the food."

"Oh, all right." He put away the C7.

"Well, thanks, Major Jericho."

"How did..." He noticed Zack staring at his name tag. "Heh, not bad. Most civilians neither know the ranks nor bother to check the name tag."

Dravs put his free arm around Zack. "We're Junior Rangers, Major."

He clapped them both on the shoulder. "Well, be excellent. See you around."

Dravs gestured with his head as he squeezed Zack. "There's more food on the other side of the pavilion. Jenny and her friend went that way."

"Well, let's go, then." Zack threw off Dravs's arm and gestured for Kaneer to follow them.

"Kaneer is not finished eating this delicious grund cow!"

"There's more over there." One of the Devoran cooks pointed. "It's sliced and ready to eat."

"Then Kaneer shall accompany you, Zack Jackson. Do not come between a Kerrolian and his food."

"You could say the same thing about Devorans." Dravs skipped past Zack and Kaneer. A nearby band ended the rhythmic tune they played and started an up-tempo, pipe-heavy dance melody.

"All Devorans, or just you?" Zack ducked under a dancer who spun a large multicolored ribbon. A group of students joined in the dance, laughing and whooping.

"Look, there's Jenny!" Dravs pointed toward the crowd lined up around a long table, obscuring the far end from view. Students, Cytherean citizens, and military personnel alike all loaded their plates with the bounty festooned upon the buffet. Jenny and Hiri stood on the near side, each holding plates laden with colorful fruits, vegetables, and what looked like smoked turkey legs, though Zack suspected whatever animal they came from never flew Earth's blue skies or wandered its verdant pastures.

Dravs waved the two friends over to one of the few free blankets in the park that dotted the area behind the pavilion. Diners, mostly students, occupied the other blankets. A trio of grey-scaled Devorans moved wheeled waste receptacles through the crowd, accepting trash from diners who had finished with their meals.

The overwhelming variety of sights and smells reminded Zack of annual cookouts his family held back home each summer, cookouts his parents would probably never again be able to hold once they moved to Vilicus. He had a sudden craving for roasted sweet corn and watermelon, but he doubted those desires would be sated at this intergalactic buffet.

~ * * * ~

Jenny and Hiri joined Dravs at the spot he procured on the park lawn. Zack and his new Kerrolian roommate helped the two young women with their plates as they seated themselves.

"I guess we should get some food, huh?" Zack looked at the crowded buffet table.

"Everything is up there more than once, so just find a free spot and fill a plate." Jenny batted Kaneer's tail out of her face as the Kerrolian spun to watch a pair of Devoran dancers skip through the crowd. The festival reminded Jenny of New Year's celebrations held on Messier Habitat, the last of which she attended before starting Cytherean Academy. It seemed the revelers here were less inebriated; however, she considered the possibility the crowd her parents hung out with partied harder.

She picked at her food while she waited for Zack to return, despite the growing hunger in her belly. Hiri had no such reservations; she halfway finished her plate by the time he, Dravs, and Kaneer returned.

Jenny stabbed what she thought was some type of fried mushroom and held it up. "Better than roasted gobelek. Right, Zack?"

He laughed at the reminder of their foraged meals on Bestic. "I think wet cardboard would taste better than gobelek."

"This one does not understand." Kaneer's ears drooped. "There is a tale to tell, yes? That we might better understand the joke?"

Jenny and Zack related the story about the Junior Ranger excursion during which they first met. She kept her description of the crash itself clinical and concise, where Zack described it akin to that of a theme park thrill ride. She told of their days in the freezing mountainous forest, scrounging for food to supplement their emergency rations, while they followed Zack's map to the only nearby city. He told of their narrow escape from predatory ferok-togs and the mercury lake.

Hiri tore off a piece of meat from the smoked leg and waved the bone in their direction. "Mmm... Ix was telling me about that the other day. You ran afoul of some weird cultists, right?"

Jenny's eyes met Zack's, and both their smiles faded. Technically, the decree forbade them only from mentioning the Athosian facility on Valtra, but Jenny didn't want to take any chances. Zack shrugged, and Jenny turned to Hiri. "Something like that. We're not supposed to talk about it."

"Really?" Dravs slurped a stringy vegetable dish. "Bariss thinks it's upsetting or something? Does it have something to do with that stuff on Valtra?"

Jenny felt a bead of cold sweat run down her spine. "It's complicated." She gestured toward several Devoran soldiers filling their plates. "They... suggested... there'd be trouble if we talked. So, we don't."

Dravs looked at the soldiers and snorted. "Pfft. You aren't Confederation citizens. What are they going to do to you?"

"It's about Athosians." Zack clamped his hands over his mouth as soon as he blurted the words.

Hiri furrowed her brow. "I don't get why—"

"Perhaps you children shouldn't be talking about such matters in public." Jenny saw the speaker's sapphire-scaled legs first. She followed them up to a shell-covered tunic and headdress that jingled as the princess shook her head.

Dravs gasped, dropped his plate, and prostrated himself. Blindly, he groped the area around himself as he tried to pull down Kaneer and Zack as well.

"Sorry about that." Zack lowered his head. "We were just talking about the time we crashed on Bestic. That's all."

The emerald-and-sapphire-hued Devoran lowered herself alongside the blanket, folding her legs underneath her. Even seated, she was as tall as Zack. "I am Valianna Hallox. I know a couple of you already." She gestured toward Zack and Kaneer before turning her attention to the rest of them. "I assume you're classmates of Zack's?"

"I'm a Junior Ranger in his troop." Jenny gestured toward Dravs, still pressing his head into the blanket. "Dravs, too. Hiri's my"—she gazed at the older girl and raised her eyebrows—"girlfriend."

127

Valianna pulled Dravs up. "You're making a scene."

"P-p-p... you're Princess V-v..."

"I am a Confederation citizen, just like you, young one." She stroked Dravs's cheek. The young, blue-scaled Devoran shuddered at her touch. "That my father was Emperor Hallox the Fifth is irrelevant. The titles no longer hold power."

Kaneer snorted. "There are many who would disagree."

"I'm Genevieve DuBois. My friends call me Jenny." She extended her hand toward the princess. "Pleased to meet you."

Valianna took her hand and pressed it to her forehead. "You are human but not from Earth, as Zack is?"

Jenny wondered if her accent or scent betrayed her. "I am from Messier Habitat."

She felt Hiri's hand slip into hers. Dravs stammered and strained to prostrate himself again before Valianna, but the princess held him in place.

"I hope you're enjoying yourselves. I understand because of this festival, they've had to cancel one of your Earth holiday observances?"

"It's not really a holiday, as such." Hiri squeezed Jenny's hand before resuming her meal.

"Halloween was once a spiritual observance on ancient Earth, but it's more of an excuse to dress up in costumes and eat a lot of really bad food." Jenny never attended Halloween parties until her first year at Cytherean Academy; no one observed the night on Messier Habitat.

"Bad food?" Dravs's jaw dropped. "All that candy and stuff? That's the best food you Earthers make!"

"Ah, youth." Valianna clucked her tongue. "There are far better things from Earth than candy."

"Like bourbon?" A man wearing an EAC military uniform stepped behind the Noble Devoran. He extended a spherical bottle as a smile spread across his face.

Valianna turned her head. She beamed when she saw him. After jumping to her feet, she wrapped her arms around him and lifted him into the air. "Hank!"

Muffling his words, the princess pressed his face into her chest and squeezed the air from his lungs.

"Dignity. Dignity."

"Of course. Sorry." Valianna released him and chuckled. "Authentic Kentucky bourbon?"

He offered her the bottle. "Is there any other kind?"

"Not legally, no." She took the bourbon, removed the stopper, and inhaled deeply. "I had no idea you'd be here."

Valianna turned toward the seated students. "May I present Lieu..."—she eyed his rank insignia—"oh, Major! Major Thomas Henry Jericho, EAC Fleet Intelligence."

He offered them a small wave, nodding toward Zack, Dravs, and Kaneer. "I've already met some of the students."

Jenny stood and offered her hand. "Genevieve DuBois, Messier Habitat, and my girlfriend Kim Hiriko, Kaku Habitat." Hiri bowed her head.

"A pleasure." He shook her hand. "If you'll excuse us, I have important matters to discuss with Madam Hallox here."

"Such formality... and a gift of bourbon. It must be serious." Valianna clasped her hands in front of her and bowed to the students. "I hope you enjoy the rest of the festival, and I hope to see you again before our final relocation. *Palla for taeno.*"

She departed with the major, leaving Jenny, Hiri, and the others to finish their meals. Zack stared at Dravs, who swayed his head in time with Valianna's steps while remaining prone.

"She touched me..." The Devoran held his hand to his cheek. "She actually touched me."

"This one thinks Dravs Sallaron has lost his mind." Kaneer pushed the Devoran with a finger. He only swayed, maintaining his unbroken gaze on Valianna until she passed out of sight and into the crowd.

"Hey..." Zack clicked his fingers in Dravs's face. "What does it mean? That thing she said? 'Palla for taeno?'"

"Uh... umm... touch..."

Jenny giggled and snorted. "It doesn't have a direct translation. 'Stars guide you' is pretty close."

"Of all the things Kaneer expected to see here, a Noble Devoran glomping a human was not one of them." Kaneer reached across the blanket and took a slab of grund cow from Dravs's plate. The Devoran didn't notice.

Hiri squeezed Jenny's hand. "Well, you can't say it hasn't been an interesting evening."

Chapter 20

Zack tossed and turned. At first, he thought the amount of food he consumed at the festival caused his restless sleep. Then, he considered it might be *what* he consumed, rather than the amount of it. Eventually, he worried about Squishy.

The Devoran military is here. The EAC military has stepped up their forces. A bunch of Devorans are staying here before they move to Vilicus, including the princess of the old empire... What if they find him? Does that thing on Venus have anything to do with why they're all here?

Apart from keeping an eye on Squishy, Zack could do nothing else to help the juvenile Athosian at the moment. A solution better than hiding him in the arboretum had eluded him. However, Zack decided to take action about the strange lights on Venus. Before he finally fell asleep, he formulated a plan.

He expected his scheme would have to wait until the next Junior Ranger meeting to implement, but his astrosciences class provided an unexpected opportunity to jump start the process.

Professor Bailey announced the midterm project after delivering a short lecture on the moons of Saturn. "As long as it's relevant to our coursework this term, you may choose whatever subject you like. We'll end class a little early, so you can each come down and tell me about your ideas."

Students rose from their seats and shuffled down the aisles toward her podium, brainstorming among each other as they waited. Zack entered the queue as quickly as possible and formulated his thoughts.

When he reached the podium, Professor Bailey glanced up from her tablet. Her greying, pixie-cut hair lay across her brow like downy feathers. "Name?"

"Zack Jackson."

She pulled up his file and raised her eyebrows, expectantly awaiting his proposal.

"I'd like to do a paper on volcanism on Venus. I saw some interesting things the last time I was operating the remote probes with the Junior Rangers, and I want to explore it a little more."

"Great!" She beamed, crow's feet appearing in the corners of her eyes. "You're the first student this term to pick a local subject."

"Maybe I could get permission to use the remote probes... to help with my research?"

"Sure. If your troop leader agrees, I'll sign off on it." She tapped her screen. Moments later, the authorization appeared on his PDA. "I look forward to reading your paper, Zack."

He bounded out of the classroom, but he didn't realize until halfway through his Devoran Cultural Studies class that he would have to write a paper on Venusian volcanism. Despite what he told Professor Bailey, he did not possess interest in the subject.

Oh well. Now I just have to convince Bariss.

~ * * * ~

A full belly and an evening of fun provided Jenny with fuel for the best night of sleep she'd had since the term started. Lingering lethargy from overeating at the Festival of Starlight stayed with her through the first several days following the festival.

To her surprise, one afternoon following classes, she found Ix waiting for her in her dorm's common area. She eyed it before nodding toward the door across the room. "Are you here for Hiriko?"

"I am not." The Valtraxian shook its head and chittered. It removed its green fez and held it in front of its torso as it bowed its head.

Ix has improved its human gestures.

"I hoped to speak with you, Jenny, if you have time."

"Sure. Do we need to go to one of the quiet rooms?" She carried her pack into her room. A napping Astrid grumbled and turned away from the door when Jenny's pack thumped against the floor. She faced Ix and, not wishing to disturb Astrid further, gently closed the door.

"I do not think that will be necessary." Ix climbed over the backrest and perched on the side of the sofa. Jenny found the holoviewer muted and flipping through channels faster than she could follow the action, so she shut it off and turned her attention toward her friend.

"Is something wrong?" Ix rarely came to visit her. Although she had known it through the Junior Rangers longer than either of them had known Zack, they weren't particularly close.

The Valtraxian wrung its upper hands and chittered before replying. "You were with Zack in those ruins on Valtra, were you not?"

"I was. Bariss told us not to talk about it." She didn't like it when adults ordered her to keep silent about something, especially when it involved her friends. "The Devoran ambassador was very upset."

"I saw a news report that suggested there was evidence at that site that the Athosians uplifted my species from our unintelligent forbearers." Ix chittered briefly before falling silent, staring at Jenny with unblinking compound eyes.

"That was on the news?" *If it was on the news, there's no point in keeping silent, is there?*

"It was." Ix bobbed its head up and down. "The archaeologists were removed from the site under protest."

"We found an artificial intelligence down there that said as much." While she no longer felt the need to be totally silent on the matter, Jenny figured discretion was prudent. She touched Ix's arm. "I'm sorry we didn't say anything. The Devoran ambassador wanted to throw us in jail just for finding it."

Ix cocked its head. "Curious. That would indicate my species owes its entire civilization, its very existence, to the Athosians."

"It doesn't change who you are, though." Jenny wished she could read emotion in the Valtraxian's unchanging expression.

"No, it does not affect my sense of self. Still, I wonder..."

"About?"

"Has Zack said anything to you?" Ix stopped wringing its hands and, instead, folded them in front of its chest.

"Not about that, no. We haven't talked about what went on there after all the adults told us not to."

Ix shook its head. "Kaneer, Dravs, Bob, and Zack seem to believe there is an Athosian on Cytherea. It came from the spherical piece of iron Professor Gladstone gifted to Zack last term."

132

Uh-oh... I didn't think that many people were involved already. "Hiri and I know about it, too." Jenny's eyes widened. "Have you seen it?"

"I have not. Have you?"

"Yes, it's in the arboretum."

"Will you take me?"

Jenny pushed herself up from the sofa. "Let's go." She took Ix's arm. "You can't say anything to anyone about this."

"I will not." Ix returned its fez to the top of its head. "The Devorans would be very unhappy to learn of this, if it is true."

To distract Ix while they traveled to the arboretum, Jenny asked the Valtraxian to explain the project it and Hiri worked on together. Ix complied with passion, and though she only understood about a quarter of what it described, Jenny noticed its joy in having an enthusiastic collaborator.

"She speaks of you often. At least, she does now."

Jenny felt her cheeks grow warm. "She and I are close."

"Yes, I understand. The type of relationship Polly wanted with Zack, I think. Though with more consent?"

Jenny laughed. "Yes, that's it exactly."

"I still do not understand human courtship."

"Neither do most humans." Jenny opened the doors to the arboretum. She pointed to their left. "Over the hill, into the trees. There's a stream."

She led the Valtraxian toward the crossing where she and Zack last found the Athosian. "It's really difficult to see in the water, so we may not be able to find it."

"I am familiar with the spot. I come here often to think."

"You do?" Jenny was surprised to hear Ix did anything so mundane as to seek out a quiet area for contemplation.

"I do." Ix scrambled to the middle of the crossing stones and pointed to a spot in the water. "Is that it?"

Jenny didn't see any object near where Ix directed her attention until she focused on the rocks beneath the flowing stream. Distorted though it appeared underwater, the shape resembled the Athosian.

"It looks like it." She crouched down on the bank to have a closer look. Upon a second inspection, she confirmed the Athosian, larger than she remembered it, moving rocks on the bed of the stream, though to what purpose, she couldn't deduce.

Ix lowered itself until its abdomen dipped into the water and lowered its head almost level with the stream rushing past underneath it. "Based on everything I have read, it appears to be a juvenile Athosian. Amazing it could come out of an object as small as that iron sphere."

"We don't know what to do with it. Zack's afraid the Devorans will want to kill it."

Ix returned to an upright posture and moved out of the stream onto the grassy bank next to Jenny. "I believe he is correct. Its existence proves their genocide failed."

"Did it? One individual can't repopulate the species, not animals, anyway." Jenny possessed more botany credits than biology, but she understood that animals required genetic diversity to grow healthy, sustainable populations.

"We should go, before we are noticed." Ix gestured toward the main area of the arboretum. "It is sufficiently difficult to detect under the water, and this is a remote enough section of the arboretum that it should be able to stay hidden for several weeks"—Ix chirped and clicked—"unless it emerges."

Jenny gripped his arm and faced him. "Might it? Why would it do that?" She imagined the panic if a group of students saw a tentacled blob crawl out of the stream.

"It was just idle speculation, Jenny." Ix stroked her arm. "I do not know what it might do."

Ix waited until they were alone in a section of the travel pod before again addressing Jenny. "Thank you. Seeing what might have been the greatest benefactor to my species was enlightening."

"Really? You think so?" Jenny grew up with simple religious observances. She couldn't imagine how she'd feel if she came face to face with her creator.

"Athosians were supposedly a hive mind; mature adults in proximity to each other operated as if they shared a brain. Seeing a juvenile at play, as vulnerable as any of us, reminds me they are just sapients like us. Mortal. Flawed."

Ix paused as a student moved through their compartment. "My assertion of individuality is often seen as a hubristic aberration by other Valtraxians, but I no longer believe this is the case."

"And here I thought all you thought about at school was engineering." Jenny laughed and put her hand on Ix's shoulder.

"I struggle with existential thoughts." Ix rubbed its hands together. "Also, I will be finished here much sooner than my friends. I am not certain I wish to leave them."

Jenny, aware Ix participated in an accelerated program, never gave much consideration to the fact that it would finish school before any of them. "Well, could you get a job here until Zack is finished? I don't know what he plans to do once he's out of school. You may not be able to follow him if he joins the Defense Force or gets a job with a private corporation."

"That is true." Ix sat and clicked its mandibles together. "Still, I feel like I should maximize the time while we are young."

"How long do Valtraxians live, anyway?" Jenny had never considered the question. She assumed Valtraxians, like most humanoid species in the galaxy apart from Devorans, lived a hundred years or so.

"Our lifespans are limited to thirty-five years. I am only nine as of my next hatching day."

"Nine? How are you this far along?" Jenny grappled with the idea that the Valtraxian was so young compared to Zack. Even more so since she was a good eighteen months older than their mutual friend.

"There are distinct advantages to being able to start education within a year of hatching. At any rate, I will undergo my final molt soon." Ix rubbed its arms together. "Perhaps I should save part of my carapace... a keepsake."

"Like your head?" Jenny giggled. The thought of Ix carrying around a hollow shell of its own head seemed a little gross.

Ix cocked its head. "It would make a good place to store my fez when I am not wearing it."

Jenny stared at the Valtraxian. "Was... was that a joke?"

"It was intended to be humorous, but I was serious about the practical application."

"Ix... that was really funny." As Jenny searched its eyes for some clue as to its thoughts, her face stared back at her tenfold, reflected in the compound lenses of the Valtraxian's eyes. Ix bowed its head and chittered.

"I have been watching many ancient earth films considered classics in the comedy genre."

135

"When do you find time for all this?" As the travel pod arrived at Anahita Dome, the doors opened to release passengers. Jenny and Ix stepped off and approached the lifts that would take them to her dorm.

"I only sleep two to three hours a night. That leaves much time for independent study."

"No one will ever accuse you of not being well rounded." It was a point so many of her teachers tried to hammer into her. To hear them tell it, if one was not well versed in many subjects and extracurricular activities, one may as well give it all up and go live in a ditch. Her parents disagreed. They often insisted one must be focused and disciplined to enjoy any measure of success.

"How are your parents, Jenny?"

She wondered if she'd been rambling about them aloud. "Improving." Finally, she could speak about them without choking up. "Papa's reconstructive surgeries are all finished, and his memory is returning. Mother has completed most of her physical therapy. She's going to stay with him until he can go home, though. Maybe by the end of the term."

"I am glad to hear that."

They arrived at Jenny's dorm. As Jenny opened the door, Ix touched her arm. "Thank you. Good night, Jenny."

"Good night."

Chapter 21

Securing permission from Bariss went more easily than Zack expected. The Devoran seemed distracted during the Junior Ranger meeting, and he let the various squads practice building makeshift shelters from raw materials, unsupervised. Kept in storage lockers in the gymnasium, the synthetic materials closely approximated what one might find in the wilderness of any given planet.

Dravs lashed together two tree branch-like poles while Bob held them. "This stuff is for if we get lost without our gear, right? Because I've never gone anywhere without a tent."

"Matter-of-fact: that is correct. Tentative statement: I don't think Zack, Mungus, Ix, and Jenny had tents when they crashed on Bestic."

"Nope!" Zack struggled to hold his poles while Jenny lashed them together. "Just our personal packs. We didn't even have any tools, just my multi-tool and Mungus's knife."

"Hold still, Zack." Jenny muttered something he didn't hear under her breath, jerked the poles, and then tied the knot. They wobbled but remained upright long enough for Ix to incorporate an additional pole to bolster them. "We'd be dead if Mungus hadn't brought his knife."

"Yes... 'knife.' Dravs punctuated the word with air quotes. "That thing is more like a sword! It's as big as my arm."

"With mocking jest: that's because you have skinny arms." Bob made a sound Zack thought might have been a laugh. "Query: how is he allowed to have such a weapon?"

Ix clicked and faced Bob. "Mungus has a cultural exemption."

Bob released the poles he held and stepped back. The tent collapsed as Dravs swore.

"Query: why are we attempting to create teepees instead of ridge tents? Would they not be easier?"

"*Mon dieu.*" Jenny slapped her forehead. She and Zack untied their poles. They helped Dravs and Bob untangle their mess before switching to a simpler style of construction.

By the time all the Junior Rangers finished creating their triangle-shaped shelters, it was time to take them down and put away the materials. Jenny returned to her dorm as soon

137

as the meeting ended, but Dravs and Bob planned to return to Ishtar Plaza with the hope of finding leftovers from the Festival of Starlight.

"Are you coming, Zack?" Dravs nodded at his friend, then at the Valtraxian. "Ix?"

"No, thanks. I have a project to work on." Zack glanced toward Bariss. The Devoran was talking via his comm implant.

The Valtraxian eyed Zack, before chittering and bobbing its head at Dravs. "I will accompany you and Bob."

"You should have been there the other night, Ix. It was great! There was so much..." Dravs waved to Zack as the three wandered off. Meanwhile, Zack loitered while Bariss finished his call and double-checked the storage lockers to ensure all supplies from the evening's exercise had been returned. The Devoran appeared distracted, oblivious to Zack as the young man tried to get his attention.

"Bariss?" Zack tapped him on the arm a third time.

"What?" Jerking his head, he snapped his teeth and then sighed. "Sorry. I'm... sorry. What do you need, Zack?"

Zack held out his C7, the authorization form from Professor Bailey on the screen. "I'm doing a project on volcanism on Venus, and my professor says if you'll sign off on it, she'll authorize VR time in the remote probes so I can do some research on the surface."

"Oh, yeah, I guess that's all right." Bariss pressed a finger to Zack's C7, authorizing the VR time. "Try not to break or lose the probe?"

"I'll be careful." He thanked Bariss and headed straight for the VR lounge. Zack approached the attendant, his PDA ready for the inevitable challenge.

The man behind the counter regarded the young man from under shaggy bangs and rubbed his drooping eyes. "There are no scheduled Junior Ranger excursions today."

"I know that." Zack waved his PDA. "I have permission from Professor Bailey. It's for a research project."

"Lemme see."

Zack tapped a few buttons on his screen to send the permission slip to the attendant. The sleepy-eyed attendant looked it over.

"Who's Bariss Tanerous?"

"My Junior Ranger troop leader." Zack tucked his PDA into the holster on his belt. "You know, the Devoran who's always in here with us?"

A nearby VR pod opened. An older student Zack did not recognize stumbled from within and straightened his shirt. He nodded to the attendant as he shuffled out.

"Huh. I never knew his name." The attendant pointed toward a nearby pod. "Three-B is ready for you. A storm is coming, so you have maybe thirty minutes before communication between the pod and the surface becomes an issue."

Zack thanked the attendant and entered the pod. The whirr of servos drowned out the VR lounge ventilation fans as the pod closed around Zack, encapsulating him in a padded cocoon of utter darkness. He shut his eyes to minimize the dazzling white flash as the interface loaded. Opening them when the link completed, he stood once again on the surface of Venus.

He moved his arms to get a feel for the probe. Spinning to get his bearings, movement felt like swimming through gelatin. From the position of the rocks surrounding him, he concluded he linked to a different probe than the one he piloted during the last Junior Ranger meeting.

On the horizon, he saw flashes of lightning illuminate the mustard-colored sky. Dark clouds loomed over nearby mountains, poising to unleash their terrible rage on the hellscape below. Atmospheric distortion interfered with the probe's instruments and thwarted his efforts to determine the distance of the clouds, so Zack focused on finding the probe he previously operated.

After expending at least ten minutes moving from probe to probe, Zack located the one he used during his last Junior Ranger exploration. He found its claw arm still outstretched toward an arrangement of odd, oblong rocks, pointing in the direction of the flat metal plate Zack had found. Turning the probe when he reached the makeshift landmark, he followed the imaginary line it drew. When he reached the hillside, he scraped at the dirt, resuming his excavation.

The sludge-like soil scattered to reveal a flat, featureless panel. More soil tumbled and covered the area Zack cleared, but he kept scraping until the flow slowed. He worked his way toward an edge and then followed it downward. Futility of his search for a corner revealed itself as he realized that the area he worked to uncover was circular and not square or rectangular.

By the time he finished clearing it, a distinct area, perhaps a hatch, almost two meters wide revealed itself. Apart from the slow wind of the thick atmosphere blowing debris across its face, the panel stayed clear. Zack focused his efforts on the frame around the circular cover.

"Skip? Can you record this?" He hoped the AI in his PDA could save video and/or images through the VR interface.

"Affirmative, Zack. These VR pods use a universal linkage interface. Recording now."

As he worked, Zack noticed a green glow beneath a patch of soil. He brushed away dirt from it. Beneath the steady light, he found a small, striped door. When he tapped on it with the manipulator claw, the cover slid open, revealing an inset handle. Zack did not recognize the continuous, looping characters that composed the inscription above the handle.

"Skip? Can you translate that writing? What is it?"

"It does not conform to any written language used in either the EAC or the Confederation. Searching archives..."

A message flashed in the periphery of Zack's vision. He ignored it. Zack's breath caught in his throat as Skip revealed the results of its search.

"Search complete. The script is Athosian."

~ * * * ~

As Jenny nursed a burned thumb, injured on a fumbled attempt to cook an egg during life skills class, Hiri snuggled with her on the sofa in their dorm. Jenny had the holoviewer tuned to a documentary about the construction and founding of Messier Habitat. She learned the basics, of course, in school there, but not to the level of detail the documentary included.

Hiri, in a desire to learn more about Jenny's origins, requested they watch it when Jenny stumbled upon it. It surprised her Hiri would take such an interest in her background—her last several boyfriends showed no such interest after they learned her upbringing didn't involve hunting or gravball.

A message from Zack pinged across her comm implant. She pulled it up. Text only, it requested her to check on Squishy because he was caught up in a class project and needed to concentrate on it.

"When this is over, want to go to the arboretum with me?"

Hiri looked up at her and yawned. "It's getting late, isn't it?"

Jenny checked the time. It was already too late, in her opinion. "Yes, but I can pass it off as a botany thing. No one will bother us."

A smile crossed Hiri's face and then disappeared. "You're going to check on that thing for your friend, aren't you?"

Jenny scowled. "Yes. He's busy with a class project."

Hiri wrapped her arms around Jenny. "Can't you say no? I have a bad feeling about that thing. He's going to get in trouble."

"Sometimes, I want to, but we're in this... whatever it is, together." She clucked her tongue, glanced at the ceiling, and huffed. "It's complicated, and I'm not supposed to talk about it. But you don't have to go if you don't want to. I won't be upset."

"No, it's okay." Hiri stretched and pecked Jenny on the cheek. "I want to spend the time with you. We can go now if you want."

Jenny picked up the remote and paused the documentary before activating her implants and locking the program to prevent their dorm mates from deleting their progress. With luck, they'd return before anyone decided to attempt mischief.

They took their time strolling hand in hand to the arboretum, talking about their plans after school. Hiri, in the engineering program, debated whether to apply to join the Vilicus team immediately after graduation or join the Defense Force for a few years first.

"I thought about that, too." Uninterested in engineering, Jenny considered herself a fair pilot—cloud gliders served as decent practice before moving to larger craft. "It's hard to decide not knowing when the EAC will become part of the Confederation."

"Yeah. You know, I wonder if it'll even matter. The EAC Defense Force or the Confederation Defense Force? I imagine what we'd end up doing would be pretty much the same." Hiri pressed the button to summon a travel pod.

Jenny found it odd none were waiting for them at the transit station this late at night. "For you, maybe. Botany, though? I think the CDF will have more opportunities for that then the EAC. I'm not sure I want to become a dedicated pilot. Ship-to-surface shuttles, maybe, but not the big interstellar ships."

Hiri grinned. "Maybe you'll get picked to be a planetary defense hotshot fighter jock." Atmospheric fighters still proved useful for defense against landing craft and small cruisers that dared to enter a planet's atmosphere, despite being unsuitable in a fight between big interstellar battleships. These days, though, such skirmishes were rare. Born after the last major conflict between powers, Jenny remembered hearing about the Callisto-Ganymede Conflict, which was settled with EAC Marines. No ship-to-ship combat occurred.

"It wouldn't be a bad assignment, would it?" Jenny tossed her hair over her shoulder. "It would be glamorous and exciting. People across the EAC would throw themselves at me. Maybe some Confederation types, too."

"You could have a guy or girl in every port!" Hiri laughed.

The transit station AI announced the arrival of a travel pod. The two young women boarded, and it whisked them toward Aphrodite Dome. They made their way to the lifts that would take them to the arboretum, but when they arrived at the top level, they found two armed Devoran soldiers blocking their way.

"The arboretum is closed"—a grey-scaled male with dark blue stripes held up a gloved hand—"by order of Marshall Voss."

Jenny noticed the Devorans wore Devoran Defense Force uniforms instead of the usual Cytherean Security uniforms. "I'm in the botany program." She gestured to the arboretum doors. "I have a project to work on. In there. With the plants."

"Sorry. No one goes in. Leave now. We're authorized to remove you by force if you do not comply."

"Authorized by whom? You're not Cytherean Security. Fine." Jenny snarled and spun on her heels before stomping away. She fought to keep her hands from trembling as they waited for the lift. *This is not good. Did they find that Athosian? Would they even tell us?*

Hiri's brow furrowed, and she kept trying to catch Jenny's eye. Jenny scanned the Cytherean News and public announcement channels for any clue as to what the Devorans were up to. She was unsuccessful in finding any information. "Jenny!"

She regarded Hiri but did not answer.

The older girl pulled her into a hug. "This isn't good, is it?"

"No. No, it most definitely is not."

Chapter 22

"Athosian?" Zack didn't have time to contemplate the revelation. The ground shook, throwing his probe backward. He kicked it into reverse and backed away from the panel as dirt and rocks rolled off it.

He watched the side of the hill erupt, showering him with sludge. The goop obscured his vision until he wiped it clean with one of the manipulator arms.

As the hill continued to rise, he realized it wasn't a hill.

It was a ship.

The vessel filled his vision, long and lumpy, like a cucumber with nodules dotting its surface. Still in reverse, he continued speeding away from it. The thick Venusian atmosphere increasingly distorted his vision the farther away from the craft he traveled.

His tracks jumped as he hit a rock. The probe tottered before it crashed on its side. As he tried to right the probe with one of its arms, a boulder the size of a scrubbot slammed into the ground before him.

Zack glanced up and realized he would be hit by building-sized, tumbling masses of stone. He blindly slapped at switches and controls in the VR pod.

Darkness engulfed his vision as the boulder smashed into the probe.

Gears whirring, the VR pod hissed open. He squinted and shielded his eyes against the glare of unexpected light. The VR attendant rushed toward him.

"Holy cow, are you all right?" He helped Zack remove his harness and helped him out of the pod. "What happened?"

"I don't know." Zack clutched the older boy's hand as he staggered out and tried to stand upright. "There was an eruption or something. The probe got smashed by a bunch of rocks."

"Wicked! I saw your feed get cut. I thought it was the storm at first, but it's slowed down and won't arrive here for another ten minutes or so."

Zack felt a bead of cold sweat roll down his back. "You aren't going to tell anyone about the probe are you? I kind of broke one last year, too."

"I have to report it, but it looked like an accident to me. It's not like they let you guys use the really good probes they conduct scientific experiments with." Alarms blared. The VR attendant's eyes widened. "I have no idea what those—"

"Attention, Cytherea residents. Please move to your designated emergency response stations immediately. Cytherean Security will direct you to the safest route. Cytherea is experiencing an emergency situation. Repeat: please move to your designated emergency response stations immediately."

The older boy swore and sped out of the VR lounge. Zack followed him, trying to remember the directions pertaining to emergency-response stations he learned in orientation last year. He assumed he should head to his dorm. One of the security guards confirmed his assumption, barking orders at him as he passed Zack.

A chattering mass of students waited at the lifts, so he pulled out his C7 while he waited and saw a text-only message from Jenny. "Zack, I couldn't get into the arboretum. Devoran soldiers had it locked down. Soldiers, not Cytherean Security."

"Squishy! Oh, that's not good." He glanced around himself when he realized he'd spoken aloud. All the students near him seemed preoccupied with their own worries and ignored him.

The announcement repeated. Several of the students shouted toward the PA system, ineffectively imploring it to "shut up."

Arriving at his dorm nearly thirty minutes after he left the VR pod lounge, he found everyone crowded around the sofa watching Cytherean News on the holoviewer. He stood next to Ix. The Valtraxian perched on the side of the couch and stroked Zack's arm.

The reporter listened to information conveyed over her implants, nodding and grunting as a screen behind her flashed the message, *Stand by.*

"All right. We've been authorized to release some information now. It appears a ship of unknown origin is rising through the atmosphere approximately twenty kilometers to the southeast of the city."

"Rising?" Ben gestured at the screen. "She's cracked. No one can fly through that toxic soup down there."

"I repeat. The ship is rising through the atmosphere. We don't have a lot of information at this time, but it appears the ship was resting on the surface. We do not know at this time how it evaded our detection..."

"That's impossible!" Alastair laughed. "Someone's having a go at us. Nothing lands on the planet. Those stupid probes we got down there don't even last a year. They weren't hidden on the surface."

Zack's heart raced. He flicked his eyes at Ix and caught the Valtraxian staring at him.

"Are you all right, Zack?" Ix cocked its head, its voice soft enough only Zack heard the question.

"It's an Athosian ship," Zack replied louder than he intended. The room fell silent, and everyone turned their heads to stare at him.

"Zacka-Zacka has lost his cracka-cracka." Polly made a circle motion near her head with one of her fingers.

"A-a what?" Ben shook his head and laughed.

Ix tapped its fingers together. "I do not suppose they have shown an exterior view of the ship?"

"No"—Barbara gestured at the screen—"just this talking head. It's still too deep in the clouds to show up on the external cameras."

The scene in the news report switched to an image of Cytherea's arboretum. "There is still no sign of the creature reported in the arboretum. Cytherean Security is working with Devoran Defense Force troops searching for what was reported to be an Athosian. Athosians were a species believed to have been wiped out by the Devorans; no sightings have been reported in centuries. A spokesperson for Cytherean Security suggests the Devorans are being overly cautious and plans to file an official protest with the Devoran ambassador for what she calls 'a gross breach of our sovereignty.'"

Zack's stomach churned, and he fought to keep a wave of nausea from overwhelming him. Over the din of multiple conversations in the common area, he heard his C7 ping several times in rapid succession as messages arrived. He checked—they were from Dravs, Bob, and Jenny.

"Zack Jackson looks unwell. Perhaps you should sit?" Kaneer scooted closer to Polly and patted the cushion next to him.

"*Baaye ofiri!*" Mickey slapped his head. "Uh, Zack, do you think that thing is what came out of your rock?"

"Thing? What thing?"

"Your rock?"

The questions assaulted Zack, and he backed away from the staring, suspicious eyes of the room. He held up his hands, as if to deflect their accusations. "I don't know anything about what's going on."

He lied, of course. The ship had been, in fact, buried on the surface of the planet. Of that, Zack was certain. Squishy's appearance almost certainly tied into it in some way, although he didn't understand how. He searched the room for some means of escape, his eyes falling on the door. Zack doubted Cytherean Security would take kindly to him wandering the city, so he turned and fled to his only refuge—his room.

After a few moments of peace, Ix entered. "I have requested they all calm down and give you a moment. It is obvious you know something, and they all think you're to blame."

Zack pointed at the broken halves of the iron star on his desk. "If Squishy came out of that thing, I have no idea how he got out. I saw that ship on the surface when I was in the VR probes, but I didn't make it launch!" *At least, I don't think I did.*

Extending four of its arms, Ix approached Zack. "I do not believe you are to blame for anything, Zack." It stroked his arm. "Remember, I was here when we returned to find the sphere broken open."

"Sorry, I know." Zack gestured toward the door. "Is anyone going to tell them that?" He shook his head. "I gotta find Squishy, Ix. I can't let those Devorans kill him."

~ * * * ~

"Have you ever seen anything like it?" Astrid stared agog at the holoviewer. The new report showed a view from one of the city's exterior cameras as the large, pickle-shaped ship pulled alongside. Clusters of glowing engine ports dominated the rear half of its bulbous form. Thrusters along the length of the

147

craft fired in sequence while the ship maneuvered to maintain a position relative to the city as it floated in the thick, acidic clouds.

"It looks like an Athosian ship." Verrak shook a clawed finger at the screen. "They should blow it out of the sky."

Wes Taylor scoffed at his Devoran roommate, "You're nuts. That close to the city? It'd wreck half of Cytherea to fire on it while it's that close."

Gabrielle curled her lip. "Athosian, my butt. How would you know, Verrak?"

"Because I know my own history, Gabby."

Ignoring their continued speculation, Jenny excused herself to the relative privacy of the bathroom. She locked the door before activating her comm system. She composed and sent a message to Zack. "Are you seeing this? I think they found your Athosian. Verrak, the Devoran in my dorm, says the ship is Athosian, too. I think you should lie low. Say nothing to anyone about any of this until all these Devorans go away."

She waited for the notification that her message transmitted, then returned to the common area, reclaiming her seat next to Hiri. The young woman slid her hand into Jenny's, resting her head on her shoulder as they watched the newscast. The picture of the ship faded to white noise before the broadcast returned to the newsroom. The reporter furrowed his brow, glancing downward as he held one hand to his ear. Then he looked into the camera.

"It seems we've lost the external feed. There's no report of malfunction. We just aren't getting a picture. We'll try to restore contact with the cameras, but for now, the ship appears to be keeping station two hundred meters east of the city. Wait—"

He held his hand to his ear again. "We're going live now to Cytherean Command for a press conference with the Devoran Defense Force commander, Marshall Voss."

The picture switched to a podium set before the EAC flag— royal blue background adorned with large gold stars. A grey-scaled, blue-striped Devoran wearing a Devoran Defense Force uniform stared into the camera from behind the podium.

"Citizens of Cytherea, we ask that you all remain calm and in your homes or places of business. This is clearly a hostile vessel, and we have summoned ships from the Fifth Fleet to the Sol System to deal with it. As this is an Athosian vessel, the Devoran Defense Force alone is equipped to deal with it in a safe and efficient manner."

"Who do they think they are?" Cait made a rude gesture at the screen. "This is the EAC, not the Confederation!"

"We're saving your butts, so shut it, Cait." Verrak glared at the redhead.

"*Trasna ort féin,* Verrak!" Cait balled her hands into fists.

Verrak stood, his hands also forming fists. "Mind repeating that? Maybe in a real language?

She smirked. "*Go n-ithe an tochas thú.*"

Gabrielle jumped between them as Verrak lunged. She shoved him backward. "Enough! I'm sure the Cytherean government has this all figured out."

Jenny nodded at the screen. "It doesn't look like it."

Major Jericho, seated at the news desk, faced the reporter covering the situation.

"I don't know what authority Marshall Voss thinks he has, but I can assure you the EAC will not allow any Devoran military vessels to engage this ship, a ship of unknown origin, I remind you, and in EAC space, let alone in such proximity to an EAC city."

The reporter shifted in his seat and cleared his throat. "Surely the Devoran authorities here—"

"The Devorans have no authority here." Major Jericho slammed his hand on the table, causing the reporter to recoil. "The Sol System is part of the EAC. Cytherea is an EAC city and an EAC facility. We are attempting to contact the ship as we speak."

"Do you think the presence of Valianna Hallox has emboldened Marshall Voss to assume he has authority here?"

Major Jericho pinched the bridge of his nose and sighed. "I have no idea what's going through Voss's head right now. Vali... Madam Hallox's presence here in no way grants the DDF any authority whatsoever. She, like the other Confederation citizens from Al-Gehara, are simply passing through as they relocate to new homes on Vilicus. Her presence here grants the Confederation no special authority, nor should it. She possesses no titles and no official function within either the Confederation or Devoran governments."

The reporter leaned toward the major. "Isn't it possible she's using EAC hospitality to shore up support in an attempt to depose the stratocracy and restore the rule of Devoran government to the Hallox family?"

Verrak leapt to his feet. "*Vasharl poos 'ta kont!* That blue-scaled *n'wah* will never take the throne."

"Sit your butt down, Verrak." Austin Sawyer, one of his roommates, pulled on his arm, dragging the Devoran to his seat. "You're blocking the view."

Jenny stood, but Hiri didn't release her hand. "I'm going to bed. Keep it down out here."

Hiri tugged on her hand. "It's early yet."

She leaned down and kissed Hiri on the cheek. "I just don't want to listen to him anymore."

"Me neither." Hiri rolled off the sofa and accompanied Jenny.

Daniel chuckled as the girls left. "Hey, the two of you keep it down while we're watching the news, right?"

Cait smacked him on the knee. "*Cúl Tóna.*"

Shutting the door behind them muffled the loudest of the obnoxious comments from the common area. Jenny sat in her chair, propping her feet up on her bed.

Hiri crawled onto Jenny's bed, lifted her legs, and rested them across her own. "So, what are you thinking?"

Jenny leaned back in her chair. "This is such a mess. I messaged Zack, but I haven't heard from him yet."

"What's Verrak's problem with Princess Valianna? She seemed nice to me."

"He's obviously loyal to the stratocracy." Jenny hoped the political squabbles of Devorus would not follow Valianna to Cytherea, but she observed not all Devorans felt about her as Dravs did. "We'd better keep him away from Dravs. I hear he still hasn't washed the part of his face where she touched him."

Hiri giggled. "He was so smitten with her. It was cute."

"If that is really an Athosian ship out there..." Jenny shook her head.

"It can't be. The Devorans wiped them all out, right?" Hiri rested her hands on top of Jenny's shins. "Thousands of years ago, right, before we were even in space?"

"If it is, it might explain why they're so eager to blow it up. They wouldn't want anyone to think they failed."

150

A message from Zack appeared in the corner of her vision. "Everyone thinks this is my fault. I think I launched the ship. At least, I think I woke it up. I'm going to be in so much trouble."

"Jenny? What is it?" Hiri patted her knee.

Jenny blinked and realized she'd spaced out with her mouth agape. She swallowed and shook her head. "I just heard from Zack. This is going to get so much worse before it gets better."

Chapter 23

What am I going to do? Over the next several days, that question became a mantra for Zack. Cytherea was all but shut down because of the Athosian ship keeping station just outside the city. Classes and all extracurricular activities were cancelled. The students could leave their dorms only to go to and from the cafeterias for meals.

Zack noted unsurprisingly that Polly dominated control of the holoviewer, keeping it glued to Cytherean News, so she, Ian, and Jamie could monitor the situation. After a day, news stations reduced their coverage to hourly updates that amounted to little more than idle speculation.

Victoria, Ben, and Alastair kept to a small table on one side of the common area, playing games, while Mickey practiced his guitar, alternating between the common area and the bedroom. Kaneer, seated on the floor with Susan, Barbara, and Ix, taught them a Kerrolian strategy game involving far too many chits and bits for Zack's taste.

Zack kept to himself, mostly. Except for Ix and Kaneer, no one spoke to him unless necessary. He worked alone at his desk, trying to figure out a solution, a way to determine if Squishy was still alive.

Relief came on the third day with an announcement from Headmaster Troughton. At Ix's behest, Zack left his desk to listen. His message pre-empted the news broadcast in the dorms, causing no small amount of protest from Polly, Ian, and Jamie.

"A compromise has been reached in the interest of security." The headmaster adjusted his antique, wire-rimmed glasses. "Classes will resume tomorrow. If there has been no change in the status of the alien vessel by the end of the week, then extracurricular activities will resume as well, and the rest of the city will be reopened."

Ben tossed a crumpled napkin at the screen. "I'm sick of cafeteria food. Open it all now, you knob!"

Headmaster Troughton droned on, "The Devoran Defense Force commander has agreed to not interfere with legitimate school-related activities. At last, we will have a return to normalcy."

"Your hair is losing its battle! Give it up already." Jamie laughed. Headmaster Troughton's comb-over had grown more obvious than when Zack saw him during Barry's tribunal at the end of last term.

The holoviewer switched to the news. A different reporter sat at the desk that morning, interviewing Major Jericho, who had been a persistent guest during the emergency. "And there we have it from the headmaster, a return to normalcy for the school, at least." She turned to face Major Jericho. "What of normalcy for the rest of Cytherea?"

"As he alluded, we and Cytherean Security are working with the DDF commander to allow citizens to resume their daily routines. Currently, there appears to be no threat from the Athosian ship. The Devorans disagree, of course, but frankly, they do not have the final say in this matter."

"What of reports that the Devoran fleet is making its way here?"

Major Jericho shifted in his seat and clenched his jaw. "They completed their Translation this morning and are en route. We expect them to arrive by tomorrow morning."

"Kaneer's family left Al-Gehara to escape those Devoran thugs." Kaneer snarled at the holoviewer. "This one hopes they fly into the sun."

"I must emphasize"—Major Jericho tapped his finger on the table—"these ships are Devoran Defense Force, not Confederation."

"What's the difference?"

"The Confederation has largely remained silent on this matter. Our ambassador suggests the Confederation wants to see us work with the Devorans to resolve the situation peacefully. They don't feel their intervention is needed at this time." Major Jericho took a breath. "That being said, the EAC Third Fleet parked in orbit over Venus this morning. Our diplomats are attempting to negotiate a solution, but in the meantime, we've been instructed to permit DDF troops access control of all transports and elevators. I've been assured the Devorans will not be allowed to trample our sovereignty with impunity."

"Do you"—Barbara covered her mouth with her hands— "you don't think they're going to have a battle above our heads, do you?"

"Pfft! Nah!" Polly waved her hand in the air. "Just a bunch of macho ship jockeys comparing their equipment. They won't do anything. It's all for show."

Zack didn't want to bet on that. The news shifted to a pair of analysts who filled the time speculating about every visible feature of the ship, drawing conclusions unsupported by what scant evidence existed thus far.

He crouched down by Kaneer and Ix. "It's dinnertime. Coming?"

"We're trying to play a game, Zack." Susan glared at him.

"This one is hungry." Kaneer stood and stretched. "We will continue after dinner."

"I understand the basics." Ix examined the chit lying in front of it. "If you wish, Susan and Barbara, we can continue while Zack and Kaneer eat."

Barbara sighed, nodding to Zack and then Ix. "Actually, I'm hungry, too. I'll go with them, I guess." She pulled herself up from the floor, ignoring Susan's death glare.

"Fine, go." Susan gestured toward the door before she rose, knocking over several pieces in her haste. "Don't come crying to me if Zack breaks the cafeteria, too."

Zack recoiled, her ire tearing into him like ferok-tog claws.

Ix drew itself up on its back two legs, towering over Susan while grinding its forearms against each other. "That is not fair. This situation is not Zack's doing."

Kaneer eyed his friends. "This one does not understand why you humans always seek to assign blame for accidents not caused by negligence or malice. It is petty and ugly."

The Kerrolian took Zack's arm. "Come, Zack Jackson, eat with friends. You will feel better."

Kaneer dragged Zack out of the common area amid his protest. Ix followed them. By the time they reached the lift, Zack extracted his arm from the Kerrolian's furry grip.

"You know, I think it might be my fault a little." Zack rubbed his arm where Kaneer had gripped it.

"It does not matter." Kaneer waved at the Devoran guarding the lift. "We're going to the cafeteria. It's time to eat."

The guard nodded and entered the code to unlock the lift. "Enjoy."

Zack chewed his lip until the elevator doors closed. "I have to find out if Squishy is still alive. If he is, I have to get him out of here, maybe onto that ship."

He felt Ix and Kaneer's eyes on him. "What?"

"This is why people blame you for things, Zack Jackson."

~ * * * ~

"Genevieve! We've been trying to contact you for days!" Jenny's mother and father leaned in close to the screen, as if proximity to it might help them see the other side. "What is going on there? Is everything all right?"

"Everything is fine." Jenny pulled back her hair and secured it with a tie. This call from her parents could not have come at a worse time. She weighed how much to tell them. "There was a security blackout, but everything is returning to normal now."

"We heard there is an alien battleship threatening the city." Her father's slow, measured cadence lengthened the sentence, and his brow furrowed after he finished speaking. It appeared to Jenny that emoting required deliberate action on his part. His expressions reminded her of a bad stage actor.

"It's not threatening anything. Don't believe everything the Devorans say." Jenny picked up her bag. "Look, I have to get to class. We don't know more than what you're hearing on the news, but listen to the EAC more than the Devorans. They are not even Confederation troops here—they're DDF."

"Be safe. Be careful." Amélie touched the screen.

"Yes, yes. Good-bye!" Jenny terminated the connection and dashed out to the common area. She barely avoided colliding in the doorway with a crouching Cait straightening her leggings. The redhead spun and grabbed at Jenny to avoid toppling over.

"Whoa there! In a hurry, are we?"

Jenny steadied herself. "Sorry. My parents called, so now I'm running late."

"Yeah, how are they doing? I heard they're getting better."

The two proceeded together down the hall toward the lift. Jenny frowned at the long line forming before the Devoran guard. "Yes, they're much better now. There's still a lot of therapy, but the danger is past. Have you beaten Verrak to a pulp yet?"

She hadn't heard much conflict between the two in the last few days, but Jenny also hadn't tried to pay attention to Verrak's pro-stratocracy rants.

Cait threw back her head and laughed. "I want to so bad. He's such a wanker."

"I thought you were going to put him to the floor the other day."

"Me old man was in the Ganymede-Callisto Conflict." Cait's brogue seemed especially thick today. "Major Jericho up there saved his life more than once. I'm not going to stand for some gung ho Devoran telling me we can't take care of our own."

The line for the lift finally advanced enough for them to board. Another guard, stationed in the lift, operated the control panel. Jenny caught him baring his teeth at Cait as she continued to speak.

"What I don't understand is why the bloody Confederation doesn't do something about it." Cait fluttered her eyes and smiled at the Devoran. "The DDF isn't their police force. They're not EAC police, and even if they were, what goes on here at school isn't any of their business."

Jenny noticed the Devoran's muscles tense, but he maintained discipline and kept his attention on the elevator controls.

"I'm sure the authorities will get it all sorted." Jenny breathed a sigh of relief when the lift opened and the Devoran remained silent as he allowed them to pass.

"Oh sure, but before or after someone gets hurt, do you think?"

Oh, you better not do anything stupid, Zack.

"Anyway, I'll see you later." Cait pointed to a nearby lecture hall. "Got to get lectured on the economic collapse of thirty-five forty. Exciting stuff!"

Cait laughed as Jenny's widening eyes betrayed suspicion of her friend's sincerity. "Yeah, I'd rather be a statue with nothing to think about. See you, Jenny!"

They parted ways. Students repeatedly interrupted Professor Wade-Smyth's lecture with questions about the current situation and irrelevant tangents rather than exploring the reading assignment, rendering Jenny's Literature and Composition class a complete waste of time. Disorder plagued most of her classes, but by the end of the next day, most of the students worked their angst and curiosity out of their systems and classes returned to the regular task of teaching.

As they'd been barred from activities except eating in the cafeterias and going to and from classes throughout the next two days, palpable relief circulated the student body when security lifted restrictions and life returned to normal—normal except for the massive Athosian ship hovering just a few hundred meters from the city.

Coach Dagon delivered bad news for Jenny's wing of cloud gliders. He stopped them in the locker room before they changed into their environmental suits. "No flying."

The entire group groaned. Joseph, a sixth-year student, raised his hand. "Are they kidding? How are we supposed to maintain our flight certifications if we're all grounded?"

"Even Cytherean Security agrees flying is too dangerous with that thing out there." Coach Dagon waved his hand toward the hangar bay doors. "Ancestors know I'm going to be the last to agree with anything the DDF decrees while they're here, but in this case, I think being cautious is prudent."

"Should we just use the simulators, then?" Jenny regarded Roger, who shrugged in reply. Simulator time wouldn't count toward their certifications, but it would at least keep their skills sharp.

"I'll authorize extra simulator time for anyone who wants it while you're grounded." Coach Dagon tapped the screen of his tablet. "You may as well go do... whatever. No point in having glider class if you can't fly out there, right? You don't need me babysitting you to fly the simulators."

Jenny retrieved her bag from her locker. Roger leaned against an adjacent locker and cleared his throat. "So, what are you going to do now?"

"Go to the library and study, I suppose. My girlfriend is still in class." She checked the time. Hiri's class didn't let out for another thirty-five minutes.

"Well, do you want to grab dinner tonight, maybe?"

She shut her locker door and raised her eyebrow. "I'll be eating with my *girlfriend*."

"Oh... OH! *Girlfriend*-girlfriend. I thought you meant a friend who was a girl." Roger chuckled and smacked himself. "Idiot!"

"It's all right. Don't worry about it." In truth, Jenny found Roger's attention flattering, despite it coming from one of the bullies who gave Zack such a hard time the past term. Since returning to school, she'd noticed a change in his disposition. She hoped it would last and that his previous attitude resulted from Barry's influence.

"See you later, Roger. Have a good afternoon." Jenny left the hangar and headed for the library.

En route, she checked her notifications to see a waiting message from Zack. "I have a plan. Can you meet me and Dravs at the Neutron Café tonight?"

Jenny knew Zack wouldn't give up on Squishy. She felt any idea he might have for finding and rescuing the Athosian from the heavily guarded arboretum would be futile at best, reckless at worst. Still, curiosity dictated she learn his plan. She sent him a reply. "Sure, but I'm bringing Hiri."

Chapter 24

"I can't believe I let you drag me into this." Dravs winced as he unslung his arm. He rested his head on his hand as he poked at the cheese on top of his pizza with a claw. "Why don't you get Bob to help you?"

Zack frowned as a portly man in a business suit blocked his view of Ishtar Plaza. If he couldn't see Jenny and her friend, they certainly couldn't see him. "You move faster than he does and know how to unlock doors to the utility corridors."

"There's literally no good reason for me to be doing this. Besides, my shoulder still aches." A string of gooey cheese stretched from the top of the pizza to Dravs's mouth. It thinned as he pulled, but it refused to break.

"We can't let them kill a baby." Zack removed a breadstick from the basket. He used it like a hook and dragged the bowl of garlic butter toward him.

"Maybe it's not a baby, huh? It could be fully grown already, and we just think they're supposed to be these huge, gross things."

"Well, maybe." Zack had seen only live juvenile Athosians. The Athosian with whom he spoke on Valtra, a holographic projection of an artificial intelligence, may have displayed an exaggerated size designed to intimidate. For all Zack could tell, the most feared species in the galaxy stood no taller than his dog.

"You should get Ix to help you."

"I tried." Zack didn't want to admit to Dravs he went to Ix first, but the Valtraxian could not take time out of its busy schedule. The lockdown put Ix several days behind on its accelerated coursework.

Dravs grunted and dropped the slice of pizza he'd been eating onto his plate. He gestured with his head toward the entrance of the Neutron Café. "They're here."

Jenny and Hiri arrived hand in hand. Zack noticed they had arranged their hair in identical three-strand braids. When they arrived at the table, the two young women sat next to each other.

"Don't you think it's dangerous to talk about this here?" Jenny waved off the server who arrived to take their order.

159

"No one will expect us to talk about it in public." Zack believed the dorms were being watched, but he doubted officials monitored all the public spaces. That seemed like too much work. "We're hiding in plain sight."

Jenny's eyebrow raised. "Is that so?"

Hiri eyed Dravs. "How's your face? Still tingling from the princess's touch?"

"No." Dravs scowled and tore into the breadstick he held like a predator rending its prey. "Coach Dagon made me wash my face."

"Is your shoulder getting better?" Hiri flicked the dangling sling.

"Good enough I can use my arm again for a little bit. Nurse Carentan still doesn't want me exerting it, but eating isn't exerting."

"Why are you going along with this?" Jenny helped herself to a breadstick and offered one to Hiri. She pointed it at Dravs as she spoke.

"Zack reminded me I always complain when I'm left out of the excitement." He washed down his breadstick with a long drink of water.

"Well, you do!" Zack refrained from reminding Dravs he had been all too eager to help and only started having misgivings while they waited on Jenny's arrival.

Jenny bit into her breadstick, savoring the buttery, garlicky flavor. "I already know what I'm going to say, but let us hear it anyway."

Zack's eyes darted at each of his friends in turn before finally settling on Jenny. He took a breath before he started, taking care to keep his voice low. "I've mapped out the utility corridors in Aphrodite Dome. Dravs can get me into them and let me into the arboretum. Just to be safe, I'm not going back out that way, though. I'll need you to distract the guards at the main entrance."

Jenny's eyes narrowed, and she placed her hands on the table. "How?"

"I don't know. Pretend you're hurt or upset or something."

Dravs spoke around the food he chewed. "Those grunts won't know what to do with a crying human girl. They'll freak out and leave their posts to get rid of you."

Jenny sat back and crossed her arms over her chest. "And you think since I'm a girl, I should do this?"

"What? No!" Zack held up his hands. "I don't care how you distract them."

"It is terrible"—Hiri shook her head—"this idea."

Zack felt his face grow warm. "We can't let them kill him."

"Did you stop watching the news?" Keeping her arms crossed, Jenny glared at him.

"I've been busy..." Zack rubbed the back of his neck. Watching a bunch of talking heads discuss the same three or four points about the situation and jumping to a succession of unsupported conclusions, felt like torture to Zack.

"Even though the guards are still here, they've been ordered not to interfere with legitimate school activities." Jenny leaned forward, resting her arms on the table. "I have course work in the arboretum."

Zack's eyes widened. "That's great! You can get in legit. Once there, put him in your pack and sneak him out to me."

"That's not—"

Hiri put her hand on Jenny's arm. "You can at least look for it. It might not even be there anymore."

Jenny turned her glare on her girlfriend, its meaning plain, even to Zack—*stop helping me.*

Zack rose from his seat. He moved around the table before wrapping her in a hug. "You're the best, Jenny!"

~   *   *   *   ~

Jenny swore to herself as Zack squeezed her. She had not intended to volunteer to become even more involved in his plans with the Athosian. Dravs slouched in his chair, grinning while he consumed pizza and watched them.

Sure, this is all good for you. After turning her baleful gaze on the Devoran and glowering, Jenny snatched a slice of pizza from the platter. She normally didn't enjoy sausage and onions, but she decided the grease couldn't possibly worsen her evening.

Later, while en route to their dorm, Hiri pulled Jenny aside onto a bench. "Hey, I'm sorry if I upset you. I was just trying to think of a way that wouldn't get anyone into trouble."

161

"I know." Jenny stared at her shoes. "I'm not really mad. I just... I should've told him no."

"Sometimes, it's hard to refuse friends." Hiri slipped her hand into Jenny's.

"It's true." Jenny checked the time. It was getting late, but there was still time to go to the arboretum. "I'm going to get this over with. You should go back to the dorm."

"Why? I can help you."

Jenny held both of Hiri's hands as she looked her in the eye. "I don't want you to get into trouble. There's no point in both of us getting suspended if things go badly."

It took a moment for Jenny's own words to sink in. *I could get suspended for this. Or worse. What am I thinking?* Hiri squeezed her hand and peered at Jenny's face, searching for answers.

After kissing Hiri, Jenny stood. "I'll be back soon." *I hope.*

Without waiting for a reply, she jogged toward the lift and headed for the transit station. Devoran soldiers rode the travel pods, but anywhere she saw Devoran soldiers, Jenny noticed EAC soldiers. The two groups never sat together and never spoke from what she observed. They just silently watched each other.

A pair of young men in the travel pod tried to engage the EAC troops in conversation eliciting only one-word answers, but the soldiers refused to divert their attention from the Devorans' every move. The Devorans, however, seemed to ignore watchful eyes and chatted among themselves in their own language about, from what Jenny understood, gravball scores, what they planned to do when they returned home to their families, opinions about the newest holofilms, but nothing sinister or secretive.

Devoran troops packed in Aphrodite Dome eyed Jenny as she made her way from the transit station to the arboretum. A pair of soldiers, a male and a female, stood guard at the arboretum doors. They held up their hands, indicating Jenny should stop.

"This area is off limits." The female stepped forward.

Jenny pointed to the doors. "I have work to do in there. I'm in Professor Hartnell's exobotany class."

"Don't care." She shook her head. Her hand dropped to the holstered weapon she wore on her hip. "Marshall Voss has ordered this area off limits."

"We were told whatever you're doing here would not interfere with school business." Jenny stepped forward, moving within the Devoran soldier's reach. "My work in there is school business. I can't finish my classwork without going in there."

The Devoran looked over her shoulder at her counterpart. "Maybe with an escort? Voss didn't say anything about students having class in there."

The male snarled and put his arm across Jenny's chest, pushing her backward. "She's lying. No one gets in."

Jenny pushed against his arm. "*Parlta!*" The male bared his teeth and hissed at the Devoran insult. "Lying? How do you think I'm supposed to work on exobiology projects without looking at plants? Are you stupid?"

The female pushed down his arm. "She has a point, Salant. I'll take her in and stay with her." She leaned closer and lowered her voice, switching to Devoran. "They're all done in there anyway. Voss is just being slow releasing us. You know that."

Jenny narrowed her eyes and glanced at each soldier in turn. She understood the words uttered by the female Devoran perfectly, but she hoped they would assume she only knew certain key insults in their language. It was not unusual for people, students especially, to know how to swear and insult people in many more languages then they spoke fluently.

"Fine, Lynai." Salant stepped away and unlocked the door. "But she's your responsibility."

"Fine." Lynai held Jenny's arm and hustled her through the doorway. Once through, Salant shut the door behind them.

"Now, be quick about it."

The dirt paths of the arboretum remained intact, unlike their trampled borders and edges. Scattered dirt from nearby flower boxes marred meticulously maintained lawns. Jenny proceeded up the path running parallel to the stream. Behind her, as the Devoran scuffed her feet on the ground, Jenny felt bits of dirt and pebbles hit the backs of her legs.

A patch of ground lay torn up, churned and muddy like a large group had struggled there or marched in place for an extended time.

"What did you do to this place?" Jenny gestured toward a charred shrub surrounded by a patch of blackened, wilted grass.

"That's not your concern." Lynai stifled a yawn. "Get busy. I'm supposed to be off duty in less than thirty minutes."

Jenny purposefully rolled her eyes before leaving the path and crossing the grass toward the stream. She heard the moving water before she saw it. A felled tree lay across the stream just down from the crossing where she and Zack last saw the Athosian. She waded into the crossing and crouched.

"This doesn't look like exobiology work."

Jenny jerked her head around to glare at the Devoran. "I was growing some Iridian water lilies here, if you must know. It was part of my midterm project. I don't suppose you've seen them?"

Lynai held up her hands and backpedaled. "All right, all right. I've never even seen an Iridian water lily."

Jenny's eyes scanned the water as she dipped her hand and made a show of checking rocks near the crossing. Something slimy wrapped itself around her hand, and she jumped before she realized she moved.

Glancing up at the soldier, she saw Lynai eyeing the area behind them, seemingly unaware of her movement. Jenny splashed the water and positioned herself so that her body blocked the view of her hand before she attempted to withdraw it.

You friend. They try kill.

The voice in her head felt like a loudspeaker in her mind, exerting pressure like someone squeezing her head in both directions at once. Jenny gasped and fell backward. The tentacle released her hand.

"What was that? What's going on?" The Devoran hooked a hand under Jenny's arm.

Jenny threw the soldier's hand off her. "Great! Just fantastic!" She uttered a string of French obscenities. "My whole project gone! Ruined. Thanks to you and your big secrets."

She scrambled to her feet, making sure to splash as much water and dirt onto the Devoran as possible as she stomped away. She heard Lynai follow but ignored the Devoran's commands to slow down.

When she reached the doors, she banged her fists on them. "Open up! Open up!"

"Just calm down, Human." Lynai caught Jenny's arm and spun her. Jenny reached up and slapped the soldier across the end of her snout.

"Don't you touch me!" She spat the words at the Devoran. A small part of her felt guilty; this soldier probably had no idea why she guarded an arboretum. Lynai snarled and opened the door before shoving Jenny over the threshold.

Jenny continued ranting as she stumbled to maintain her footing. "All my work so far this term is wasted. Gone! What am I supposed to do now? I was lucky to get them in as early as I did, now there's not enough time to grow new ones!"

She spun on the Devorans guarding the door. "You can bet Major Jericho will hear about this. You weren't supposed to interfere in schoolwork. You certainly weren't supposed to destroy it!"

Jenny turned and strode away, ignoring them as they shouted for her to stop, and she darted into the travel pod as the door closed. She fell into one of the chairs as it lurched into motion.

As the pod whisked her toward Anahita Dome, she concentrated on breathing slowly and steadily to calm herself, then she laughed. *With a performance like that, maybe I should start taking drama classes.* Shaking, her laughter turned to tears. Jenny forced herself to regain composure until the travel pod stopped. Tears streamed down her face as she sped on foot to her dorm. She glanced around the common area just long enough to confirm Hiri's absence.

The full enormity of the danger she risked by slapping an armed soldier hit Jenny like a gravball to the gut. She flew past her roommates. Locking herself in the bathroom until her tears abated, she waited until she heard her remaining dorm mates go to bed.

A single thought reverberated in her head: *Stupid. Stupid. Stupid. Stupid.*

Chapter 25

Zack shut the door of the quiet room behind him. He found Jenny pacing and wringing her hands. He wasn't keen on meeting before classes like this, but at least she met him in Hathor Dome.

He sat down and wasted no time coming to the point. "So, you're going to check on Squishy today, right?"

Jenny shook her head. "I went last night. I found it, and it *talked* to me."

"He can talk?" Zack tilted back in his chair until the front legs left the floor. He clutched at the table to keep from flipping over.

"It was telepathic, like when Bob touches you. *He* touched me when I had my hand in the water." Jenny flexed her fingers before crossing her arms and leaning forward. "I don't think my Devoran escort noticed. You don't think he... indoctrinated me or anything?"

"Well, what did he say?" Hardly an expert, Zack learned all he knew about Athosian indoctrination from the Devoran who tried to kill him on Bestic. He was under the impression it required the Athosian to attach itself to one's head.

"He said I was a friend and told me the Devorans tried to kill him."

"That's all?"

Jenny nodded and frowned. "It was like he squeezed my mind when he spoke. It didn't bother me at first, but I have an awful headache today, Zack."

"Oh." He never got a headache when Bob spoke to him telepathically. He hoped Squishy didn't hurt Jenny, but he suspected individuals reacted differently to mental stimuli. "Maybe you should talk to the nurse."

"The Devorans said they were waiting to get the order to leave. It might be safe to go see him tonight. Tomorrow would probably be better."

"We have to get him out of there, Jenny." Zack chewed his lip. *But where? Where are we going to put him? Does that big Athosian ship have anything to do with this?*

Jenny shook her head and slid away from the table. "I'm done. I'm sorry, Zack, it was too dangerous. Those Devorans had guns."

"Okay. Okay." Zack fought to maintain a neutral expression. He hoped Jenny would agree to help him, maybe use her cloud glider to transport Squishy to the Athosian ship. He tapped his foot as he tried to think of another way to get Squishy to the vessel. He assumed someone piloted the ship and that it wasn't just a drone. He couldn't think of a logical reason someone would have programmed an ancient ship to fly up to and park outside a city that didn't exist when it was buried.

"Thanks, Jenny. I'll think of something." He patted her shoulder as he left the quiet room. He didn't have time to sit and eat breakfast before classes, so he settled for a sticky bun and a glass of juice. He chuckled to himself as he imagined his mother berating him for his choices, but more nutritious offerings proved difficult to eat while walking to class.

He finished his breakfast while waiting for the lift. Devoran guards still gummed up the works, and most of the students were no longer discreet with their complaints.

"Moira told me Kelly told her about a friend whose brother saw a *thing* in the arboretum, and that's why these Devorans are all up in our business."

Zack didn't recognize the voice of the student talking behind him, but her accent sounded like one from Texas. Her friend grunted in response.

"She said it was all gross and covered with tentacles, like an octopus."

"Do these Devorans like calamari or something?" The boy's thick accent sounded Eastern European, by Zack's estimation.

"Idiot. Calamari is squid. Octopus is octopus. Anyway, they weren't eating it; they were shooting at it."

Shooting? At Squishy? At least they missed.

"Crazy. There's nothing in the arboretum but trees and flowers."

The girl behind Zack tapped his shoulder and pointed ahead. He'd been so busy eavesdropping he hadn't noticed the line had moved forward.

"Whatever it was, I think they got it. I heard they're reopening the arboretum tonight."

"Do you think *they'll* go home now?" The boy's statement conveyed his obvious contempt for the DDF.

The soldier guarding the lift doors clicked his teeth together. "Don't count on it, kid."

He continued staring at the boy behind Zack until they all boarded the lift. Zack didn't have to speak the other student's language to guess the slur he shouted at the Devoran guard as the doors closed. Fortunately, the intimidating DDF troops limited their activities to the business and operations areas of Cytherea and avoided the school. Zack made it to his first class just in time.

All morning, he schemed to liberate Squishy from the arboretum and transfer him to a place safe from Devoran soldiers, Zack's classes zipped by in a blur. Despite his efforts, by lunchtime, he remained bereft of a plan, unable to develop a realistic scenario since his meeting with Jenny. As he consumed his chicken parmesan, Xal plunked his tray on the table and sat across from him.

"Zack, I have a favor to ask."

"Hmm?" Chewing, he noticed the chicken felt more rubbery than usual. In Zack's experience although the flavor tasted the same, meat from an animal that had wandered a farm often possessed a tougher texture than vat-grown meat. Sometimes, however, processing facilities over-tweaked the settings controlling fat and moisture content, creating rubbery meat.

"In Kova Kasi tonight, try to pair up with me."

Zack almost forgot that class was that night. His plan to sneak into the arboretum and rescue Squishy would have to wait. *Maybe I can go there after Kova Kasi.* "Why?"

"Our first ranking test is tonight, and I can throw you around easier than Dravs. His tail gets in the way."

Zack found sparring with Dravs difficult, too, for the same reason. Although Dravs weighed less than he and much less than Xal, the Devoran learned early on to utilize his tail as a sort of third leg to give him greater balance and even greater leverage when resisting throws or trying to throw an adversary.

"Okay, I'll try. We may not get to pick our opponents."

"I noticed something about Kifu Raneri." Xal leaned forward, glancing from side to side as if he thought someone might eavesdrop on their conversation. "He pairs sparring partners by proximity, and never pairs adjacent students. If we each stand on either side of Dravs, and we stand at either end of the class, he'll pick us to spar against each other."

"Huh. I never noticed that, but now that you mention it..." Zack had a thought. "What if someone is absent tonight? And Dravs may not be able to participate because of his shoulder."

Xal's mouth hung open. "Um, well, let's try to line up on the left. He usually starts picking from the left, right?"

"Sounds good. Have you talked to Dravs about it yet? Is he even going to be there?"

"I didn't want to upset him. He might take it personally if I don't want to spar with him for the test."

"Good point." Dravs hated sparring with anyone except for Zack or Xal. Zack hoped the Devoran had not figured out their kifu's method of selecting sparring partners. "Hey, I can't stick around after practice, though. I have something important to do."

Xal lowered his head and softened his voice. "You be careful with that, Zack. I heard these Devorans almost killed a student the other day."

"Where?" Zack hadn't heard of any incidents between the DDF troops and students, just a lot of mutual insults thrown both ways.

"In the arboretum. I heard they were ready to incinerate everything in there until Headmaster Troughton and Major Jericho stopped them."

It was the third version of what occurred in the arboretum that Zack heard. In the absence of facts, the students of Cytherean Academy seemed to fabricate stories to suit their fancies. Regardless of the truth, Zack needed to get Squishy out of there that night.

~ * * * ~

Jenny and Hiri sat at the most secluded table in Heisenberg's, a restaurant in Ishtar Plaza specializing in food from across the galaxy. A popular refrain repeated by customers "You can never be certain where today's special will be from at Heisenberg's" flashed beneath the sign.

The day's special hailed from Ersid—roasted glommy bird with tubers. One of Hiri's favorites and large enough for two, they ordered the glommy bird to share.

169

What is it with glommy bird and mes amours? Mungus loved it, and apparently so did Hiri. *Maybe being with me makes people crave it.* Jenny didn't dislike the fowl. It reminded her of both duck and pork. The meat itself was tough, but she couldn't tell if it was vat-grown or from a live animal. *Maybe that's part of the mystery.*

"So, I heard about last night." Hiri pushed food around on her plate with her fork.

"Which part?" Jenny braced herself for the recitation of outlandish rumors.

"The part where you ran in sobbing and locked yourself in the bathroom until everyone went to bed." Hiri's big, green eyes stared expectantly. "Your parents? Is everything all right?"

Jenny chuckled and cut into her glommy bird. "It had nothing to do with them. I did something stupid and scared myself. It was dangerous and stupid. I knew better."

"Helping Zack?"

She nodded as she chewed. "I'm fine now. I was scared, angry at myself, and just... it was just a release, that's all. I told him I couldn't help him with that stuff anymore."

"So... what now?"

What now? "Nothing, I guess. He can do his little schemes, I'll see him at Junior Rangers, and the rest of the time I'll concentrate on school."

Jenny relaxed in her chair and released a long, slow breath. "My parents are better, my classes are going well, and I have you. It's all good."

A smile brightened Hiri's face. "Very good, I'd say."

As if on cue, Jenny's comm implant registered an incoming call from her parents. *Again? I asked them to use my terminal a dozen times if I asked them once.*

"What is it? That's not the face of all good."

Jenny scowled and sipped her water. "My parents are calling."

"Go ahead. It's fine." Hiri tapped the table's embedded screen. "I'll look at the dessert menu."

Jenny accepted the call, angling her head toward the wall to conceal her conversation via implants from other diners. "Hello?"

"Jenny." Her father's tone reminded her too much of Bob's. "How are you?"

170

"I'm fine, Papa. I'm having dinner with my girlfriend right now."

"Oh, I'm sorry. I just wanted to talk to you for a bit. I will call back later."

"No, it's fine." Jenny wiped a tear from her eye. Her father never called just to talk to her, not before the accident. "How are you, Papa? Getting better?"

"Yes. I am better." His avatar turned from side to side. Despite the small picture, she observed his skin appeared natural. "I look... human... again. Things are still difficult, though. I remember much more, but I don't... feel. I remember feeling, but don't know how."

Jenny furrowed her brow. "You mean like when you touch things? Are the cybernetics they gave you working properly?"

"I mean emotions. I feel sensation, better than before, but not feelings. I remember loving you and Amélie, but I can't feel it."

Jenny squeezed her eyes shut and brought her hand to her mouth. She felt Hiri touch her arm. "I'm sorry, Papa. I don't know—"

"It is all right. They told me talking about it might help me remember."

Jenny nodded. "You said you were proud of me earlier."

"Yes. I remember feeling that... before. I never told you. I'm sorry. But I should go. I know I'm upsetting you, and I don't want to ruin your evening with your friend. Things will be better, Genevieve. I promise I will be better."

"I love you, Papa."

"I... love. You. Good-bye." He frowned and ended the call. After pulling herself together, Jenny told Hiri what he said.

"Is that normal? I mean, after your operations, did you forget how to feel?"

"No, I didn't." Hiri moved her plates aside and took Jenny's hands. "But that doesn't mean anything. Every patient's response to such extensive surgery is different. Remembering how to feel emotions might be part of his healing."

Jenny wiped her nose on her napkin. "But he will remember, right?"

"I... I don't want to lie." Hiri looked away. "I honestly don't know. Probably?"

171

While Jenny appreciated Hiri's honesty, it didn't make her feel better. She knew what would, though—a chocolate sundae, and Heisenberg's made the best in Cytherea.

Chapter 26

Noting every part that ached, Zack changed out of his gi and into his regular clothes. Xal watched him with sidelong glances.

"Does it hurt much?"

"Only when I move." Zack winced as he pulled on his shirt. Kifu Raneri made Dravs sit out tonight because of his shoulder, however Xal and Zack both passed the ranking test and earned their black-striped yellow sashes., Zack suspected he'd be feeling his bruises more than Xal felt his and almost envied his Devoran friend. He double-checked his pack, securing all the items he needed for later, before he headed with Xal toward the cafeteria. As much as Zack wanted to get started on his search for Squishy, his stomach begged for food.

A sign advertised tonight's cafeteria special, meatloaf, one of Zack's least favorite meals. He used to think the mashed-together lump served as an excuse to utilize leftovers. However, recently, his mother taught him people made meatloaf on purpose and not just to avoid throwing away food.

He selected a barbeque bacon cheeseburger and fruit salad. Xal selected a double helping of meatloaf with a side of roasted potatoes.

"I wish they had more Ersidian food."

"Isn't there a restaurant in Ishtar Plaza that serves Ersidian dishes?" Zack heard other students talking about it, but of the three restaurants in Ishtar Plaza, it was the one he hadn't tried. It seemed too fancy for his taste.

"Heisenberg's." Xal sat across from Zack at one of the long tables. "But you never know what their specials are going to be from day to day."

"Ow." Zack tossed his pack under the table by his feet and grimaced as he sat, recalling the moment when Xal threw him and he landed on his butt, hard. His glutes felt tender as he placed his weight on them.

"I'm really sorry. I really had no idea I'd hurl you out of the arena and into the sidelines like that."

"It's okay." Zack chuckled. "Dravs broke my fall."

Xal poked at his meatloaf. "Do you think he'll be okay? He was howling like crazy."

Zack grimaced. "I think it re-dislocated his arm."

173

"Ouch. Now I really feel bad." Xal pushed away his tray, leaving his food uneaten.

"You're bigger and heavier than most everyone in the class. I'm surprised it didn't happen sooner." Zack pushed Xal's tray toward him.

"Hey, have you heard..."

Lost on Zack, the rest of Xal's sentence faded into the background as Rio approached them. Zack's eyes fixed on her instead of Xal. Unaware of Zack's inattention, the Ersidian chattered on. Rio noticed Zack's gaze and stopped at their table. As her smile grew, she sat next to Xal, her eyes locked with Zack's.

"...anyway, that's what they were telling me. Oh! Hi, umm... I don't think we've met." The Ersidian startled when he noticed someone alongside him.

"This is Rio. Rio, Xal." Zack concluded her eyes were silver, at least in the lighting of the cafeteria. Like navigational beacons set against her dark skin and hair, they called to him.

"Nice to meet you, Xal." She offered him her hand. "You're my first Ersidian friend."

"Oh." Xal wrapped his big, furry paw around her hand and chuckled. "Thanks. Are you a first-year?"

"No, second. I transferred." She turned toward Zack. "What are you doing tonight?"

"I'm... umm..."—he struggled to describe his evening without revealing his plan—"I have an important thing to take care of. It's personal."

"I see." Rio's smile faded as she stared at her own cheeseburger and fruit salad. "I could help you, you know. I don't mind."

Zack froze, his burger suspended halfway between his plate and his mouth.

"It's about that thing, isn't it? That creature that fell out of the ceiling on Ryll Bob?" Rio met his gaze. "Dravs told me how you were looking out for it."

"*Dravs* did?" Zack spoke through clenched teeth. *He blabs too much!* "I don't know... we could get in trouble. I don't want to be responsible for that."

"He says you want to help it." She placed her hand on his. "If that's true, then I want to help you. We're supposed to help each other, right?"

174

Xal cleared his throat. Zack glanced up at the Ersidian who shook his head as he shoveled meatloaf into his mouth. As much as Zack didn't want to involve anyone else, he needed assistance. Dravs was hurt, Jenny was freaked out by her encounter with DDF soldiers, and Xal was too afraid of getting in trouble.

Rio offered to aid him. She seemed smart, and Zack wanted to get to know her better and maybe spend time with her.

He licked his dry lips and nodded. "Okay, let's finish eating, then we'll go to the arboretum. It should be open now."

~ * * * ~

Jenny and Hiri held hands as they walked through the park in Ishtar Plaza. Some signs of the Festival of Starlight remained, such as trampled patches of muddy grass and the odd streamer stuck in a tree or shrub, but by and large, the area seemed more subdued than it had been since the Devorans arrived.

The visitors kept to their tents for the most part, talking among themselves, playing games, or debating with their family and neighbors. Jenny wondered how much of their inhibition was due to DDF and EAC soldiers now patrolling the plaza.

Sitting in the middle of the other pavilions, Valianna's tent stood out as the tallest structure in the park apart from the trees. Now, Devoran soldiers surrounded it, a wall of scaly flesh preventing passersby from lingering. Jenny felt their eyes on Hiri and her as they passed.

"Hey! I know you!" A soldier stepped out of ranks and seized Jenny's arm.

Jenny pulled Hiri behind her as she broke Lynai's hold. "Don't touch me!"

Lynai drew her pistol but kept it at her side. "Stay where you are." Tapping her temple, she activated her communications implant. "I have the student who assaulted me in custody in front of Hallox Pavilion."

Jenny's dinner threatened to escape. Hiri squeezed her arm and pulled her close. Jenny clenched her fists to keep from trembling.

Other DDF soldiers in line put their hands on their weapons, and from the nearby tents, scaly snouts poked out to see the cause of the commotion.

"I checked with the school." Lynai pushed her toothy maw close enough Jenny smelled what the Devoran ate for dinner. "There have never been Iridian water lilies in that arboretum. They won't grow in an oxygen-nitrogen atmosphere."

Merde. I didn't think of that. Jenny clenched her teeth. Caught in the lie, she wanted nothing more than to flee, but facing a dozen armed Devorans stole her nerve.

"Jenny?" Hiri's voice was a choked whisper.

"Quiet!" Lynai reached for restraints attached to her belt.

"What's going on out here?" Valianna pushed her way through the soldiers ringing her tent. Lynai turned and bowed before the Noble Devoran.

"I caught the human who assaulted me last night." She turned and snapped her teeth in Jenny's face. "She was foolish enough to walk around in the open."

"This human?" Valianna gestured toward Jenny. "Assault you? A trained DDF soldier? And she is a large enough threat you need to restrain her and hold her at gunpoint?"

Valianna pushed Lynai out of the way and eyed Jenny. "My, my! These human children are monstrous, aren't they? I don't believe we've faced such a dire threat since the Damos Uprising of Forty Fourteen."

A chuckle circulated the troops while Lynai fumed and curled her lips. Valianna took Jenny's arm and led her through the troops toward her pavilion. "While you're calling for backup, summon Major Jericho and Cytherean Security, as well. This is their jurisdiction, not ours. Come, my dears, let us wait where it is comfortable."

Valianna pulled back the tent flap and gestured inside. Jenny held Hiri's hand as they entered. The princess invited them to sit. "May I get you a beverage while we wait?"

"No, thank you." Though Jenny's mouth was a desert, she was certain anything she took into her system would unlikely remain in her stomach.

Hiri shook her head, pulled her seat close to Jenny's, and continued holding her hand.

"Assault is a serious charge." Valianna poured herself a drink in a tall goblet and sat across from them, crossing her legs as she regarded the pair. "Frankly, I find it difficult to believe you attacked that armed soldier. We can talk about it, or we can wait until Marshall Voss, Major Jericho, and whomever Cytherean Security sends arrives."

"She was dragging me around by the arm, like I was some criminal. I slapped her and told her not to touch me." Jenny squeezed Hiri's hand. "That's all."

"Where did this occur?"

"Jenny, maybe we should wait until human authorities arrive?"

"I was in the arboretum. For school." Jenny considered waiting as Hiri suggested, but Valianna seemed reasonable when they met during the festival, and she seemed more curious than angry or vindictive tonight, not like Lynai.

"I see. How did you get in?"

"That Devoran and her cohort let me in." Jenny pointed to the pavilion tent flap. "You aren't supposed to interfere in legitimate school business."

Valianna sipped her drink. "Ah, we must clear up a misunderstanding immediately." She pointed at herself. "I have nothing to do with Marshall Voss's attempt to usurp control of Cytherean Academy from your administrators. I'm sure he'll have quite harsh words for me for even speaking to you."

She circled the two humans. "The unfortunate truth is there's a large contingent of Devorans both here and at home who feel the stratocracy is not the best choice to lead the Devoran Empire into the future. They wish to see the throne restored to the Hallox family. There are others, of course, who disagree."

"Thus far"—Valianna returned to her seat—"I've been able to cajole, convince, coerce, enthuse, however you like, many of the soldiers assigned to me into treating me as someone with influence. It is a great irritant to Marshall Voss."

Valianna gestured toward the area outside her tent. "These soldiers aren't guarding me, they're officially here now to prevent me from mingling"—she pointed at Jenny and Hiri—"with the likes of you."

Uninterested in Devoran political squabbles, Jenny wanted nothing more than to return to her dorm with Hiri, crawl under the covers, and not emerge until every DDF soldier headed home.

"Why were you really in the arboretum?"

Jenny's stomach leapt into her throat. Cold sweat beaded on her forehead. "I told you, school."

Valianna shook her head. Her seashell earrings clinked together as they swayed. "I read Lynai's report. Iridian water lilies?" She clicked her teeth. "Careless."

"Don't say anything else, Jenny." Hiri tugged at her arm.

"Nonsense. This isn't a court of law, and I'm not a judge. Lynai deserved a slap for treating you like a piece of meat. But I know you're lying, Jenny, isn't it?" Valianna leaned forward. "Yes. I know. I can see." She tapped her temple with her finger. "My implants detect by your physiological responses that you're lying."

Jenny shut her eyes and clenched her teeth. One could accurately assess if a person they knew was lying if one used one's optical implants to scan the person's body heat, respiration, and pulse. It became a more challenging prospect with unfamiliar species.

"I spent a lot of time around humans. It's part of the reason the stratocracy are not my biggest fans. They feel I'm unfairly biased toward your species." She chuckled and relaxed in her chair. "Maybe I am. I find humans fascinating. You're so adaptable and open-minded."

"Maybe you should tell me why Devorans were shooting up the arboretum." Jenny didn't expect Valianna to offer information about that, but she figured it couldn't hurt to ask. Certainly, it wouldn't make her situation any worse. "There's nothing secret in there. It's an extension of the school."

"A Devoran student reported a sighting of an Athosian in your arboretum. He even sent a holovid."

Jenny's jaw fell open. Hiri leaned in. "I'll bet it was Verrak!"

"It was not. A friend of yours?"

"One of our roommates." Jenny shook her head.

"You knew about the Athosian. Interesting."

Jenny glared at Hiri.

"Oh, don't deny it. It's written all over your faces. Where did it come from?"

Shaking her head again, Jenny crossed her arms and slumped in her chair.

"Fine." Valianna raised her goblet to her lips. "We'll wait."

Chapter 27

"What will you do if the arboretum is still closed, Zack?" Rio walked beside him, her hands clasped behind her back. They'd already passed several pairs of Devoran soldiers en route from the transit hub to the lift, but the hallway to the arboretum seemed clear.

"Maybe one of the utility corridors will be unlocked." He pulled out his C7, inserted the earpiece, and opened the map he downloaded earlier. A maze of utility corridors ran underneath the arboretum, and he located one of the entrances nearby. "Up there, in that nook."

Just off the main hallway, the hatch sat in the floor of the nook. Like the one he and Dravs entered behind the cafeteria's recycler, it had a control panel. Impossible to determine at a glance whether the door was locked, the two approached the complex display.

He and Rio rounded the corner to see two DDF soldiers guarding the arboretum doors. Leaning against the walls and facing each other, they conversed in Devoran. When they saw the two students approaching, the one nearer the handle opened the door.

The one holding the door snorted when Zack thanked him as they entered. Rio brushed one of her braids over her shoulder. "I wonder why they're still there if they're just letting everyone in?"

"Beats me." Zack led Rio up the path and onto the lawn toward the stream. They observed gardeners working the flower beds, repairing the path, and digging out charred shrubs. In the distance, he heard the roar of a chainsaw and grinding metallic teeth chewing through felled trees. The air carried the acrid stench of charcoal layered under the scent of freshly cut grass.

"What I want to know is why they gave up their search after going through the trouble of shooting the place up?" Zack crested the hill near the stream's crossing. As they approached it, he pointed at a fallen tree lying across the water just downstream from the crossing.

"I don't see anyone around, do you?" He put his hands on his hips as he scanned the foliage for gardeners and other students.

179

"There's no one near us." Rio caught up to him and hooked her arm into his. "Where should we begin looking?"

"Between that log and the stone crossing, I think." That's where Jenny told Zack she found Squishy the night before.

"What does he look like?"

Zack peered into the stream. "Well, he's kind of hard to see in the water. He's transparent and small."

After searching the water near the crossing for twenty minutes, Zack gave up and moved downstream. Back home, he could have ordered hip waders from the fabricator and searched the middle of the stream. He didn't find them listed in Cytherea's system, however, and he considered he'd likely appear conspicuous parading around the city in waterproof overalls.

"I don't see anything living in this water. What does he eat?" Crouching at the opposite bank of the stream from Zack, Rio probed the meter-deep water with a stick.

"That's a good question." Zack's attempts to learn more about Athosians had been stymied by unknown parties removing and blocking his access to the information whenever he searched. "The Devorans have worked really hard to remove all the information there is about them. All I've been able to find out is that they're supposedly all dead and they were all very bad."

Rio peered across the stream at Zack, tilting her head. "That seems... unusual. No species is born bad."

"I know. I think they're just hoping people will forget they ever existed."

"I found something!" Rio pointed at a spot in the water. She moved her stick closer. It jerked in her hand, and then bowed as if under a weight. As she withdrew it from the water, Squishy clung to the end of the stick like a blob of goo. He reached up the stick with his tentacles and wrapped them around her hand.

Zack ran up the stream to the crossing, leaping from stone to stone until he reached the other side. Rio offered him the branch with Squishy clinging to it.

"He's touching you! Is he talking to you?"

Rio shook her head as she passed Squishy to Zack. The Athosian latched onto Zack's hand before releasing Rio, crawling up the stick and onto his arm.

Zack felt a weighty sensation in his mind. He staggered as his vision faded, and then returned.

Friend. Help.

"We're going to get you out of here, Squishy. I just haven't figured out how, yet."

Ship.

"How did you learn how to talk?" Zack tossed the stick to the ground once the Athosian fully gripped his arm. Rio helped him remain steady as the mental invasion left him a bit unbalanced. She helped Zack make his way to one of the large, nearby boulders on which to sit.

Others are close. Take me. No harm.

Zack squeezed his eyes and shook his head, before focusing on Rio. "He says there are others close."

"Others? Here?" Rio's eyes widened, and she looked around the clearing. "I don't see anything. There are some workers several hundred meters away, but no one closer."

Others in ship. They help. They good.

"We have to get him to the ship." Zack pulled off his pack and opened it. "Hide in here."

Squishy released Zack's arm and crawled into the pack. After closing it, he stood and swung it over his shoulder. "We should go."

"Zack, how are we going to get it to that ship? It's not docked, and they're not going to just let us take a shuttle."

Heavier than Zack expected, the pack with Squishy in it bulged at the bottom, and he hoped it wasn't too obvious something alive occupied it.

Zack's mind raced as he considered his options. "Do you know if all the cloud gliders are still grounded?"

"I think so." Rio pointed ahead. "Someone's coming. I hear them just ahead."

Two Devoran soldiers with slung rifles came over the hill, appearing from behind some shrubs. Zack froze a moment before resuming his pace. He shoved his hands in his pockets and gazed at the trees, trying to appear as though he was just out for a walk. Rio put her arm through his and rested her head on his shoulder as they strolled.

"Hey, you two!" The Devorans unslung their weapons and advanced toward Zack and Rio. "Have you seen a human and Devoran skulking around the stream?"

Who are they looking for? Zack furrowed his brow and shook his head. "No, I didn't see anyone else." He turned to Rio. "Did you?"

"Just some of the gardeners. None of them were Devorans, though."

"You kind of look like the human we're looking for. Zack Jackson. The Devoran is Dravs Sallaron."

Zack chuckled. "Oh, them! Yeah, I know who they are, but I haven't seen them since class this morning." He hoped having Rio on his arm and his other hand jammed in his pocket would prevent the Devorans from seeing how much he shook.

"Really?" The taller Devoran narrowed his eyes. "Hm. Why isn't your ident chip transmitting?"

"I don't have one. I'm from Earth, we're not allowed to get implants until we're sixteen."

The other Devoran stared at his companion. "Rio Canción. You have implants. Not from Earth?"

"I was born on a ship. I've never been to Earth."

The taller Devoran gestured toward Zack with his rifle. "Name?"

"Um..." His first impulse was to give them Steve's name, but if they checked, they'd see he was from Rigel Kent in the Alpha Centauri system. "Jamie McCrimmon." He was pretty sure Jamie was from Earth.

"Wait here while I check that." The Devorans turned their backs to Zack and Rio while they discussed the situation in Devoran.

Rio pointed toward the tree line and mouthed, "Run?"

Zack shook his head. The Devoran spun to face them. "You don't look like your picture on file."

"Yeah..." Zack forced a laugh. "Those are always awful, right?"

"It also says you have a class three medical implant. I don't see it on my scan."

Uh-oh. "Well, you know..." He dropped his jaw and pointed past the soldiers. "Look out, it's the Athosian!"

The Devorans raised their weapons and turned in the direction Zack pointed as he charged for the tree line. Rio released his arm and followed. Shouts from behind him indicated his bluff failed. He ducked under a low-hanging branch, grunting as it snagged on his C7's earpiece, yanking it out of his ear. He ignored its loss and turned toward the crossing, hearing the Devorans behind him.

"We are in pursuit. Requesting permission to engage with force."

Force? Are they going to shoot me? He jumped over a shrub and dared glance backward to locate Rio, where he found her keeping pace with him and, indeed, threatening to overtake him. Cursing followed the snapping of branches behind them. Much larger than the human teens and encumbered with military gear, the Devorans stalled at the dense foliage, unable to continue their pursuit.

Rio reached the crossing ahead of Zack and pointed upstream. He suspected she intended to go to the maintenance hatch near the stream's source. According to the maps he consulted the other day, it lay just up ahead obscured by bushes.

Kneeling at the control panel, she had unlocked the hatch by the time he arrived. It slid open, and she gestured inside. "Quick, get in!"

"How did you—"

Rio pulled Zack by the arm and ushered him through the opening before sliding in after him and stopping only to shut the hatch behind them. Motion-sensitive lights flickered on. The grinding whine of power saws and diggers from the arboretum faded as the hatch sealed.

"Don't stop!" She pushed him forward, and they continued to run.

~　*　*　*　~

Tears streamed down Jenny's face as her stomach clenched like a too-tight knot in her gut. She felt like she might vomit. "That's all I know. He just wants to the creature. He doesn't believe a baby is dangerous."

Major Jericho sat next to Valianna, his hands folded in his lap as he listened to her. The Noble Devoran's brow furrowed, and she glanced up at Marshall Voss. The Devoran commander refused to sit and towered over her, his protruding teeth glistening in the light of the tent. He held his hand up to

183

his temple. "Search the arboretum for a human and Devoran student. Zack Jackson and Dravs Sallaron. They're in collusion with the Athosian. Report in when you've found them."

"That's a little extreme, don't you think?" Major Jericho's lips became a thin line. "Collusion with an infant?"

"You humans are ignorant of the true danger even one Athosian represents. If there are any on that ship, it is no mere infant we're dealing with." Marshall Voss returned his gaze to Jenny and stepped forward, his snout mere centimeters from the top of her head. "Your cooperation ensures your continued attendance at this school. I will make sure the headmaster understands Zack Jackson was the mastermind of this plot."

"That's enough." Major Jericho rose and pushed his way in between Jenny and Voss. "I will remind you this is an EAC facility in EAC sovereign space. You have no jurisdiction here. If your people harm any of the students"—he pushed Voss backward, away from Jenny—"there will be repercussions."

Hiri hugged Jenny from behind. "It'll be okay."

No it won't. Zack will never forgive me. She wanted to remain strong, to say nothing to the Devorans. She hadn't expected they would threaten to have her expelled.

"You don't know Headmaster Troughton and the Cytherean Academic Advisory Board the way I do." Voss's lips pulled away from his teeth in a sneer. "They won't risk their Confederation funding to protect a couple of mediocre students."

"Get out." Major Jericho pointed toward the tent entrance. Voss's eyes flicked toward Valianna. She nodded once.

Spinning on his heel, he snapped his teeth, and exited the tent. Major Jericho returned to his seat and glared at Valianna. "You could have done something."

"Like what?" She cocked her head. "Thrown my weight around, perhaps? Exerted all the influence I do not officially have to brush the actions of a couple of students under the proverbial rug? There are larger issues at play, here, Hank. You know that."

Major Jericho crossed his arms. "You know what's going on here. 'Mastermind,' really? It isn't right to punish Zack and Dravs for doing the right thing."

Wracked by sobs, Jenny buried her face in her hands. She felt a clawed hand on her shoulder.

"You did well, child." Valianna's soft and sibilant voice soothed her. "They will understand in time, as will you. You have become involved in something that could change the galaxy, but it will not be easy"—Valianna removed her hand from Jenny's shoulder—"for any of us."

Jenny wiped her eyes. Valianna faced Major Jericho. "You know what you must do."

"That's not why I came to Cytherea." The human officer crossed his arms over his chest and frowned. "This situation has gotten out of control."

"I wish you would just say what you mean!" Jenny stood, her hands balled into fists. "This could ruin our lives. Mine, Zack's, Dravs's." She regarded Hiri. *I'm so sorry I got you involved.*

"You're a very clever human." Valianna smiled and steepled her fingers. "We could speak more plainly, but with discretion comes a certain amount of plausible deniability. You will understand in time. The language of soldiers and diplomats is often not plain by design."

Major Jericho rose and guided Jenny and Hiri toward the pavilion's tent flap. "Return to your dorms. Speak of this to no one. I promise you, I will do everything I can to ensure your friends' safety."

Chapter 28

"Do you think they're following us?" Zack checked behind them regularly, but detected no sign of their Devoran pursuers.

"It's possible, but I changed the passcode, so it should delay them."

Zack stopped and faced Rio. "What? How did you do that? How did you know how to even open the hatch?"

"I'm very good with computers, Zack." She touched his cheek. "Very. Good."

Zack set his pack on the floor and knelt beside it as he opened the flap. Squishy poked the top of his body out. A tentacle snaked out and wrapped itself around Zack's hand.

"I have no idea how to get you to the ship." Zack eyed the Athosian. He was covered in fuzz and lint from the inside of Zack's pack. "They're not docked to the city."

Go now. Will be soon.

"We need to get to the docking level." Zack pushed Squishy down into his pack and closed it before slinging it over his shoulder.

"What will we do there?"

Zack pulled out his C7 and consulted the map. Cytherea's docking level sat deep enough in the city that it allowed contiguous access to each dome. Discouraged from visiting it, students were not officially informed it was off limits. It was used only when ships too large to land in the hangar bays needed to offload people or materials.

"He thinks the Athosian ship will have docked by the time we get there."

"How? The city won't let them, will they?"

Zack paused at the T-intersection and checked his map again. He found a ladder well to the right, a few hundred meters away. "I wouldn't think so, but what do I know?"

They stopped at the ladder well. Zack descended first, in case someone waited for them at the bottom. The corridor appeared empty, and he gave the "all clear."

He showed her the map when she completed her descent. "According to this, there's a jackobot hub about four hundred meters away. From here"—Zack pointed to another ladder well leading to the Kalogeros level utility corridors—"we should be able to go straight to the docking ring from there."

"Which docking port, though?" Rio pointed to his screen and moved the display to each of the four ports in turn. "Alpha, Beta, Gamma, or Delta?"

"Probably, this one." He zoomed in. "K-Gamma. I think that's the closest to where the ship's been hovering."

"That makes sense."

Zack turned off his C7's screen. "Hey, you have comm implants, right?"

"Yes, why? We probably shouldn't try to contact anyone."

"Can you listen in without giving us away? I want to know if they've alerted security or anything like that." Eluding a couple of Devoran soldiers would be easy compared to evading all of Cytherean Security in addition to DDF troops. He gestured down the corridor, and they proceeded past bundles of conduit and power cables. A whiff of rotten eggs punctuated the stale scent wafting on the thick, dry air.

"Do you smell that?" Rio sniffed the air. "It smells like sulfur."

"A leak, maybe?" Seals along each level kept Cytherea airtight, impervious to the Venusian atmosphere. In the bowels of the city, though, it was possible maintenance was lax, especially since these utility corridors were intended for various types of service robots.

"Maybe."

Squishy squirmed in Zack's pack, and he shifted it to the other shoulder. He let his free hand brush up against hers. As if by instinct, Rio grasped his hand. Footsteps echoed in the corridor. Zack recognized the sound of claws clicking on metal. He listened to their footsteps as they walked; neither his shoes nor Rio's were capable of making the sound he heard. He dared glance behind them.

The corridor lay clear, but distinct footsteps echoed, even when he and Rio remained motionless. He tugged at her hand. "We've got to move faster."

~ * * * ~

Major Jericho escorted Jenny and Hiri through Ishtar Plaza. His withering glare, aided, no doubt, by the warm embrace Valianna gave him before they departed, discouraged Devoran troops from obstructing them.

Jenny waited to talk to Hiri until after Major Jericho ensured they boarded the lift that would take them to the transit hub. Jenny pressed the button for Skolio level instead.

"I'm going to Zack's dorm. Maybe he's contacted Ix."

Hiri tapped her temple. "You could call him."

"No." Jenny shook her head. "They might be monitoring comms."

To her relief, no Devoran soldiers were stationed in the halls of Hathor Dome's dormitories. She paused a moment and put her hand against the wall when she realized what that meant.

"What is it?"

"They've pulled all the troops out of the dorms to hunt for Zack and Dravs."

"Your friend has gotten himself into some big trouble."

Jenny pulled herself together and marched to Zack's dorm. Polly answered.

"Hey, Zack Attack ain't around." She leaned against the door jamb, twirling a strand of purple hair around her finger.

"We're here to see Ix." Jenny didn't see the Valtraxian in the common area.

Polly stepped aside to let them in. "He... it's in their room."

Jenny led Hiri through Zack's dorm cluster. A comedy show from Ersid played on the holoviewer, but no one seemed to be watching it. Polly's sister and the Kerrolian student played a game containing more pieces than Jenny had ever seen. She thought games with physical pieces existed only in museums or as antique collectibles.

Zack's room sat to the right of the entrance. Jenny knocked on the door and waited. She heard Mickey's voice from the other side.

"Come on in!"

Ix sat burrowed in its bedsheet nest, reading on its tablet. Mickey sat cross-legged on his bed, tuning his guitar. His eyebrows raised when the two entered.

"Uh... Zack's not here."

Jenny pointed at the Valtraxian. "We came to see Ix."

Ix lowered its tablet. "Jenny. Hiri. What do you need?"

They took Zack and Kaneer's chairs and sat before the Valtraxian. Jenny kept her voice low. "Ix, do you know where Zack is? Has he told you anything?"

"He normally eats with Dravs and Xal after Kova Kasi. Have you tried The Neutron Café?"

The piercing screech of city alarms cut through the air like a ripsaw. They all ran into the common area where the talking heads of Cytherean News replaced the comedy show that had been playing.

"The ship is moving now, approaching the city. In several languages, it is requesting permission to dock." The reporter seated behind the desk droned about this news as if describing the drying of paint, despite the screeching city alarms in the background. "We have been assured that at this time, there is no cause for alarm."

"Well, why are you sounding the alarms then?" Polly flung a cushion at the holoviewer. "Idiot!"

As if on cue, the alarms stopped. The reporter held his earpiece, nodded, and then continued. "City administrators apologize for the alarms you've been hearing and tell us they were tripped by overzealous DDF personnel who have been removed from Flight Control. We're going now to Major Jericho in Flight Control. Major?"

The scene switched to Major Jericho, now wearing his dark blue, casual duty uniform. "The ship began its approach prior to transmitting its request for permission. We've fixed that problem now, and we expect docking to commence in the next five minutes. I urge everyone to go about their business; there is nothing unusual about a ship docking with the city, and we are confident there is no threat to the security or safety of Cytherea citizens, despite what you may hear from the DDF. As you know, the EAC's official position is to extend the hand of friendship to new species whenever we encounter them, rather than immediately treating them as a threat."

The reporter's voice cut in. "But Major, the Devorans have claimed this is an Athosian ship. A species which waged war on the galactic civilization for hundreds of years."

"Yes, I am aware of the DDF spin on the situation. There is no evidence that this ship was involved in that conflict. After more than a millennium, I think we can afford to at least hear them out when they say they wish to peacefully negotiate."

Jenny turned to Hiri. "We have to find Zack." She ducked into Zack's room for some privacy and pulled up his comm address. Before connecting, she had second thoughts. If the DDF were looking for him, they might be able to trace a transmission to his comm unit. She called Xal instead.

The Ersidian answered right away. "Jenny? Why are you calling me?"

"Xal. Where's Zack?"

"Umm... I... uh..."

"He and Dravs are in big trouble."

"Dravs? He's not with Dravs."

"*What?*"

"Dravs got hurt in Kova Kasi, so we didn't even get to eat together." Xal cleared his throat. "I might have accidentally thrown Zack into Dravs and hurt his shoulder. Again."

Jenny plopped into Zack's chair. Hiri rapped lightly on the door and peeked in. She entered when Jenny gestured for her to come in and sit. "So, he's by himself? Where did he go?"

"No, that new girl went with him. I think her name is Rio? He took her to the arboretum."

Jenny slumped, covering her face with her hands. "Okay, thanks." She disconnected before he had a chance to respond. *What is he thinking? Is he thinking? And now he's dragged someone else into this mess?*

"Jenny?"

She looked up. Hiri reached toward her, her brow furrowed in concern.

"It's all right. I just... I have to do something." *He wants to get that Athosian to the ship. Did he contact it somehow?*

"What can you do?" Hiri rolled her chair closer and put her hand on Jenny's knee. "If you go looking for him, you'll be in the same mess he is."

"It's my fault they're looking for him." The thought that she was responsible for repercussions on Zack because of this situation clenched her stomach in knots. She rose from her seat and took Hiri's hand. "Come on, let's get back to our dorm."

She sought the dorm for Hiri's benefit. Jenny needed to stop there before putting her plan in motion, and she refused to put Hiri in jeopardy.

~ * * * ~

Zack clamped his hands over his ears as the metal walls of the utility corridor amplified and concentrated the city alarm. "Ow! What is going on?"

He and Rio arrived at the ladder well that would take them to Kalogeros level. Her eyes became unfocused, like he had noticed Jenny's became when she'd check for information or messages on her implants.

"The ship is moving closer to dock."

Zack stopped with a hand on the ladder and one foot hovering above the precipice. "How do they even—"

"Do you think they're watching us?" Rio craned her neck to look both ways down the hallway. The alarms drowned out the sounds of their pursuers, but there were still no visual signs of them.

With an abrupt squelch, the alarms stopped. Zack dug into his ear with a finger. "Maybe... I... it doesn't matter. Squishy needs to be with his people, not with these Devorans, and I'm going to make sure he gets there."

He mounted the ladder and half-slid, half-climbed down to the next level. When he reached the bottom, he stepped out of the ladder well and waited for Rio to catch up. He consulted the map again while he waited.

"Where to now?" Rio followed him as he strode down the corridor.

"There's a maintenance hub just ahead. They're supposed to have little travel pods that can get us to the docking ring. It's two kilometers if we have to walk, so hopefully the pods won't be locked down. Only service personnel are supposed to have access to this area anyway, so they may not be secured." It was a good idea, in theory. His father had told him stories about how after local kids broke into the unfinished areas and messed with all the unsecured equipment in one of the big arcologies he worked on in San Angeles, the company he worked for had to start locking down construction equipment. He hoped Cytherea was just as lax within its secure areas.

Rio tugged on his wrist to stop him. Her eyes searched his. "If we're caught..."

191

"You can go back if you want." Zack didn't blame her if she feared expulsion or worse. He hoped she stayed, but he would proceed alone if he must. He could not leave Squishy to the Devorans. It wouldn't be right.

"No." She threw her arms around his neck and hugged him. "I started this with you. I'll finish it."

Chapter 29

Jenny waved a greeting to her dorm mates as they watched with rapt attention the latest updates on the holoviewer. In the time it took Hiri and her to travel from Zack's dorm to theirs, the ship docked. As yet, no contact had been reported between Cytherean Security and the crew of the ship. She paused a moment, hanging back near the door to listen in.

"While the docking tube has made a secure connection with one of the ship's hatches, it has not opened. Major Jericho is on his way to K-Gamma to meet our new arrivals. In a terse exchange with the DDF commander and Cytherean Administration, Major Jericho reinforced his claim as the highest ranking EAC fleet official and the only person authorized to negotiate a first-contact situation on behalf of the EAC. Marshall Voss refused to speak with us on the matter, but a spokesperson for the DDF said they considered this an example of human hubris and arrogance—the Athosians are well known already, their lack of formal contact with the EAC during the last war notwithstanding."

K-Gamma. That's where the ship is. Right under this dome! Jenny dashed into her room and changed out of her school clothes. She flung them onto her bed as she looked for some attire that might encourage the adults to take her seriously. After contemplating an evening dress, Jenny decided to don her Junior Ranger uniform. *At least this way, if Zack gets us into a real mess, I won't be messing up clothes I actually like.* Hiri gasped as she walked in on Jenny mid-change.

"What are you doing? There's no meeting tonight." She scratched her head. "Not this late... is there?"

Jenny finished buttoning her shirt, lifted her pack, and pulled Hiri in for a kiss. The other girl tensed initially, but then relaxed, sighing in resignation as she returned the embrace.

"I'm going to help Zack."

"Well, then I'm coming with you."

Jenny shook her head. Hiri cut off her reply by pressing her finger to Jenny's lips. "No arguments. Let's help your friend."

Nodding, Jenny hugged Hiri, before the two dashed away, heedless of their dorm mates' shouts. The lift at the end of their hall would take them only as far as the transit hub, but another lift there would carry them to the docking ring on Kalogeros level.

As she expected, Cytherean Security stopped them at the transit hub. One of the armored, uniformed security guards, a human, held up her hand. "Hold it right there, ladies. This area is off limits for now."

"Because of the Athosian ship docking. I know." Jenny clasped her hands behind her back, relieved she didn't have to deal with another Devoran soldier. "I have a message for Major Jericho. It's about Zack Jackson. It's very important."

"It can wait." The guard lowered her hand, hooking her thumb into her belt.

Hiri crossed her arms over her chest and shook her head as Jenny frowned and tucked a strand of hair behind her ear, pulling her honor braid to the forefront. *This guard probably doesn't even know what this is.* "It really can't. My name is Jenny DuBois. Call the major. Tell him I have a message regarding Zack Jackson. I promise you, it is important." She hoped her Junior Ranger uniform would lend at least some credibility to her claim.

The guard sighed and activated the comm unit in her helmet. "Get me Major Jericho, please. It's urgent. There are two students here, one a Junior Ranger... what? Yes, sir." She glanced at Jenny. "What was your name again?"

"Jenny DuBois."

"Jenny DuBois, sir. She says she has information for you regarding Zack Jackson. Does that mean anything at all to you? It does. Very well. Yes, sir. Right away."

The guard motioned for Jenny to follow her. "Sorry about that. We're just trying to keep everyone safe. The major says to send you right down."

Jenny fought to keep her expression neutral, but inside she jumped for joy and cheered her successful ruse. She and Hiri moved forward until the guard blocked Hiri's way.

"Just you, Ms. DuBois. The major specifically said to allow only you."

Jenny's heart sank and she turned to Hiri. "I don't think I'll be able to change his mind."

"I want to help. There must be something I can do."

194

The guard put her hand on Hiri's shoulder. "Return to your dorm, miss. Ms. DuBois will be safe with Major Jericho." She gestured toward the lift at the end of the hall as she nodded at Jenny. "Press the button for Kalogeros level. He should meet you there."

"You have to stay here, and I have to do this." Jenny gazed into Hiri's emerald eyes.

"No... no, look, if Zack is with the major, he's safe. You can just stay in the dorm tonight."

"I'll always be grateful for your kindness and help with my parents' situation, and I really want... this to work out. But I know Zack needs my help now. I hope you'll still be here when I get back."

"Don't go..."

Jenny kissed her before leaving Hiri alone with the guard.

Jenny entered the lift and followed the guard's instructions. While the lift descended, she composed a quick message to her parents telling them not to worry if they didn't hear from her for a few days; school was busy, and she had a lot of tests to prepare for. By the time she finished the message and sent it, the lift door opened on Kalogeros level.

Attired in his dress uniform, Major Jericho waited in front of the lift. Behind him, a dozen EAC soldiers wearing heavy armor stood in formation. The docking ring resembled Cytherea's transit hubs, except cargo assembly areas took the place of berths for travel pods, and a striped section of floor led to the docking hatches. Windows looked out of Cytherea, though the bulbous, dappled spaceship that occupied the docking ring blocked the view of the Venusian clouds. In the diffuse amber light, the ship resembled a diseased pickle.

"Ms. DuBois. *Now* you have something to tell me?" His eyes scrutinized her from head to toe. "You changed clothes. Please tell me this isn't some prank."

"I'm here to help Zack." She stepped out of the lift. "It's my fault the Devorans are after him. What happens to him, happens to me."

"Your loyalty is admirable, but there's really nothing more you can do here."

She scanned the area, finding it devoid of both Devorans and Zack. "Where is he? He must've gotten word to the ship somehow. How did they know when to dock?"

Major Jericho rubbed his temples. "The DDF hasn't found him yet. The last I heard, he was with another student and thought to have gone into the utility corridors. The Athosians, if that's what they are, are being tight lipped about the timing of their docking. Look, if you want to help your friend, just go home. Rest. He's going to need friends when he's brought up on charges. Maybe you can think of ways to get him leniency."

He led her to a row of seats overlooking the ship. She took his arm. "He's doing the right thing. If those Athosians in that ship are friendly, for whatever reason, he's doing the right thing. You know he is."

Sighing, he sat down next to her. "It won't matter what either of us thinks if the Devoran soldiers catch him."

"Then we have to find him before they do." She rose and scanned the area for the nearest hatch into the utility corridors, locating it behind them, just to the left of the lift. "I'll go."

He squeezed shut his eyes. Pinching the bridge of his nose, he sat motionless for several moments. "Valianna was right about you two. She noticed those Ersidian honor braids, too, you know. Honor before reason, just like an Ersidian. Fine." He stood and held a finger in her face. "You go find your friend and bring him here, to me. If you're caught by the DDF, I know nothing. You slipped away from us in the confusion, understand?"

"Yes." She stood up straight and nodded. "I won't get caught."

In her mind, her responsibility to Zack rendered irrelevant the risk of being caught by the Devorans. Major Jericho accompanied her to the utility corridor access hatch and gestured to one of his troops. "Get it open."

"Sir?"

Major Jericho snapped his fingers. "Now, Corporal."

"Yes, sir!" The man knelt at the hatch controls. Within moments, it slid open. Jenny ducked inside, pausing to regard Major Jericho. He nodded once before motioning for the corporal to close the hatch. It slid shut, leaving Jenny alone in the darkness, with only emergency lights to show her the way.

~ * * * ~

"Are you sure you know where we're going?" Rio looked over Zack's shoulder as he consulted the map on his C7. Without his earpiece, he dared not risk using Skip to dictate the directions to him as they walked, and he suspected the Devorans would trace his C7 when Skip connected to the Hypernet. Offline mode seemed much safer.

"I'm pretty sure, yeah." Turning in the direction they came, he traced the route on the map with his finger. Then he remembered something from the trip to Bestic—the information he brought with him was well outdated. "Do you think this map is old? Maybe they've added or removed sections since they last updated this."

"I don't think they have. I read up on Cytherea before I transferred here. They haven't done any construction in years." She turned her head to look at the map sideways. "We must have missed something."

"Hey, I haven't heard the Devorans recently." He looked past her down the corridor. "Do you think they got lost?"

Rio turned her head toward the corridor and listened. "Maybe they went the way we were supposed to go."

"Nuts. They could be waiting for us in that maintenance hub." Zack checked his map again. "Aw, look. There's a hatch we missed. See? Here?"

They retraced their steps, traveling a few hundred meters, and discovered the hatch designed to blend in with the other wall panels. The door release lever lay hidden behind a smaller panel off to one side. They found it hanging open, and the layer of dust on the button seemed recently disturbed, smudged.

"I'll bet the Devorans came through here." He shut the door release panel and consulted his map again. "There's got to be another way around."

"Here." Rio pointed to a square room just ahead of where they realized they were lost. "It looks like it's a refuse collection hub. This might be a scrubbot conduit we can use to go alongside the travel pod track. It'll be slower to walk, but I'll bet it's too small for the Devorans to use."

Her suggestion gave Zack an idea. "Are you good enough with computers to hack a scrubbot? Maybe we could ride one and save us some time."

She grinned. "It can't hurt to try."

They hurried in the direction of the refuse collection hub. As they approached it, the sounds of machinery processing city waste grew loud, as did the stench. Zack wrinkled his nose in disgust and pulled his shirt up to cover it, but he gave up after the third time it fell.

"Organic waste is disgusting!" Rio waved her hand in front of her nose as Zack straightened his shirt.

"No kidding." They continued until they reached a door labeled "Waste Reclamation." Like many others in the utility corridors, it was secured with only a simple push-button mechanism.

The opening door unleashed an odiferous assault upon them, bludgeoning them with the worst stench of rotting meat and rancid oils. Zack retched, biting his tongue to keep from gagging. He took a moment to steady himself against the door before he pushed forward.

"You'd think these machines would be sealed so all this stink wouldn't get out." He found talking difficult; Zack tasted the smells that permeated the air. Each word, each breath, threatened to bring up his cheeseburger and add it to the nasty tapestry of odor.

Across the room, he saw a charging rack containing two parked scrubbots, each possessing a single blinking green light. They resembled squat, round suitcases, about a half-meter across. Rio approached one and knelt before it as Zack searched for the conduit they saw on the map.

Behind a clanking recycling unit, he found the duct. It opened into a narrow corridor, just wide enough to accommodate the width of a single scrubbot and tall enough that he and Rio could walk it, if necessary. The dim lights of the Waste Reclamation room illuminated only the first meter or so, and the passage did not appear to have lights of its own.

Shaking her head, she brushed off her pants as she stood. "No good." Rio tucked her dark braids over her shoulders. "There's no control panel to access for reprogramming."

"I found the conduit." He pointed to it. "It's large enough for us to walk in it, but there are no lights."

"I guess the bots don't need it. Your C7 has a light, right?"

"Yes, but I've got a better one in my pack." He crouched down and took off his pack, opening it to get the flashlight inside. "Hey, Squishy. We're working on getting there as fast as we can. Are you all right?"

The Athosian's tentacle brushed against the back of his hand. *Dry. Help soon. Others close now.*

"He's drying out. Is there a faucet or something in here?"

Rio searched for one while Zack tested his flashlight. The beam of light cut through the darkness, revealing the conduit to be little more than a long rectangular corridor with a smooth metal floor over which the scrubbots could travel. Pipes ran overhead, parallel to the floor.

"Over here!"

Zack flicked off the flashlight. Rio stood alongside a tall stack of metal crates by the wall. "I can see what looks like a faucet behind these crates. Help me move them?"

"I think so, yeah." He moved around to the opposite side and wriggled his arm behind the stack. He felt Rio's fingers from the other side as she did the same.

"On three. Ready?" He waited for Rio to acknowledge. "One... two... three!"

Together, they shoved against the boxes. A metal banshee screeched, for a moment drowning out the machines, as the crates scooted forward a few scant centimeters and permitted Rio to reach the faucet.

"Get your bag. I don't have anything to put the water in."

Zack ran to the spot where he left Squishy. Clutching his pack, he turned and noticed the top of the stack teetering.

"Look out!" His shouted warning came a moment too late as the stack collapsed. Zack fell backward, raising his arm to shield his face. He crashed into the scrubbot rack. Rio screamed and disappeared behind a clatter of metal and dust.

Chapter 30

Though the lighting system in the utility corridors provided dim, yet sufficient, illumination, Jenny adjusted her ocular implants to improve her low-light vision as she searched for Zack. The result wasn't quite the same as a sunny day, more like an overcast one, but it prevented her from stumbling and kept her hands free.

As she traveled, she pulled up a map of this level's utility corridors on her implants. She overlaid it on her vision, and it updated her position in real time as she walked. Jenny kept her pace slow and deliberate as she programmed the map to show the most direct route from the arboretum to here. Several kilometers with few side treks, she'd likely find Zack along it.

She noticed a maintenance travel hub on the map under the arboretum. The travel pod track leading away from it terminated in a robot repair bay not too far from her current location. Jenny flagged that route, and picked up her pace. As she got closer, crisscrossing cables and conduits choked the utility corridor, covering the floor like thick weeds.

The young woman walked on top of them, keeping a hand on the wall to help maintain her balance. It was obvious this corridor was used only by humans, and rarely at that.

An incoming call flashed in the periphery of her vision: Major Jericho.

"Yes?"

"What's your status?" The bags under his eyes appeared especially pronounced on his avatar, since it consisted of just his head and filled most of her vision. She tried and failed to adjust it to a more comfortable size, chalking it up to some military override of comm system settings. She paused and leaned on the wall.

"I'm near a bot maintenance bay. It has the terminus of a travel pod track. I think Zack might try to use it to save time."

"Good thinking. There should be a log computer nearby. You can use it to see if there's anyone en route. I'll have our tech on this end get you temporary access."

"I'm trying to hurry. I want to find Zack before the Devorans do." Jenny suspected the Devorans were under no orders to bring Zack in safely and would shoot through him to get the Athosian, if need be.

200

"Don't bother." His face disappeared for a moment and reappeared. "We've just received word that the DDF pulled out all their personnel about twenty minutes ago."

"They left Cytherea?" Jenny took a moment to pull back her hair, twisting it into a makeshift braid she hoped would keep it out of her way while she searched for her friend.

"Apparently. I don't trust that Marshall Voss doesn't have something up that scaly sleeve of his, but for now, no one else is looking for Zack and that other Devoran."

"Dravs should be easy to find. I'm sorry, Major. I assumed Zack and he were together, but they're not. Dravs was injured during their Kova Kasi class. Zack's with another student. I think her name is Rio." At this point, Jenny didn't see the point in being less than honest with the major. He seemed fair and interested in helping them. In her estimation, being forthright could only serve to help their situation.

"Human? From the EAC?"

"I think so. I don't know her."

"We'll see what we can dig up on our end. If they're both EAC citizens, that makes keeping the Devorans out of our hair easier. Valianna will back me up on that, too. Thanks for the update."

"I'll let you know when I find him."

Major Jericho nodded and terminated the call. Jenny let her implants readjust to the low light and proceeded toward her destination. When she reached the maintenance bay, more lights flickered on, illuminating the expanse. Scrubbots, jackobots, and even security bots lay scattered across the bay in various stages of disassembly. Tool benches and hydraulic racks formed a maze of machinery through which Jenny navigated. Her map didn't show a level of detail to help her find the other side, but by climbing up on several workbenches along the way, she spotted a small travel pod hanging from a track.

A thin layer of dust and grime covered the pod; it hadn't been used in a few weeks by the look of it. She found a nearby control panel and activated the system. While it loaded the activity log, Jenny consulted her map. The track from which the travel pod dangled was the most direct route between her current location and the area through which Zack likely proceeded.

The log showed no current activity, indeed. As she suspected, it hadn't been used in several weeks. Jenny noticed the control on her end included master commands, so she set a notification to alert her if the system activated within the next day. Once the command executed, she turned the system off and searched for an alternate route Zack might have taken.

Nearby, Jenny located a scrubbot conduit running parallel to the travel pod track. If he traveled from the direction she guessed, it was the second most likely route. Her ocular implants compensated for the darkness in the conduit by overlaying a grid over the map and rendering the conduit in grey, so she closed the hatch behind her and moved on.

~ * * * ~

Two tentacles reached out of the pack resting on his chest to touch Zack's face. *Loud noises. Safe?*

"I'm okay, Squishy." Zack moved his pack off his chest and onto the floor before dusting himself off. He pushed himself to his feet and shoved a crate out of his way. It teetered on its edge before falling and busting open, revealing wrapped parts Zack assumed were for repairs.

He left his pack and Squishy by the scrubbots as he made his way through the debris. "Rio? Rio!"

"I'm over here."

The crates littered the corridor. Many lay busted open, scattering their contents on the floor, making the path through them treacherous and uneven. Picking his way over and through the field of machinery parts, he found her sitting on the floor, her legs pinned under a pair of crates. Her head leaned forward, resting in her hands, her braided hair covering her face.

Zack wormed his way next to her and brushed her hair to the side. She lowered her hands and tilted her head.

"I should have anticipated that."

"Are you hurt?" Zack couldn't see her legs under the unsealed crates that rested upon them.

"Yes, I think so. I've been better, certainly." The lack of inflection in her voice worried him. If crates fell on top of him, he didn't think he'd be as calm.

Reaching forward, she shoved the crates off her legs. Her pants and skin were shredded. Gleaming metal shafts surrounded by twitching, pinkish muscle, oozed blue fluid. The azure-colored liquid pooled beneath her legs, spreading across the floor like melting ice cream.

Rio touched his face. He turned to her, his mouth agape. "I'm sorry, Zack." Her bottom lip trembled. "I can't go with you anymore."

"You have cybernetic legs?" He felt simultaneous relief and horror. If she possessed legs of flesh and bone, the damage would send her into shock and she would bleed to death before help arrived.

"No." She took his hand. "Look at me."

He searched her grey eyes. Tears welled in their corners. "I was not permitted to reveal myself."

"What? What are you talking about?" He tried to pull away. *I wish I'd brought all my Junior Ranger gear, maybe the first aid kit would help.* He pushed some of the debris out of his way. "We have to get help."

"Zack. Please." Rio swallowed and shook her head. She took his hand again. "I am a bio-replicant."

Her words took a moment to register. "An android? That can't be. Your eyes... Steve told me..."

"I am an advanced prototype, LC series four. I was sent here, to school, to test my social interaction skills, to see if I could fit in." She sniffled. "I wanted to do this with you. To help. To be part of what you're doing with this Athosian."

"You still can be." He tried to put his arm around her, under her arms to lift her up, but she pushed him away.

"My legs are too damaged. Get the water, and then get your Athosian to its people." She wiped her face, leaving streaks of blue android blood behind. "I'll be all right. When you're gone, I'll activate my implants and call for help. I just... I didn't want you to find out about me like this. No one was supposed to know."

Zack was torn. "I don't want to leave you." If he hurried, he figured he could give Squishy to the Athosians and return to her before the authorities arrived.

203

"You have to." She reached up and pointed to the faucet. "I can't be the reason you fail. Get your friend water and go. I will be fine. I promise. I won't bleed out, I just can't keep up with you anymore."

He coughed to disguise the sob that overtook him and lurched toward his pack. Zack brought it to the faucet. He splashed some water on Squishy before closing it and slinging it over his shoulder.

"After I get Squishy where he needs to go, I'll send help." He knelt by her. "I promise."

Rio craned her neck and kissed him. "Thank you for being my friend." Then she pushed him away. "Go. Save your Athosian friend."

Zack stumbled toward the scrubbot conduit, wiping his eyes. He snatched up his flashlight off the ground and turned it on as he plunged into the darkness.

Chapter 31

Zack's legs ached from running on the hard, smooth surface used by the scrubbots. He didn't keep track of how much distance he covered; he found it difficult to read and run at the same time, but he missed Coach Dagon and the track upon which he ran laps. It was much easier on his feet and legs.

Fortunately, the entire length of the scrubbot conduit followed a straight line, except for curving slightly to follow the outside arc of the dome. As he ran, his thoughts drifted to Rio with her legs mangled, lying in the scrubbot corridor. He hoped she would be all right. *Maybe the Devorans or some of the city maintenance crew found her.*

"Who's that ahead?" a familiar voice called out from the darkness.

"Jenny?" Zack stopped and shone his flashlight along the conduit. Emerging from the darkness, Jenny approached, holding up her hand to shield her eyes from the glare of his light.

"Zack! Thank goodness!"

He lowered his flashlight. "What are you doing here? Why do you have your Junior Ranger uniform on?"

She pulled him into a hug. "I'm sorry, Zack. I'm so, so sorry."

"What for?" He squirmed out of her grip.

"Where's the girl you were with?" She looked past him down the darkened conduit.

"Oh, Rio's hurt." Zack touched her arm. "A bunch of metal crates fell on her. I didn't want to leave her, but she said it was more important I get Squishy to his people."

Jenny pulled him in the direction from which she approached. "She's right. They've docked now, and Major Jericho and his people are waiting for them to open the hatch. Why didn't you call Emergency Services for her?"

Zack shook his head. "The Devorans might trace the signal from my C7. They can't be that far behind me.

"Major Jericho told me the Devorans gave up. They pulled out and left Cytherea altogether."

He wrinkled his face. "That doesn't make any sense. After all the fuss they made?"

Jenny agreed with Zack's assessment, but she also trusted Major Jericho had not baited them. "That's what he told me."

"They could still be listening in. Rio's at the Waste Reclamation room at the end of this conduit." Zack ran alongside Jenny. "She's okay for now, but, I have to get Squishy to safety. We'll have to send someone for her."

"We'll let the EAC know when we get there. They'll send someone for her." Jenny slowed her pace to allow Zack's shorter legs to keep up.

"How did you know the Devorans were after us?" *Is that what she was apologizing for?*

"Everyone knows, Zack."

Onward they ran. They settled into a rhythm, jogging in sync until they reached the end of the conduit. Jenny opened the hatch leading to the maintenance bot repair facility. Once Zack passed through, she secured the hatch behind them.

"How did you know where to find me?"

She tapped her forehead. "You're not the only one with maps. I knew you were coming from the arboretum. There are not that many routes on this level from there." She pointed at a travel pod hanging from a rail. "I'm surprised you didn't take that, though."

Zack frowned as he eyed the pod. "We missed the turn to take us there, I guess. It sure would've been faster." His aching legs agreed.

"Come on. It's not far now." She led him across the repair bay and into a utility corridor thick with wire and conduit, a jungle of plastic vines and metal roots. She held a low-hanging cable out of the way while they picked their way across the myriad of power conduits strewn across the floor.

"The bot tunnels are much easier to walk in." Snagging his shoe on a rope-like bundle of cables, Zack stumbled. Jenny caught him before he fell.

"I ran into one of the Devorans who gave me trouble last night." Jenny's voice was soft and flat. Zack strained to hear her. "They detained us and made me tell them what you were doing."

Zack stopped in his tracks. "They made you? How?"

Jenny faced him, tears in her eyes. "They said they'd get me expelled, then arrest me for assault, and ship me off to prison. A Devoran prison. Sycorax."

"Sycorax?" Even in Wamsutter, Wyoming, stories of Sycorax were the stuff of legend. It was a hostile world, a death planet of choking fumes, molten rivers, and vicious predators. The prison was safe, relatively, but escape meant surviving with little to no gear on a world which most sapients were ill equipped to survive. The air was poison, the plants had razor-sharp leaves and were toxic to mammals, and the prisoners were the worst dregs the galaxy knew.

"I didn't believe the part about prison, but all that talk made Major Jericho angry. I think if Princess Valianna hadn't been there, he would have throttled Marshall Voss."

"I'm sorry, Jenny. I don't want you to get expelled."

Shaking her head, Jenny chuckled and sniffled. "I guess it doesn't matter now." She tugged at her shirt. "I tricked the EAC troops into letting me pass to talk to Major Jericho by telling them that I'm helping you. I'll bet the Devorans won't just let it drop. We're in this together now."

He adjusted his pack on his shoulder. "Let's get it done then."

~ * * * ~

"It's not far now, Zack." Jenny urged him to pick up the pace.

"Good, we can get help for Rio." He followed along beside her, hopping over the conduits and cables that snaked across the floor.

He pulled out his comm unit. "Okay, I'm going to call her now. If they don't talk to me, I don't have to lie about where I am."

Jenny urged him to keep walking as he spoke.

"Rio? I found Jenny! She said Major Jericho told her the Devorans called off the search. I don't know why, but it's probably safe to call Emergency Services now. I'd do it, but they'd ask where I was, and I still have Squishy. No, it's okay. I'm sorry you got hurt, I really am. Okay, I'll tell her."

He stopped and put one hand against the wall. "What? Oh... I... umm... yeah, I... sure. I guess we'll have to see what happens when all this is over. Okay. Bye."

207

Jenny's implants detected increases in Zack's heart rate and respiration.

"Is everything okay?" She motioned down the corridor, and they continued walking.

"She wants me to take her to the Yule Celebration. It's still months away. I said 'yes'... oh, Jenny! What if I get suspended because of all of this?" He backed away from her and slumped against the wall.

"If she's talking about the Yule Celebration, she can't be hurt that badly." Reluctant to further discuss the consequences they were likely to face, she stuffed those concerns into a deep corner of her stomach. Worrying about them now wouldn't help them accomplish their task.

"She is, but... well, I shouldn't talk about it. She wouldn't want me to." He stuffed his hand in his pockets and stared at the floor.

Jenny wrinkled her nose. "That's strange. Where did she get hurt?"

"Her legs, they're... broken, I guess."

Jenny put her hand on Zack's shoulder. "You like her, don't you? I mean, really like her? Like Polly."

"No, Polly was more into me than I was into her. She's okay, you know, but not really... no, I didn't want to do things with Polly so much."

"But Rio's different."

He nodded, keeping his eyes fixed on the floor. "Yeah."

"If we get out of this, we'll go double, Zack. Rio and you, Hiri and me."

Zack looked up at her, a half-smile on his face. "That sounds fun."

"Let's get moving." Jenny led him onward. The whirr of machinery increased as they passed a well-lit junction. They felt a breeze blowing across the intersection, heading deeper into the city. According to Jenny's map, one route led to part of the massive air-handling system that circulated air throughout the city. The opposite path led toward the city's edge and the maneuvering jets that helped the city maintain its position in the clouds.

A bridge crossed the junction, the handrail on the right side of which split where a ladder led down to the underpass. Zack paused to look down.

"It's a long way."

"We're not going that way, though. Straight across." Jenny glanced over the side as they walked. Down below, a jackobot welded a piece of machinery. Staggering, Jenny shut her eyes against the glare as the brilliant white glow from the robot's welder arm briefly overwhelmed Jenny's implants.

"What's that up ahead?"

Jenny blinked her eyes until her vision cleared and squinted to see what Zack pointed at. A humanoid shape blocked the corridor, but at this distance, even Jenny's implants couldn't view it clearly.

The shape raised a hand. "Private Colt, Delta Squad. Is that you, Miss DuBois?"

Jenny moved forward. "Yes, I found him. Come on, Zack."

A young man, the soldier appeared to be only a few years older than Roger. Wisps of dark hair poked out from around his helmet. "I found them, Corporal. Bringing them in now."

"Where are you taking us?" Zack stood his ground as the private gestured for them to follow him.

"Back to Major Jericho. He was concerned with how long it was taking you."

"I wasn't gone for..." Jenny checked her chronometer. Two hours. *I didn't realize so much time passed.*

"He disagreed, miss. Let's go where it's more comfortable. We'll get you cleaned up. I think there's grub, too, if you're hungry."

The three of them walked together for ten minutes before reaching the hatch through which Jenny first entered the utility corridors. Private Colt ushered them through the door before coming through himself.

Zack stared through the observation windows at the Athosian ship. His eyes were dinner plates. "Wow... that's really big. I knew it was big, but that's really big."

Major Jericho interrupted his conversation with a dark-haired woman, another soldier, and approached them. "Good job. Now then"—he put his hands on his hip and turned to Zack—"what are we going to do about you? Do you have any idea the trouble you've caused?"

Zack shrugged the pack off his shoulders and opened the flap. The little Athosian's head, covered in fuzz matching the color of the pack's interior, poked out. "I couldn't let the Devorans kill him, Major."

"No, I suppose not." He looked them over. "Need anything to drink? Eat? Are either of you injured?"

Jenny declined food and water for the time being. The option she really wanted, sleep, was not offered. Zack threw his pack over his shoulder. "I'm fine, but my friend Rio was hurt. She's in a Waste Reclamation room. Her legs are broken."

"You just left her there?" Private Colt snarled as he removed his helmet.

Zack glared at him. "She made me! She said getting Squishy to safety was more important."

"All right." Major Jericho held up his hand. "That's enough, Private. You're dismissed. We'll have someone get your friend."

"She's already called Emergency Services."

"Fine, we'll follow up."

"Major!" One of the soldiers near the docking port pointed at the hatch. "It's opening!"

"Come on!" Major Jericho motioned for the two youths to accompany him. He took a spot directing in front of the hatch and gestured for Jenny and Zack to stand behind and to his right. The squad of soldiers moved into position. They stood in ranks behind and to Major Jericho's left.

Jenny breathed deeply and regarded Zack. She stretched a trembling hand out toward his. Zack's eyes widened, and his face split with a grin, like he was about to meet a rock star for the first time. She bit her lip. *They better be friendly.*

Chapter 32

Rivulets of water ran down the walls of the stark-white interior of the hatch as it slid open with the hiss of equalizing pressure. The Athosian revealed within wore a bullet-shaped environmental suit, topped with a clear, fluid-filled dome. Small round ports ringed the suit, two of which bulged before extending tentacles as the Athosian exited the ship. The alien reached toward Major Jericho as two more of its kind exited the spacecraft.

Offering his hand to the first one he assumed to be the leader, Major Jericho stepped forward. The tentacle coiled around it. "On behalf of the Earth-Alpha Centauri Alliance, I welcome you to Cytherea."

The Athosians bobbed up and down, and Zack noticed they floated above the floor plates.

"Thank you."

A slight echo accompanied the sound of the leader's voice. Zack saw no evidence of a speaker on the environmental suit. He felt neither pressure in his mind like when Squishy communicated with him, nor a similar sensation like he felt when Bob spoke to him telepathically.

"We are Alpha Primus of the Athosian Nomocracy. We greatly desire to speak with the highest authority available."

"I am Major Thomas Henry Jericho, EAC Fleet Command. I'm authorized to speak for the EAC in this first-contact situation."

Alpha Primus withdrew their tentacle. "Very well."

"Am I speaking to a collective or an individual?" Major Jericho clasped his hands behind his back, a drop of slime or water, Zack couldn't determine which, falling from his fingers and splashing on the floor.

The Athosian's ten eyes blinked in sequence, and the alien made a quarter-spin within their environmental suit. "We share a hive intelligence, though we are capable of acting individually. We request you refer to us as 'they' as your gendered pronouns are inappropriate. We are certain you have many questions. However, we wish to take custody of our polyp prior to any such negotiations."

"Polyp? Oh! The juvenile. Zack?"

211

Zack stepped forward and opened his pack. Squishy poked out his fuzz-covered head. "Here, I tried to take good care of him, but I really didn't know what I was doing."

Four tentacles snaked from the suit, reached into Zack's pouch, and withdrew Squishy. More tentacles appeared as Alpha Primus passed the juvenile around their body to one of the Athosians behind them. The second and third Athosians' environmental suits appeared nearly identical to Alpha Primus's, including placement of the tentacle ports, except they hovered at a lower height, giving the impression that Alpha Primus was taller.

"The polyp has told us of your assistance." Alpha Primus tilted their environmental suit toward Zack. "We wish to know how they came into your care."

"Actually, I'm rather curious about this myself." Major Jericho turned and faced Zack.

"Oh, um..." Zack's face grew hot as all eyes focused on him. "Professor Gladstone gave me this thing, a round bit of iron in a case with oil all around it, last year. He said it was a fragment from an iron star, but it shouldn't exist. It broke open after... when I got back from a Junior Ranger thing one night. It was hollow, and we saw a trail from whatever was inside going to our air vent. Later, Squishy fell out of the ceiling in the cafeteria. I tried to catch him... them? Th... they got away, so Dravs and I had to go into the utility corridors later to find them..."

Major Jericho rubbed his temples, while the Athosian focused on Zack. "Where did Professor Gladstone acquire a polyp's stasis pod?"

Zack struggled to recall that conversation. "He was on an EAC exploration ship? I don't really remember. He gave it to me as a gift. He said they found it near Etta care... carinay, I think?"

"Eta Carinae." Major Jericho rubbed his chin. "I remember reading about an expedition out that way when I was at the academy. FTL drives were much slower when that ship left. It's a supernova remnant approximately seventy-eight hundred light-years away, visible from our southern hemisphere, or Earth's rather. I suppose it would be visible from here without the cloud cover."

"We are familiar with the location. Do you still have the fragments of the stasis pod?"

Zack patted his pockets out of habit. "I do, but it's still in my room." He looked up at Major Jericho. "Ix could bring it down for me, if it's important."

The major held up his hand and shook his head. "We don't need any other students involved."

"Ix knows about Squishy and the Athosians already. It's a Valtraxian!"

Alpha Primus spun to face Major Jericho. "We deem the recovery of this pod important. We also greatly desire to speak to a Valtraxian."

"Oh, for goodness sake." Major Jericho pinched the bridge of his nose. "Typically, in first-contact situations, we do not involve a group of school children."

Zack regarded Jenny. Both returned their attention to Major Jericho. He muttered to himself and sighed. "Fine. Holt, go get the Valtraxian."

"I'll let Ix know to expect you." Jenny nodded at Corporal Holt as the man snapped to attention, then trotted toward the lift. She leaned down to Zack. "Anything you need?"

"I kind of wish I had clean clothes."

Jenny smiled and nodded. "I'll let Ix know."

"All right, look, now that all this is out of the way, we have a conference room prepared." Major Jericho gestured toward the far end of the docking ring.

"We would prefer to have the discussion aboard our ship." Alpha Primus spun another quarter turn. "These environmental suits are bulky and uncomfortable."

"If our environment is unsuitable for you"—Major Jericho returned to his parade-rest stance, clasping his hands behind his back—"why would your environment be suitable for us?"

"We modified several sections of our ship to accommodate both our species, so we may all be comfortable while we interact."

"I'll bet that's why they sat out there for so long." Zack nudged Jenny, careful to keep his voice low so it would not disturb Major Jericho.

Alpha Primus bobbed. "That is correct, Zack Jackson."

"Very well." Major Jericho nodded. "We'll proceed once the Valtraxian is here."

~ * * * ~

"Jenny, this is going to be so cool!" Zack bounced on his heels as she finished composing the message to Ix telling it to be ready for EAC Corporal Holt and to bring Zack's Junior Ranger gear, uniform, and the remnants of the iron star.

When she finished with that message, she composed a second one to Hiri. "Found Zack, everything is fine for now. This is going to be historic; can't wait to tell you all about it."

Major Jericho approached and crouched before them. "Okay, you two. This is unprecedented, and personally, I think you should not be here. But I have orders to the contrary. I expect you to behave, be quiet, touch nothing, and do as I say. Understand?"

"Of course."

"Yes, sir!" Zack beamed at Major Jericho.

He held a finger in Zack's face. "I'm serious. If I say 'run,' you run. No questions. No hesitation, all right? We have no idea what to expect, and I'm not in the habit of bringing children on my ops."

Jenny stiffened.

He glanced up at her. "Yes, children. You have no military training, and you're not diplomats. What happens today will affect the course of galactic history."

"I know, Major." Jenny raised her head. "I also asked Ix to bring Zack's Junior Ranger uniform, so he can change into clean clothes. I doubt he has a suit lying around, and we don't have time to have something new fabricated."

They both eyed Zack. His pants hung covered in dust and grime from the utility corridors, and his knees had chalky, azure stains from android blood.

He chuckled. "Yeah, my mom would say I'm not presentable."

Major Jericho nodded. "Yes, I appreciate that. Very well."

He stood as a woman wearing the rank of sergeant approached him. She carried her helmet tucked under one arm, and a rifle hung from her other shoulder. She stood at attention until he acknowledged her.

"What is it, Watley?"

"Delta squad is ready to escort you in, sir."

214

"An armed escort." Alpha Primus floated closer to the two human officers. "I assure you that is not necessary."

Sergeant Watley opened her mouth to retort, but fell silent when Major Jericho raised his hand. "It's a matter of protocol, Alpha Primus. Our regulations require dignitaries entering potentially hostile territories, even under a flag of truce, to do so only under armed escort."

"Hostile?" The Athosian bobbed backward. "We are scientists. Our ship has no weapons."

"I can appreciate your reluctance, but look at it from our perspective. We've had almost a thousand years of the Devorans telling us... well, frankly, very bad things about Athosians. That we're even speaking to you is making them very... shall we say, anxious?"

"We understand. Will two escorts be acceptable?"

Major Jericho thought a moment. "Yes, that will suffice." He turned to Sergeant Watley. "I want Herd and Coulson."

From the corner of her eye, Jenny saw two soldiers in the nearby formation stiffen.

"Sir, Herd is a pilot, not infantry."

"I am aware of that, Watley."

"Yes, sir!" Sergeant Watley snapped to attention and gestured to the two soldiers. A dark, athletic woman wearing an officer's insignia on her flight suit and a pale, wiry man wearing light combat gear adorned with chevrons hustled toward them and stood at attention.

"Lieutenant Herd reporting."

"Sergeant Coulson reporting."

Major Jericho snapped his fingers. "Watley, give Herd your rifle."

He took the soldiers aside to speak to them while they waited on Ix. Jenny let out a long breath and checked her comm implant. The message to Hiri was still pending, although the one to Ix had been received. She flicked through the options to discover her transmissions were being blocked.

She regarded the assembled troops until she observed one serviceman plunking away at a terminal. He noticed Jenny watching him and threw her a salute. *So, he's monitoring communications.*

Alpha Primus floated closer to them. In their environmental suit, the Athosian stood easily two meters taller than Major Jericho. They hovered in front of the students, spinning in a slow circle as the suit hung rock-steady in the air.

Zack cleared his throat. "Did your ship reactivating have anything to do with Squishy's pod opening?"

The Athosian bobbed up and down. "The stasis pods are programmed to open when a particular signal reaches them from one of our ships. We were in close enough proximity to trigger it."

Zack shuffled his feet and stared at the floor. "Um, can you tell me about indoctrination?"

Jenny's eyes widened, and she kicked Zack's foot.

The Athosian lowered themself until the base of their environmental suit almost rested on the floor. "A technique used by the Conquerors to control lesser species. It is relatively easy to accomplish, but requires physical joining of the host Athosian and the subject until a link is established. How do you know about this?"

"Zack!"

"What?" He waved a hand. "Major Jericho didn't say we couldn't talk to them while we waited."

Zack retrieved his C7 from his pocket and pulled up the images he acquired on Bestic. He held it before the Athosian. "A Devoran tried to put a juvenile Athosian on my head to indoctrinate me. He said he was part of the Cult of Athos. Huh... they're upside down in these tanks, aren't they?"

"Indeed. This was recent?"

"Almost two years ago." Zack examined the image again. "These only have eight tentacles."

"It is not uncommon for individuals to exhibit eight to ten tentacles and eight to ten eyes. Standard genetic variation among Athosians, similar to human eye color or possessing straight or curly hair." Alpha Primus's eyes blinked in sequence around their body. "Even this long after their defeat, the Conquerors' influence causes discord. Where did they come by that polyp? What are the coordinates of Bestic?"

"I don't know. It's pretty far away."

"I doubt the Devoran soldiers that arrived after we escaped kept any of those polyps alive." The truth of the outcome of that situation seemed obvious to Jenny considering DDF troop behavior ever since the Athosian ship revealed itself.

"We fear you are correct. Nevertheless, we will investigate in due time."

"We found a lab on Valtra, too. The hologram said your people uplifted the Valtraxians."

"Zack!" Jenny kicked his foot again. "I'm not sure we should be telling them everything right now! We're not supposed to talk about that."

Zack shrugged. "What are the Devorans going to do to us now? We're talking to a live Athosian. They're going to really hate us just for that. Anything else will be peanuts to them. Besides, shouldn't the Athosians already know about their own labs?"

"I... well, I guess you have a point. Still..." Jenny considered it unwise to discuss how much the Devorans wanted to kill all Athosians while they stood before Alpha Primus.

"We did uplift the Valtraxians. The Conquerors sought to use them in their battles. Fortunately, they were defeated prior to putting that plan in action. It was an act of desperation, though few would admit it at the time."

"All right, enough." Major Jericho approached them. "Stop bothering Alpha Primus."

"It is no bother, Major. We approached them. Children possess a forthrightness many adults lack."

"Yes, it takes years to learn discipline and discretion." He pointed Zack and Jenny toward a rack of chairs facing the observation windows. "Why don't you two go wait over there? We'll need to get started shortly."

Jenny dragged Zack away from the Athosian.

Once underway, he shook his hand free. "We may as well make the best of it!"

She fell into the chair and cupped her hands around her face as she grunted a reply, "We are going to be in so much trouble."

"Trouble?" Zack laughed. "Who cares? Jenny, we're making history!"

Chapter 33

"Come on Ix, where are you?" Zack twisted in his seat to check the door across the loading bay. Alpha Primus hovered at the entrance to the docking port, clasping tentacles with another Athosian who emerged from their ship a few moments earlier. Like the others he'd seen, this new Athosian wore an almost identical environmental suit.

Zack jumped up from his seat when the lift door slid open. Ix skittered out, followed by Corporal Holt. Jenny seized his arm to keep Zack from running to his friend. The corporal led the Valtraxian to Major Jericho before escorting it to Zack and Jenny. As if mesmerized, Ix fixed its gaze on the Athosians as it passed them.

Corporal Holt ushered Ix past the Athosians. "And here are your friends."

Ix offered the broken halves of the iron star to Zack, while keeping its eyes fixed on the Athosians. "I brought your sphere, Zack."

"Thanks!" Zack took it from him and put it in his pocket. "Did you bring my gear?"

Tossing a canvas bag to him, the Valtraxian nodded. Zack opened it and looked inside. "Thanks."

He glanced at the surrounding area. "Is there a bathroom or something? I need to change."

Corporal Holt pointed toward some cargo crates. "Change over there. No one will see you."

Zack ducked behind the crates, stripped off his grungy clothes, and changed into his clean Junior Ranger uniform. By the time he finished, Major Jericho, his escorts, Jenny, and Ix assembled in front of the docking port and Alpha Primus. The rest of the EAC troops stood in formation some distance away, except for one soldier holding a holocamera.

Major Jericho regarded his squad. "All right, can we get on with this now?"

"The delay was not an inconvenience for us." Alpha Primus gestured toward the docking port. "Shall we proceed?"

"On behalf of the Earth-Alpha Centauri Alliance"—Major Jericho stood at attention—"I accept your invitation. My superiors eagerly await news of a new, mutually beneficial relationship between our peoples."

"This way, please." Without turning in his suit, Alpha Primus moved away from Major Jericho and into the docking tube.

The major motioned for his entourage to follow him, first Zack, Jenny, and Ix, followed by Lieutenant Herd and Sergeant Coulson bringing up the rear.

Cytherea's docking tubes were like all the others Zack had passed through on his various trips—semi-circular in cross-section with bright white overhead lighting and grated deck plates. The sides were composed of flexible, self-patching tear-resistant material, strengthened with metal struts to facilitate extension and retraction.

This docking tube bunched up near the expansion joints, typical of those not fully extended. The hatch to the Athosian ship lay open a few meters away, revealing the interior of their ship, and opening into a room that resembled a bubble with a flat floor and light grey curved, translucent walls. Through the walls, Zack observed large tubes through which silhouettes of Athosians traveled.

"We have modified this portion of our ship to accommodate you. Our species is most comfortable in an aquatic setting, which, as you might imagine, makes interactions without environmental suits difficult." Alpha Primus led them through the foyer, down a semi-circular corridor, and into a long, capsule-like room.

Several ports lined the walls. Unused environmental suits like the one Alpha Primus wore lay affixed to the ports. Alpha Primus maneuvered their suit into one of the empty ports, as did their companions. Mechanical clicks echoed in the room as the suits locked into place before Alpha Primus and the other Athosians vanished with a whoosh.

A section of the ceiling faded and gradually became fully transparent. An Athosian regarded them as a voice echoed throughout the room. "Exit this chamber through the door at the far end. In the next room, you will find accommodations we hope you find comfortable. We will meet you there."

He swam away, leaving the students with Major Jericho and his bodyguards. "All right, let's keep moving."

"Do you think their whole ship is filled with water, sir?" Sergeant Coulson's mouth hung agape as he marveled at the shapes moving behind the translucent walls.

"We'll find out soon enough." Major Jericho ushered them through the chamber and into the next room. A half-moon shaped table curved in front of a glassy bubble with a dozen chairs positioned along the table's length. An Athosian, whom Zack assumed to be Alpha Primus, bobbed in the liquid contained by the bubble.

Major Jericho claimed the seat directly in front of the Athosian, flanked by Herd to his right and Coulson to his left. Jenny sat next to Lieutenant Herd, and Zack slid the chair next to her away, leaving room for Ix to settle in between them.

"When I left the hive, I never expected to ever stand aboard an Athosian ship." The Valtraxian slid its fez from its head and held it in front of its thorax.

"Are the accommodations acceptable?"

Major Jericho shifted in his seat. "Yes, fine, thank you."

Zack scooted backward in his seat and discovered his feet did not touch the floor. The material from which the seats were constructed enveloped him like a bead-filled cushion, hugging and gripping him. The absence of armrests gave him trouble; he wasn't quite sure what to do with his hands, so after fidgeting a bit, he interlaced his fingers on his stomach.

Alpha Primus rotated slowly as they regarded the humans and Valtraxian. "We're certain you have many questions. We also have many questions. It is our hope we can use this time to learn about each other, before discussing items of a political nature."

A pair of Athosians passed behind Alpha Primus. To Zack's eyes, apart from physical size, they seemed identical. He scanned the room, trying to determine from where Alpha Primus's voice emanated. He saw nothing that resembled a speaker grill or any other sort of audio system.

"Indeed." Major Jericho folded his hands on the table in front of him. "Why did you choose this particular time to reveal yourselves, and why were you hiding on Venus?"

Alpha Primus's eyes blinked in sequence. "We chose this world to hide upon because we knew there was a minimum level of technology required before your species would be able to discover us. We sought a refuge from the war. Twelve hundred years ago, many of us in the scientific community—"

"Excuse me," Major Jericho held up a finger. "Twelve hundred years? You were hiding on Venus for twelve hundred years?"

"Yes. We were in suspended animation. Our ship is capable of sustaining us in that state for quite some time with minimal energy requirements."

"That's..." Major Jericho threw up his hands. "That's astonishing!"

Zack looked past Ix at Jenny. When she finished counting with her fingers, she leaned toward Zack. "That's before Rigel Kent was established."

The EAC's main colony in the Alpha Centauri system, its first extrasolar colony, Rigel Kent was barely a thousand years old. The Athosians had been to the Sol system centuries prior to that, before humanity became an interstellar species.

~ * * * ~

To think, they've been here longer than we've been out there. Jenny's mind reeled.

"Your species showed promise. We hoped when you were advanced enough, you would be willing to listen to reason rather than immediately attacking, as I understand the Devorans would have you do."

"How in the name of Hades did you hide a ship on Venus?" Major Jericho ran his hand through his short-cropped hair. "We were certainly spacefaring a thousand years ago."

The Athosian turned a different set of eyes onto the human. "Your technology cannot monitor the entire solar system at once. It was trivially easy when Venus was in superior conjunction to Earth."

Major Jericho laughed. "You hid... you landed when Venus was obstructed by our sun."

Back then, humanity concentrated on the moon, Mars, and the Galilean moons of Jupiter, and Titan. Rigel Kent, in the Alpha Centauri system, wasn't established until nearly three hundred years after manned exploration of the solar system begun in earnest, before Cytherea was founded, in fact.

"Not every Athosian agreed with the Conquerors. They sought to destroy the Devorans and their allies, just as the

221

Devorans sought to destroy us. However, like you, like the Devorans, like every species in the galaxy, we are not a monoculture."

Zack tugged at Jenny's sleeve. "What's that?"

She leaned over and whispered. "They don't all believe the same politics and things like that."

Alpha Primus rotated more quickly in their bubble. "The Conquerors controlled our society, and they felt, as a superior species, they should scourge this galaxy of lesser lifeforms. We disagreed."

"So you were at war with each other, as well as the Devorans?" The major bit his lip and sighed. "It's an old story."

"But not accurate. We did not war amongst ourselves. When it was clear the reasoned approach would not work with the Conquerors, we reached out to the Devorans." Alpha Primus's eyes blinked simultaneously. "But they would not listen. The Devorans were destroying us indiscriminately. Warriors and scientists, adults and polyps, alike. Battleships and unarmed research vessels, it did not matter."

"Yes." Major Jericho nodded. "The Devorans are quite proud of their campaign of genocide."

"We knew the only way to preserve our species was to withdraw and hide." Alpha Primus's tentacles gestured to encompass the ship. "This vessel contains sufficient individuals and genetic material to repopulate our species, if need be."

Major Jericho gestured around the room. "This ship is all that's left of you?"

"There were others. We do not know if they survived."

"Others? Here on Venus?" After blurting the words, Zack clamped his hand over his mouth as Jenny nudged him. "Sorry."

"No, in other places, spread across the galaxy."

Major Jericho steepled his fingers in front of him. "Are there other ships like this one in any systems within twenty light-years? What about warships—did you hide any of those?"

"We cannot speak for the Conquerors. Those of us who seek peaceful coexistence and cooperation hid only scientific research vessels with stasis capability."

"The Conquerors, huh?" Major Jericho sat back in his chair. "The Devorans are confident they wiped out all of them. They waged a five-hundred-year campaign after the war officially ended." He scoffed. "They were still at it when the EAC first encountered the Devoran Empire."

"Then it is likely they were successful. Devorans can be quite thorough."

The ship lurched and rocked. Jenny gripped the edge of the table as the lights in the room flickered.

"What was that?" Zack pulled himself upright on the edge of the table.

Ix rose and held the table with its second set of arms. "It felt like an impact of some sort."

Alpha Primus spun in a rapid circle. "We are under attack."

Major Jericho leapt from his chair. "Everyone back to Cytherea. Now!"

After darting to Jenny, he pulled her from her chair before he reached across and did the same to Zack. He pushed them forward. "Coulson, get them out!"

The ship rocked again, accompanied by distant rolling thunder.

Jenny took Zack and Ix's hands. Together, the three of them were more stable than each individually in the lurching, rolling ship. Ix tugged at them as it skittered ahead, but Jenny kept a tight grip.

Another boom dropped the ship at least a meter. Jenny and Zack sprawled to the floor. The Athosian shapes behind the walls darted to and fro. Rough hands grabbed her and pulled her to her feet.

"Are you all right?" Coulson brushed Jenny's hair out of her face. She fumbled for the hair tie that came loose and refastened it.

"Yes, fine." She shook off his grip and grasped Zack's hand again. They ran through the environmental-suit room and into the foyer.

"What the..." Coulson turned and faced them. "Sir! The hatch is closed."

Jenny fell to the floor again as the ship accelerated.

"Jenny?" Zack reached out to her.

Major Jericho stumbled into the room, but he was thrown against one of the environmental suits as the ship shuddered under another impact and banked. "You have to take us back to Cytherea! Now!"

223

Alpha Primus's voice reverberated in the room. "We're sorry, Major. That's not possible at this time. We're taking heavy fire from orbit."

"The Devorans? Cytherea Control! This is Major Jericho aboard the Athosian vessel. Who is firing on this ship? We're still aboard. Civilians are aboard. Children!"

"The Devorans are shooting at us?" Zack's grip became a vise, crushing Jenny's hand. She winced and extracted her fingers from his iron claw.

Ix clung to one of the environmental suits and looked backward at Zack and Jenny. "This is not an ideal situation. Perhaps you should return to the chairs. They may provide a modicum of protection."

"The Valtraxian is right." Major Jericho pointed toward the conference room. "Get back in there. It's safer."

Jenny crawled until she reached the wall and then used it to pull herself to her feet. She reached for Zack, seized his outstretched hand, and held onto it while he stood.

The lurching stopped for a moment, and then Jenny felt the familiar stretching sensation that accompanied a faster-than-light Translation. She glanced over her shoulder at Major Jericho. His eyes and unvoiced curses on his lips confirmed her suspicion.

The Athosian ship was leaving the Sol system.

Chapter 34

Zack's stomach felt squeezed before stretching like a taut rubber band. He tumbled backward, smacking into the wall.

A great weight pressed against him, and then the room spun. Rainbows burst in his sight, a kaleidoscope of colors wheeling around him, spinning, twirling into infinity.

He forced his head to move, to look for Jenny. He glanced down and noticed he missed a belt loop on the back of his pants before he noted a scuff on the heel of one of his shoes.

My back? Upon realizing his head faced backward, Zack tried to scream, only to taste the sound of tearing metal. He squeezed his eyes shut against the sound of purple-and-green cold. A sense of calm overcame Zack, and for a brief moment, he felt as if he floated in a mist. *Nuts, I forgot to reply to Mungus.* The absurdity of his non sequitur thought brought a smile to Zack's lips.

Zack's eyes snapped open as someone brushed his fingers. A noodle-armed Jenny reached toward him, her arm stretching across several meters of room.

Coulson and Herd were as one, spinning like a pinwheel around Jenny's noodle arm. Major Jericho pounded at the door, hanging on for dear life as each blow of his fist caused rainbow ripples to cascade around the room.

Time stopped.

~ * * * ~

As soon as she felt the stretching sensation, Jenny turned to run for the conference room. Even without restraints, the form-fitting chairs there would be safer than standing during a Translation.

Her head throbbed with the screams of orange ceilings. As she grabbed for Zack's arm, he seemed to move farther and farther away from her. His head spun like a scene from an ancient horror film she once watched.

Ix melted into the environmental suit to which it clung. Beyond, through the translucent wall, Jenny saw Athosian silhouettes caper and prance through their liquid medium.

Jenny's vision shrank to a pinpoint, and the way her head throbbed, she realized she tumbled head over heels. She braced herself for impact.

~ * * * ~

Zack's stomach felt like it twisted and tied itself into a knot. He rolled over, keeping his eyes shut out of fear the room would still be spinning if he opened them. He suppressed the urge to vomit. The floor felt stable enough, so he lay still, cheek against the cool, smooth metal floor.

"Hey." He felt a hand on his shoulder, shaking him. "Zack!"

He turned his head and cracked open an eye. Major Jericho knelt at his side. Thus far, the room did not violently spin. Zack turned and looked for Jenny. She sat in the corner, hugging her knees to her chest. Her hair covered her face like a curtain of gossamer chocolate. Ix scampered to her and tentatively touched her knee.

Zack sat up and cradled his head. "Ugh, that was worse than my first Translation."

"I'm not going to argue with that." The major helped Zack to his feet. "I think we've actually landed."

"That was the worst Translation and landing I've ever experienced." Jenny used the wall to pull herself to her feet. Her skin appeared ashen and her breathing shallow.

"Where?" Zack looked around the foyer. The stark light grey walls had not changed, despite all he remembered seeing during Translation. Lieutenant Herd tended Sergeant Coulson, who sat moaning and holding his head.

Major Jericho banged his fist against the wall. "Hey! We're still alive in here. Where are we? A little communication would be nice."

After the ambient light dimmed, a rectangular section of the wall glowed. An Athosian face appeared. "Apologies." The voice was not that of Alpha Primus. "Centuries of corrosion affected our drive engines. Damage from the attack also affected our systems. Arrival at Athos rougher than anticipated. Atmosphere breathable by human standards."

"Athos? Your home world?" Major Jericho stepped away from the viewscreen.

"Mon dieu." Jenny fell against the wall and wrapped her arms around herself.

Zack's discomfort at the rough Translation faded as he fought to keep a grin from crossing his face. The image on the viewscreen shifted and displayed a star map of the local area.

Major Jericho tapped on the map. "Can you zoom this out? Where are we in relation to the Sol system?"

The map zoomed out. The Athosian system was revealed to be part of a scattered cluster of stars. It kept zooming, revealing that cluster to be part of a fuzzy conglomeration of stars neighboring a second, smaller smudge. The zoom continued until a spiral was shown at the top of the screen. A green line traced the route from one of the arms of the spiral, through the vast gulf separating it from the large fuzzy cloud.

Major Jericho stumbled to the docking hatch and started pounding on it. "Let me out. Open up!"

Zack squinted at the star map. His head still ached from whatever method the Athosians used to propel their ship, but he forced himself to focus. According to the map, it appeared the ship traveled an impossible distance in a short time. Jenny shuffled to his side and traced the line with her finger.

The hatch upon which Major Jericho pounded slid open with a hiss. A ramp extended toward the ground, embedding itself in the loamy soil. Stepping backward as it opened, he then ran through it. Zack, Ix, and Jenny followed.

Ix chittered and clicked as it clambered down the ramp. It plucked a blade of grass and held it up for inspection. "It feels waxy. The edges are sharp. Be careful."

Thick and full of moisture, the air felt like a liquid to Zack— warm, fruity soup. He heard water lapping nearby, as if a shore lay near. Stars speckled the sky above, yet night didn't appear as dark as he expected. He tilted his head up to find the source of light.

"My God." Major Jericho fell to his knees as he gazed upward.

The field of stars seemed less dense than Zack viewed in Wyoming, but he could never have seen the object that dominated the sky from his home.

Not in the way he currently viewed it.

A vast spiral stretched across the sky. The glow from its center appeared far brighter than the full moon, and it cast shadows across the ground. It was at once clear, bright, fuzzy and unfocused. Although it was full of stars, he could not single out one.

"Take a good look, kids. We're the first humans to ever see this."

Zack dropped to his knees before rolling onto his back and facing the great object in the sky above. The sharp-edged ground cover irritated his skin, but the view more than made up for his discomfort.

"That's home, isn't it? The Milky Way?" Jenny's voice broke.

Zack gasped, his stomach a rock in his gut. All of his excitement about being on a new planet vanished in that moment.

"Yeah. Over one hundred and fifty thousand light-years away." Major Jericho lowered himself to the ground fully and reclined. "Our fastest experimental ships would take almost six years to travel this far, and they can't carry enough fuel for a Translation of this distance, anyway. We can't even talk to them from here."

Zack glanced at the Athosian ship. Illuminated by the galaxy hanging in the sky above them, it resembled a beached whale, a vast hulk blotting out the horizon behind them. A closer look revealed it was, in fact, not beached, but bobbing in water. "But they can take us back home, right? I mean, we're not stuck here, are we?"

"I hope so." Zack strained to hear Major Jericho's whisper.

Zack pulled out his C7 and turned on the screen. As expected, there was no signal. He held it up to the sky.

"Don't bother." Major Jericho folded his hands on his chest. "Everyone we know will be dust and ashes by the time any signal reaches home. I doubt that thing can even transmit out of the system."

"Skip, get pictures of this." Zack smiled at Jenny. His parents could keep him from going to Ersid, but now that he lay on Athos, looking across the vast gulf of space toward the cosmic pinwheel that was home, he endeavored to make the most of it.

Zack regarded his friends. "It's like Major Jericho said— we're the first humans to ever see this. No one is going to believe us when we get back."

Zack Jackson will return in *The Ruins of Athos.*

www.ingramcontent.com/pod-product-compliance
Lightning Source LLC
Chambersburg PA
CBHW060428180626
46817CB00007B/2716

*9 7 8 1 9 4 4 9 9 9 0 5 6 *